Animus mundi

TALES OF THE SPIRIT OF PLACE

Edited by
Jaym Gates

Published by Outland Entertainment LLC
3119 Gillham Road
Kansas City, MO 64109

Founder/Creative Director: Jeremy D. Mohler
Editor-in-Chief: Alana Joli Abbott
Senior Editor: Gwendolyn Nix

ISBN: 978-1-947659-46-9
Worldwide Rights
Created in the United States of America / Printed in China

Editor: Jaym Gates
Cover Illustration & Design: Jeremy D. Mohler
Interior Layout: Mikael Brodu

Visit **outlandentertainment.com** to see more, or follow us on our Facebook Page **facebook.com/outlandentertainment/**

CONTENTS

Introduction, **Alana Joli Abbott**..5

Coaltown, by **Heather Clitheroe** 7

Blackthorn, by **B. Morris Allen**..17

The Forgetting Field, by **Caroline Ratajski** 24

Reef, by **K. C. Norton**..28

Ouroborus in Orbit, by **J. Daniel Batt**...................................34

In the Water, Underneath, by **Damien Angelica Walters** 37

Scab Lands, by **Wendy N. Wagner** 41

Cactus Flowers and Bone Flutes, by **Mercedes M. Yardley** 51

The South China Sea, by **zm quỳnh** 54

The Other Shore, by **Rebecca Campbell** 67

The Threadbare Magician, by **Cat Rambo**...............................78

Imperator Noster, by **Sonya Taaffe** 108

Long Way Down, by **Seanan McGuire**....................................111

Second Verse, Same as the First, by **Stina Leicht** 121

Twilight State, by **Gemma Files** 153

Heartbeat, by **Laura Anne Gilman** 171

— INTRODUCTION —
Alana Joli Abbott

There are places in the world that feel alive. The ancients--and plenty of moderns--were well aware that, while we humans may think ourselves separate from the natural world, we are shaped by it. In some cases, recognizing the spiritual power inherent in the land led to building structures to interpret that power: avenues of standing stones, tombs and cairns that prohibited straight lines to keep spirits from escaping, and holy buildings of all sorts.

Sometimes these sites of power... aren't so nice.

As a young academic, I served as a teaching assistant on a number of mythology study tours, and it was both a delight and a terror to see many of these sites firsthand. In Avebury, England, I walked with undergraduate students along the West Kennet Avenue. Scholars have debated the purpose of the stones; the mythographers on our tour hypothesized that it was an Avenue of the Dead, and that while the ancients might have walked along the avenue outside the stones, the center of the path was for the spirits of the dead, hence the reason it was formed in a straight line. (It was believed that spirits could not turn corners and needed a direct path.) There, we also visited a hill where a human constructed ledge would create a double sunrise: one for those who stood at the peak, and one for those who stood on the ledge, when the sun crested the peak of the hill. Again, the students posited the idea that this double sunrise was for the benefit of the spirits: the landscape itself had been changed by its residents in order to honor the otherworld they knew lived alongside them.

In Turkey, I visited the ruins of the Roman city of Ephesus, where their theater—not necessarily a place moderns would associate with spirit—is constructed as though it is the mountains in miniature. The theater's hemisphere is a faint echo of the mountains behind it, the same shape as those hills closing in to the water. Because of its placement in the landscape around it, scholars of sacred geography have compared it to a womb: here is the place where a child is released into the world, or where ideas are born. But for some, including me, there is a more visceral reaction to the site, one that scholars might be at a loss to explain. When I visited the first time, I was so overwhelmed that the view brought me to tears, emotion welling within me to bursting. There is something about the spirit of that place to which I connected on a level that a clinical analysis cannot explain. The power there is too emotional to fit neatly into logic.

Likewise, some of the world's darker places create an emotional reaction that's hard to explain through impersonal observation. There are stories of people traveling to a waterfall in Massachusetts without an offering, and suffering nightmares until they return. There are cenotes in Mexico that draw people to their edges; once used for sacrifice, these sinkholes have visitors who claim they are still hungry things, waiting for tourists to jump into their maws. There is a cave I visited in Ireland which, beyond any rational reason, felt as though it wished to eat me. For some places, that personal, emotional response has been felt by generation after generation. The ancients, and those moderns still open to such response, know that there is something *more* to a place, something beyond, something powerful.

The stories in this collection feature those powers, some benevolent and some cruel, so deeply connected to their landscapes and locations. The humans who encounter them sometimes come out ahead, sometimes worse for the wear, and sometimes just a part of the balance that ties their communities to the world around them.

The earth has power.

Traverse it wisely.

Alana Abbott
July 2018

— COALTOWN —
Heather Clitheroe

In North America, our lives are inextricably entwined with the coal and oil industries. While many people make an effort to use solar or other alternative energies and otherwise conserve energy, the reality is that most of us rely in large part on oil and coal to keep our lights on, heat our homes, and fuel our cars.

A coal mine is a strange place. In these tiny, poorly lit, dusty and dirty spaces, it's impossible not to be aware that you are underground and you may not live to see the surface. Miners around the world tell stories about spirits who live in the mines. Miners from the United States tell of Tommyknockers, who steal tools and food, and who knock on the walls of a mine right before a cave-in. The stories of the knockers were brought to the USA by Welsh and Cornish miners. Some miners see them as evil spirits, who knock on the walls to weaken them and cause disaster. Other see the knocking as a warning, and leave small bits of food as a thank you to the spirits.

According to Bureau of Labor Statistics, mining is the second most dangerous occupation in the United States (as of 2006). Miners face risks of injury and black lung disease, and they work long, physically and emotionally taxing hours. When we talk about the hidden costs of our energy sources, we tend to speak of them in environmental terms. But there are other costs to consider.

In Clitheroe's story, "Coaltown", a town relies on the local mine for their economy. All the families in the town are dependent on the success of the mine, but its success comes with a cost. In the story, Clitheroe uses fantasy to challenge us to consider the real costs of the resources we rely on.

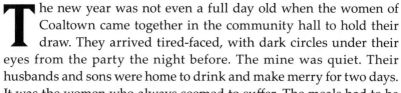

The new year was not even a full day old when the women of Coaltown came together in the community hall to hold their draw. They arrived tired-faced, with dark circles under their eyes from the party the night before. The mine was quiet. Their husbands and sons were home to drink and make merry for two days. It was the women who always seemed to suffer. The meals had to be got and the children looked after no matter how much their heads might ache. And if some of the women had drunk as much and made as merry as the men, it was only because they had tried very hard not to think about the draw to be made the next morning.

The wind was cold. New snow had fallen in the night, and it covered the hills and rimmed the naked trees. The sky was sullen and heavy with cloud as the women walked silently through the slush. They crowded into the hall, stamping their boots clean as they came inside. Every one of them with something precious to lose, something to fear.

This year, one hundred and ninety-seven women would put their name into the draw. They knew who they were. They didn't need reminding that they were to stop at the table at the entrance to carefully print their names on slips of paper. Several old women sat and took the slips gravely, placing them into an old, battered box with a slot on the top and a lock across its side.

Edda Helms walked in behind her mother-in-law. Heavily pregnant, she bent awkwardly to write her name, then gave the slip of paper to her aunt.

"How are you, dear?"

"Oh, can't complain," Edda said. She would have liked to. She'd been up all night. First with heartburn, then a leg cramp, then the snores of her husband after he'd finally come to bed, stinking of sour whiskey and running urgent hands over her body. Her back ached and she had a headache, and there was still the laundry to do. Piter worked the second shift at the mine. He left early in the morning, before the sun was up, but at least he was home every night in time for dinner.

"Come over after the draw," her aunt said. "Come have a cuppa tea with me. I haven't seen you all week long."

"Maybe tomorrow?"

"You look tired." The older woman cast an appraising eye at Edda's stomach. "The baby dropped. Not long now, eh?"

"No," Edda said. "That's what everybody says." It felt like the baby was almost between her legs these days. She only had two weeks to go. Maybe three. She ought to have kept better count…well, there was nothing for it. The baby would come when it was ready.

She'd never thought she'd marry a miner. There had been talk of sending her away the city, to learn to be a teacher. She could come back and teach the little ones while their fathers were underground and their mothers were hard at work at home, trying to wash the coal dust off the furniture. She was supposed to have a better life.

But then she'd gone and fallen in love with Piter. A miner, just like his da. He could barely read. Could sign his name but not much else. He left school early to go and work in the breakers, picking through slate and slag as lumps of coal rolled on by on the belt. Then he'd been put on as a door boy, opening up for the carts and the men. And after that, mule boy, driving the tired old beasts down into the mine. By the time he was thirteen, he was 'prenticed to his uncle, learning how to swing his pick and set a charge just so, bringing the coal down but not the roof. His skin was pitted with black dust, pale from so much time spent in the down under. He'd come to court her with his skin raw from washing, scrubbed so hard it was pink when he'd come to stand at the bottom of the porch step to ask her aunt if he might take her to the hall for a dance.

It touched her. It touched her powerfully.

One thing led to another. She found she was late. There had been a wedding. As was so often the case in Coaltown, the wedding dress passed down to her had an extra panel sewn in around the belly, with clever darts and lace work that hid her thickening waist. Her aunt only said that she hoped Edda would be as happy as she had been, that she wanted her to have a good life. There was no more talk of going away to be a teacher.

Piter bought up a house—the papers on it were owned by the company. But it was *theirs,* with a small front room that he filled with furniture bought on credit, and he carried her over the threshold as she laughed. They made love in their new bed, ate the dinners she cooked. She scrubbed at the floor and the bed linens to get the coal dust out, just like Piter's mother did for his da. Just like her mother must have done. A married woman now, Edda was putting her name in the draw for the first time.

Her aunt took the slip of paper and pushed it through the slot and into the box. For a wordless moment, the sour sick came up the back of her throat, her heart pounding. "Come and see me tomorrow, love," her aunt said. "I'll fix you up a nice lunch when Piter's gone down."

"I…" What to say? The sweat prickled down the small of her back, the fear hissing in her ears as she struggled to compose herself. She blinked hard, tried to take a slow breath and choked.

Her aunt's callused hand closed over hers. "No worries, my girl," she whispered. "Don't count your sorrows until they're drawn."

Edda walked into the hall, trying to smile at the women she knew. Some of them patted her shoulder or looked on with sympathy. The others just smiled vaguely back at her, lost in their own worries.

There were no chairs set up. No need. There'd be no lingering, after. When they were all there, the boxes were carried up to the front, and she held her breath with one hundred and ninety-six others. Nobody was missing. Only Tessa Adams was at home, nursing her da after his stroke, but Tessa's oldest daughter stood as proxy, put her name in for her. Edda leaned against the wall to try to rest her back and waited for the draw to begin, one hand on her stomach while the baby rolled and stretched.

She went home in a daze, her mother-in-law and her aunt walking alongside her. Five names drawn, and one of them her own. Of the five, she was the only one roundly pregnant. In her pocket was the first envelope of money they'd given her. "To help with the baby," they'd said. "To thank you for your service." The other women had the same envelopes, but they weren't afraid. One look at Edda and they were reassured; she'd have the baby before they were even puking up in the morning. She'd be the one to carry it down to the mines before she could even cross her legs comfortably. The mine only needed one.

A good omen, to have a baby to take down so soon. That was what people were saying.

By the time Edda was home, there was a covered basket waiting for her. Her aunt picked it up as Edda opened the door. "Somebody's brought you dinner," she said, lifting the cloth to look inside. "Stew."

"Fine," said Edda, tonelessly.

"Why don't I make you some tea?" Her mother-in-law was already into the kitchen, reaching for the kettle.

"No," said Edda. "I have to start the wash."

"Just a cup," said her mother-in-law. "Sit down."

Her aunt helped her to a chair, then sighed. "Don't cry," she said. "There will be other children, pet. There will be. But I wish it weren't you."

Her mother-in-law glared at her aunt. "Don't say that," she said. "It's an honor, that's what it is. She should be proud."

"To give up her first to be a canary?" her aunt snapped.

"Don't use that word," her mother-in-law said. "It's vulgar. Her husband is a miner. She knows what it means to be drawn. She should be glad."

"Glad," Edda's aunt muttered. "It's barbaric."

Edda let them bicker. She sat, with her hands resting on her belly. Breathing in and out slowly, waiting to feel the baby move. There. A fluttering kick. Another. *I'm so sorry,* she thought. *Oh, god, I'm so sorry.*

When the labour pains were close together, she sent Piter to get the midwife. The roof creaked as the wind blew. It was snowing again. Edda waited in her bed, her hands twisting the sheets into lumps. She tried not to groan from the pain, to stay calm. She could imagine curtains stirring as women went to their windows to watch Piter dashing through the snow.

Everybody was waiting on Edda. There'd be no long months of hoping for one of the five to get pregnant. She came with a baby ready-made, and all she had to do now was to push it out. The front door rattled and she raised herself up to her elbows. Was that Piter? Was he back already?

No. Just the wind. She let herself back down, groaning as another contraction seized her.

Coaltown produced the very best. It came from deep inside the hills, way down far. Their coal burned hot and bright. A good, smokeless blue flame that gave the best heat. There was always steady work here. You could work for the mine or you could do something to help the mine stay running. Nobody went hungry in Coaltown. It was a poor life, always in debt to the company store, but at least you could feed yourself and your own and have a little left over to save for another day.

And other mines didn't have canaries. They were dangerous. Nobody sang to the things that came up from the down below to keep them from attacking the men. Heard but not seen, the canaries held off the firedamp that could tear the men apart, too. They sang to keep the rocks from falling on them. They saved the men from the afterdamp that would smother them. Coaltown's men made coal, and its women made canaries and the next generation of miners.

The house shook with a savage gust of wind, and she started to cry with fright and dread.

The hours were lost to her. The world contracted into a ball of pain, wracked her until she was shivering and sweating at the same time. The midwife spoke soothingly to her at first. Then sternly. Then sharply to Piter. "Get my bag." Edda was dazed, lying limp in the new bed that she and Piter shared. Spent. But still the pains came. She didn't want to push. But her body had its own reason and logic that she did not, could not resist.

The clanking of metal stirred her from her misery, and she spoke. Her voice was raw. "W-what's that?"

"To help the baby," the midwife said. "Lie back."

The wind roared loud around the house as she heaved and pushed and sobbed. The ground trembled in time with her contractions. The hills waited with the women of Coaltown, who, at home in their beds, thought sorrowfully of Edda Helms and what she was going to have to do.

She was weak and pale from the blood she'd lost, but she'd memorized every line of his face, every wrinkle, the soft folds on the back of his neck. They let her have that. Then her aunt and her mother-in-law got her up from bed and helped her dress and wash, braiding her hair. They told her it was time.

Piter sat in the rocking chair in the kitchen, holding his son. The baby was swaddled in flannel. The coal fire was lit; the room was warm. Piter's eyes were red-rimmed and swollen, but he gave the baby to his mother. Edda put on her coat and slowly wound a scarf around her neck. She leaned on her aunt, and together they slowly walked out the door. "Be strong, my girl," her aunt said softly. Piter choked back a sob.

The sun was just rising, a splash of feeble light edging over the hills. Her breath came in a ghosting cloud. It had grown cold, and the slushy snow had frozen into hard ruts along the road. Women were waiting for them. They came hurrying out of their front doors, some standing on their porches or in their front yards, expectant and hushed. They began to fall in step behind Edda as she walked past, keeping a respectful distance behind her. Edda could feel them watching, their gaze a pressure that settled between her shoulders. She walked up from the rows of houses into the winding, tree lined road that led to the mines, followed by the mass of women.

Here the trees were thick, clustered close together so that the branches formed a tight woven canopy. In the early spring, when the leaves first came out, the bowered path was pretty. "Just how like looking through water," Piter said one night, in the dark, while they lay in bed together waiting to fall asleep. "It's the prettiest thing I ever seen," he said. And then he corrected himself. "Except you." She'd laughed, her head resting on his chest, listening to the steady beat of his heart.

It did not look friendly now, or pretty. The branches twisted together, gnarled limbs making fists that clenched. A gust of wind rushed suddenly down the hills, and they shook. Edda heard somebody coughing wetly behind her, wondered who it was that had come out to risk pneumonia for her. Her aunt took her arm as they began to climb, breathing more heavily, and Edda put a hand on hers. "If it's too much…"

"I'll come the whole way with you, pet," her aunt said.

Her mother-in-law walked beside them, carrying the baby. He was wrapped warmly. Her head was down, and from time to time, she twitched the blankets back to look at his small, perfect face. There was a red mark on his forehead from the forceps, but it was fainter than it had been, no longer swollen. Edda's boy slept.

The road gradually levelled, and they emerged into a clearing. The outbuildings were here, a bit of smoke rising from a narrow chimney of the company office. The wind blew harder now, whistling in her ears, but Edda refused to shiver. *I won't*, she thought. She walked on, careful not to stumble, and then she saw the men. It nearly brought tears to her eyes.

They were standing along the road, lining it. A hundred of them. Maybe more. Some she knew, many she didn't. Men with beards blackened by the dust, men who shaved their chins smooth, men who were still slender youths, their shoulders already stooped from the time they'd spent crouched underground, ducking through shafts with their charges and picks. Piter had the same way of standing: canted slightly, his neck a little broader on one side from the muscles that came from holding himself at an angle for hours. They looked at her with open pity, these men, but with gratitude, too. Some of them nodded at her. Others wiped their eyes. Her cheeks felt hot and she turned her head to look up at the sky.

A company man came out of the office, and several men stepped aside to let him by. He wore shoes—so silly, in this weather, with this much ice on the ground, Edda thought. Hobnailed boots would be so much more practical. His lovely overcoat was the most fanciful thing she'd seen, beautifully cut and swirling around him as he walked. He was taking something out of his pocket. An envelope. She stopped in the yard. The women behind her halted.

It was quiet in the clearing. There were no birds this morning, not even the little dun sparrows that hopped and chirped all the year round. The hills crouched all around them, and the sun touched half the clearing where it could cut through the rock escarpments that ringed the mine. The sky was achingly blue. A perfectly clear January sky wrought from the icy cold of her despair.

She went in alone. That was how it was done. Her aunt embraced her, holding her close and rubbing her back. Her mother-in-law's chin trembled and tears dripped off the end of her nose, but she gave the baby to her and whispered, "I'm proud of you." Edda wanted to scream. The baby stirred with a funny, chuffing grunt. She took him in her arms and looked at him once more in the sunlight, folding the blanket back so she could see his whole face.

The company man gave her a small lamp. He handed the envelope of cash to her aunt. "Once you get inside, you'll be fine." He spoke with a city accent, his words clipped and graceful. He talked to her like she was simple. She said nothing, and his face turned red as she looked at him and thought, *you don't know anything about us.*

As she reached the entrance, a voice called out behind her, strangled with grief. "Tell my girl I love her!" She shuddered and kept walking, holding onto her small boy. She stretched out an arm to touch the wall to steady herself as she stepped over the steel tracks and wooden ties, feeling her feet sinking into loose stone. Sunlight glinted on a streak of quartz in the wall. The ground began to slope downwards, and it grew darker as she walked. She couldn't see more than a few metres ahead, and she felt her heart quicken. She held her baby close, the lamp swinging from the crook of her arm.

The darkness closed around her as she walked on. It was warmer inside the mine. Water dripped. She passed narrow entrances to other shafts, the canvas curtains rustling as her hand trailed across them. The air grew thick and heavy. She stopped, her breath rattling in her chest. She waited.

She hugged the baby close. She was deep inside the hill now, deep down. She could feel the pressure of the earth above her. It pressed down on her. It was hard to breathe. Sweat trickled down the small of her back. She wanted to turn and run out, to take her boy and race home to Piter. They could leave. They could. They could leave and go somewhere far away, where he wouldn't go down into the shafts and she could raise her boy in the sunshine. She whimpered. And then Edda wept, too afraid to go any further, unable to go back. The light from the lamp was feeble. The mine was blacker than black. As black of coal.

She heard a soft crackle. Rock grated. A shiver of stones fell from the ceiling. They pattered down around her, striking her head and shoulders, and she bent herself over her baby to shield him. When it stopped, she raised her head and her breath caught in her throat. Her hands tightened on the baby, convulsively.

Something scuffled in the rock nearby, but she couldn't see what it was. She heard a faint humming, a thrum that ran through the rock and came up through her heels. It was one voice. Then another joined it, the wordless song swelling around her, coming close. Something touched her, and she jerked herself away, gasping in terror. Another touch, a feeling of a small, rough hand on hers, another on her back, something touching her shoulder. They were coming to her. There were small hands on her back, pushing her forwards. She took a staggering step, then another, letting them lead her.

This was the way it had to be.

This was what she had to do.

She could finally see the small shapes around her. The children were long limbed, lithe and slender. Their skin was scale and rock, and dust shivered from them as they ran towards her. They scampered gracefully on their arms and legs in the dusty gravel, their mouths open as they sang. Heads turned to her, squinting with black eyes at the light from her lamp. Quartz teeth flashed as they smiled. They danced in a circle around her, plucking at her clothes. One stood on its legs—she could not tell if it was a boy or a girl—and touched her hair. It laid a cool hand on her face, pressed a finger to her cheek. "Your mother says she loves you," Edda said. Her voice echoed. The child threw its arms around her, laid its head briefly on her shoulder, and then backed away. "Your mothers love you," she told the children. "All of you. They miss you and they love you." They crept closer, heads turning side to side as she spoke.

Edda sat down carefully on the floor, up against the wall, and stretched her legs out, cradling her son in her arms. She told them about their mothers, about the sunshine and the blue sky. She talked until her throat was dry and hoarse. The baby woke and began to cry, a thin wail that bounced off the walls, and the children gathered around her to look at him, their heads pressed together.

She looked past them, down the shaft, and she could see something coming slowly out of the walls. It moved ponderously. It had the same shape as the others, but the legs were broader, the shoulders wider.

One of the children ran towards it, and the creature stretched an arm to it and took the child's hand.

Edda undid her jacket, lifted her shirt and nursed her son. One of the children lay on the ground beside her, its head in her lap. She hesitated, and then she gently stroked its cool shoulders. The child turned its head, sighing, and patted her leg as it snuggled closer. It sang to her. She wiped her nose on her sleeve, licked her lips. The rock wall embraced her, shifting to support her back. The song ran through the walls and into her. The old creature shuffled towards them, and Edda saw how it touched the children as it passed: a loving caress for each one. She saw how they leaned into it, heard the song grow happier.

"We all love you," she said to them. She looked at her son. His eyes were open. "Don't forget me," she told him.

When she walked out into the sunshine, she was empty and numb. Somebody took her by the shoulders to lead her away, down the hill and home again. She'd left the blankets behind, all except the flannel that had been wrapped around his small body. Edda held that in her hands, and from time to time, she lifted it to her face and inhaled the sweet, dusty smell of her boy.

— BLACKTHORN —
B. Morris Allen

The mărțișor (pronounced roughly 'mart-sea-shore') is a symbol of spring. In Moldova (between Romania and Ukraine), friends give each other a mărțișor on the first day of March. It's not a valentine—there's no romantic element— and the exchange doesn't have to be bilateral. It's just a gift to a true friend. The mărțișor can be hand-made (like this one) or purchased. The recipient wears the mărțișor throughout March—pinned to a lapel, perhaps. On the last day of March, you tie each mărțișor you received to the branch of a tree.

Romania and Bulgaria each have variants of this tradition (in Bulgaria, it's called a мартеница), and there are dozens of origin stories. The story on the other side is the one told in the village of Tomai in western Moldova, just by the Romanian border.

The story of the mărțișor
There was a time like no time; if it hadn't happened, we wouldn't tell about it. One year, on the first day of March, the beautiful Spring came to the edge of the forest. There, in a clearing under a blackthorn bush, she saw a bright white snowdrop. Naturally kind, Spring decided to help the little flower, and she started to move away the snow and break some of the thorny branches. Winter, seeing this, was angry and called the wind and cold to destroy the flower. The snowdrop immediately froze. Spring tried to warm the flower by covering it with her hands, but she cut her finger on a thorn. A drop of blood spilled from the wound and trickled onto the snowdrop. The warm blood revived the flower, defeating Winter. The colors of the mărțișor symbolize the snowdrop and the blood of Spring.

———◖●◗———

There is a black thorn bush up on the hill above the village, where the slope is too steep to farm, and too bare for deer. The branches of the bush are splintered and thin, its core twisted and rough. The bush crouches in a rocky clearing at the edge of the forest, naked to the wind and sun, its roots clinging to cold stone and the little bit of soil it has gathered. The bush has been cut, burned, buried in filth, but it clings to life, such as it is. The locals call it Winter's Bush, and revile it for having made Spring bleed.

It was a long time ago, in the village of Tomai, in Moldova, back when it was Bessarabia, or maybe even before that, when it was no country at all, just a region between the Danube, the Dniester, and the Black Sea. A time when the land didn't belong to anyone in particular.

In those days, the seasons were more free than the rigid periods we think of now. Summer wandered the land, a pale thin man with golden hair, and the air was warm and dry wherever he went. When Autumn came in her rich dress of brown or red or orange, the berries ripened, and the trees dropped their bright leaves out of respect. Spring... it was Spring that everyone loved. A plump brown girl dressed in the blue of the sky laced with the thin silver of distant clouds. Wherever she passed, the land shone green with the grass that reached up to cushion her feet. The trees stretched out their leafy hands to brush her hair. Flowers sprang out in all the colors of the rainbow just to light her path with beauty.

Spring sang as she walked, and the breezes stirred shrubs to accompany her voice with a rustling, whispered melody. Birds warbled their happiness, and squirrels chattered a chorus of delight. Spring smiled, and the world smiled back, for she loved it, and it loved her. Everyone was happy when Spring was near. Except for Winter.

Winter was a strong and handsome man, dressed all in white, from cloak to belt to boots. He smiled and danced as he walked, and touched the land with the lightest of touches. All agreed that he was the most beautiful of all the seasons, pure and clean and so pretty that it gave you chills just to look at him. Yet, much as they admired him, people couldn't wait for him to leave. They welcomed him and threw festivals when he came, but if he stayed for long, they grew dark and distant. For with Winter came snow and cold and ice, and while those are beautiful, some kinds of beauty are hard to bear.

Over the years, Winter became sad, for he loved the land and the people, and he longed for them to love him back. He spent hours designing snowflakes one by one—each a miniature work of art, perfect but ephemeral. He taught the frost to spread in fancy patterns across roofs and walls and glass. He froze streams into playgrounds, and waterfalls into sculpture. The people oohed and aahed and praised him, but then they went back into their warm homes, and didn't invite him in. When he had gone and another season wandered by, his art melted, and the ground warmed, and the people came out to rejoice. All the seasons had this warming effect, yet the people loved Spring the most, so that when Winter eventually lost his patience, it was Spring he was angry with. He determined to ask her why she destroyed his work, and why the people loved her but hated him.

The world is large, and the seasons didn't often meet. This was before the calendar was quite so rigid, and sometimes Summer would follow Spring, or Fall would follow Winter, depending on how they happened to wander. So when Winter went in search of Spring, he didn't quite know where to look. Spring, for her part, knew nothing of his search, and wandered the land as the whim took her. As he searched longer and longer, Winter nurtured his hurt into a cold fury, so that he walked in a blizzard of wind and snow and hail, and the people avoided him even more than before.

The village of Tomai was large, for a village, with a population of over a thousand men and women. It lay in a valley with a small stream at its heart, the simple houses held in by low hills crested by trees. High on the western hill, just below the forest, stood a lonely thorn bush. It grew on ground thick with stones, the remnants of a boulder shattered by years of cold and heat. The soil was thin, the rocks jagged, and little grew.

The thorn bush did what it could. It spread its roots wide, and wrapped them around fragments of rock. It stretched its spindly branches to the sky, or spread them in a little fan to catch some leaves when Fall passed near and the wind was in its favor. Each leaf became a little bit of soil to cover its roots. The trees of the forest tried to send the leaves toward the bush, and little animals sometimes carried bits and pieces of forest debris to it. They felt sorry for the bush, because they all agreed that it was ugly. Where other bushes grew straight and tall, waving their leaves or needles like flags, or painting themselves with flowers, the thorn bush was black and gnarled and rough, its flowers small and grey and sparse. And it was covered with thorns.

The bush wanted to be smooth and glossy, broad and green and inviting. But no matter how hard it tried to grow straight, its little trunk twisted round and round, and its fragile branches snapped and cracked in the wind. Where it tried to produce bright flowers and lush leaves, it mostly grew thorns—long, sharp weapons of dull black. The bush strove for peace and plenty, but it was built for war and dearth.

The bush did best when Summer was nearby, for its sparse foliage and long thorns let it thrive when water was scarce. Yet the heat only accentuated its difference from the rest, and made it sad. While the bush liked Summer well enough, what it really loved was Spring. When the forest came to life, even the little bush felt it might be able to grow straight and green like the other plants. But no matter how it tried, it grew only longer, sharper spikes, until the birds stopped landing, and even the squirrels kept their distance. Nothing grew around the bush, and though it gradually accepted its lot, it was lonely.

One day, a strange bird came by, and, knowing no better, came to land on the thorn bush. The bush was happy for company, and, with all its might, twisted its thin branches so that all the thorns pointed down. It hurt, and it felt its fibers tearing, but with a quiver in its voice, it said to the bird, "Welcome! Make yourself comfortable and tell me the news." The thorn bush thought that if only it had some news, it might be able to attract others into conversation, and maybe friendship.

The bird was a starling, and a little rude, for he was far from home and from his flock, which made him nervous. "Your branches are thin and shaky, bush, but I thank you for your welcome, whatever its shape. I am tired, for a wind blew me off course while I was collecting seeds. Now I must get my harvest back home to my children, for the wind was cold and hard, and Winter is on his way."

This made the bush unhappy, for all the world knew by now that Winter sought Spring, and that he was angry. "You must warn Spring," the bush said. "She was here not long ago, just over those hills." It pointed one small branch to the east, and when it unfurled, its thorns glinted cruelly in the evening light.

"Thank you," said the bird nervously. "For your kindness I will give you one of my seeds, but for your thorns I will leave you now and go on my way." So saying, he spilled one small seed from his beak, and fluttered away to the east.

The bush was sorry and hurt that the bird had been afraid, but it valued the news, and told everyone that would listen "Winter is coming. Grow your warmest fur and bark and prepare. Winter is coming." Most of all, the bush treasured the bird's little gift. With one of its thorns, it dug a little hole for the seed, and swept over it the best loam it could gather. Since winter was coming, it circled its branches round and round and made a little mound over the soil to keep off the snow, and to ward off the wind. It turned the thorns out so that whatever grew would not be harmed. The twisting hurt its branches, but the bush bore it quietly, and held them in place until they grew together into a dark, jagged shield.

As Winter passed through the lands, he brought with him the storm of ice and cold that had become his habit. The snow fell thick and deep before him and behind, covering the land with a shining carpet of smooth, soft white. He asked everywhere for Spring, but no one answered him back, and he went on his way alone and angry. When he came at last to the village of Tomai and to the forest on the hill, he stopped, and spotting the thorn bush just above the snow, said to it, "Little bush, I see you are like me—sharp and beautiful and disregarded. Tell me, have you seen Spring? I would speak with her."

The bush might have blushed, if it could, for no one had ever called it beautiful, and Winter was handsome indeed. But it was sad that even Winter, who gave it compliments, also saw the thorns. Even worse, the bush was ashamed that this cruel and beautiful season saw its loneliness so clearly. It was proud and sad at once, but it loved Spring more than it loved Winter, and it gave no answer.

Winter grew angry that even this lowly, spiky bush thought itself too good to speak to him. He stormed away, leaving behind a thick crust of snow and ice that covered the bush completely. Under the snow, the bush's little mound of twisted, painful branches held against the snow, and warmth of its roots kept the patch of ground from freezing. Beneath the soil, the tiny seed began slowly to grow, sending out shoots and roots of its own to probe the dark ground.

It happened that Spring came back through the village soon after. The snow melted before her, the birds sang, and the plants grew green. When she neared the forest, she saw the thorn bush, still strewn with snow. As she approached, the little bush shook itself so as to look its best, but the snow it shook off it tried to gather around its thorny mound, so that the little seed would have plenty to drink in warmer weather. As it did, the seed itself sent up its tallest shoot, and with it a little white flower, for the seed was a snowdrop—one of the flowers that reacts the fastest to the approach of Spring.

When Spring saw the little flower behind the shield of thorns, she felt sorry for it, for it looked as if it were trapped. She reached in to clear away the snow and give the snowdrop room to grow. Fearing to hurt her, the thorn bush twisted its thorns even further, so that they faced not toward the snowdrop, nor toward Spring, but outward and inward, in a rosette that pierced the bush's own branches through and through. From their wounds, they dripped sweet moisture down upon the flower. The bush strained its fibers to the utmost to keep from harming flower or season, though the pain grew to torment and then to agony.

Meantime, Winter had not gone far. He had stopped in the next valley over to sit sullenly and sulk. "Even a thorn bush," he said, "disdains me," and thought that he should have covered it with ice as well as snow. Or instead of snow—just a thin coating of ice along all of its branches and thorns. It would make a striking pattern, for the bush was graceful in its own desolate, poignant way. It had been so determined, on ground so bleak, so forlorn and alone, despite its graceful, delicate thorns.

At last, Winter said to himself, "If even the thorn bush that no one loves, and that grows in such rough terrain, can find the heart to love Spring, can I do less?" If everyone loved Spring, but did not love him the same way, that was perhaps not her fault. Perhaps it was simply the result of her nature, just as his was to be quiet and lonely. He felt better for letting go of his anger, but he also felt a little ashamed of himself and his actions. He realized, too, that he had been cruel to the thorn bush, a creature as lonely as himself, and he turned slowly back to apologize. He thought to layer it with a pattern in his thinnest, finest frost—a small tribute to the bush's unusual beauty. As he thought this, the blizzard around him gradually calmed, until he walked in a paradise of white and silver.

He walked back through the forest, branches thick with snow, and he smiled at their beauty as he went. As he drew closer to the top of the hill, he saw icicles developing as the snow slowly melted with Spring's proximity, and refroze with his. He stopped to admire them. Together, he realized, he and Spring could create a beauty different than either could create alone.

When Winter at last came down to the edge of the forest, he saw Spring kneeling before the thorn bush, and he rushed forward to speak to to apologize for his anger and jealousy. But as he neared, he saw her shoveling aside the snow he had created, and that would help the bush survive drier times. Seeing this, he grew angry again, and the cold wind chilled the flower's fragile new stem so that it began to droop.

"What are you doing?" he cried.

"I am saving this flower," Spring said without looking up. She took hold of the thorny rosette that had shielded the snowdrop, and broke it apart into sharp segments. The thorn bush jerked as Spring broke its spindly branches, and one of its thorns pricked her finger.

"You are hurting this bush," cried Winter, for he loved it now as a kindred spirit.

Blood from Spring's finger slowly dripped onto the snowdrop, streaking its wintry white with patches of scarlet. It's warmth thawed the flower a little, and it turned toward the bush for comfort. As she watched, Spring saw the bush do its limited best to form a shelter with the little stubs of its branches. She turned to Winter, and saw his anger and his pain and his love for the little bush.

"I am ashamed," she said. He saw the sorrow in her eyes, and took her hand to wash it with clean snow. When the bleeding stopped, he drew her away to the hilltop, and they talked long and deeply.

The villagers still avoid Winter, but he still decorates the land for them. People say that Spring defeats Winter, but in fact, the two seasons are the closest of friends, and they arrange to meet every year to celebrate their love for each other and the land. Their natures are so different that they cannot be together long, but when they are, they make a special kind of art. Each year Spring brings strength to the thorn bushes to show Winter that she remembers how they met, and Winter gives Spring snowdrops to show that he knows how deeply she cares for even the smallest life.

In Tomai, the villagers wear little red and white pins to honor Spring's rescue of the flower. They don't know the full story, and still blame the thorn bush for harming Spring. The thorn bush bears the abuse silently, and the thorns protect it from serious violence. Often, there are snowdrops nearby, and the children ask their parents to let the bush be. When the villagers are gone, the bush relaxes and unwinds its branches, and prepares the snowdrops' beds for Spring's next visit. For, misunderstood as they may be, the soft flower and the spiny bush are the closest of friends, and you will often see them together at the edge of the forest, twined together under a blanket of snow.

— THE FORGETTING FIELD —
Caroline Ratajski

In the Regency and Victorian Eras, flowers were assigned meanings, which could turn a bouquet into an elaborate message. Many flowers were assigned multiple and sometimes contradictory meanings, so if you were trying to communicate with a lover through the language of flowers, you had best hope that you were both consulting the same flower dictionary. The more common flowers were defined in fairly standard terms. For example, a red rose meant romantic love, as it still does today, while the mimosa represented chastity because its leaves close at night and when touched.

Prior to the Victorian Era, floriography was used in art, literature, and common culture all around the world. In the 1600's, Turkish people used flowers to convey meaning much like the Victorians did two centuries later. The Bible makes frequent use of flower symbolism. In Hamlet, by William Shakespeare, Ophelia famously recites flower meanings: "Here's rosemary, that's for remembrance. Pray you, love, remember. And there's pansies, that's for thoughts."

In 1818, Louisa Cortambert (using the pen name Madame Charlotte de la Tour) wrote Le Languge de Fleurs, the first flower dictionary, which kicked off the Victorian craze. Artists made use of the symbolism of flowers to enhance their art, and lovers made use of it to declare their feelings.

In this story by Caroline Ratajski, flowers have meanings, and hungers, and desires that humans cannot begin to imagine. These flowers have made their own dictionary.

———— ❦ ————

Chrysanthemum, for loss.

We flowers eat what we are hungry for.

The two-leg stoops, takes a knife to the blossom base. The blade is dull and it tears rather than slices, but we have no hole for screaming.

This one's guilt comes to us when it presses our childmaker to its mouth. It had pollinated with more than one, and loss followed. We have never understood the two-leg fixation on pollination.

But this flower does not hunger for lost love. We have eaten much of the darker feelings, the ones that turn inward and slice with sharper stone than this two-leg carried. It took a petal between its teeth and tears it from us, disappearing it into the body.

And with a small taste, we remember, and for one last time, it remembers too. More than remembers. It relives.

We see the memory it wants gone almost immediately. It is slightly aged and sitting just at the top, rubbed smooth like a stone in the river. It has reviewed the memory often. But that is not what we are hungry for.

Too long we have gorged ourselves on the two-legs' bitterness, taking their pain into this field, our act of mercy. We fed so fully it has faded us. Our blossoms are not so vibrant as they once were, purple and red faded to grey and brown. Other animals do not come to us anymore, and we wither.

This one has a sadness for another two-leg, but also a great happiness, buried beneath. We feed on that instead, pulling this one through the happiness of a bright spring day when it was fresh and new and the world was full of possibility. Laughter and long hair and cool water on bare toes. It asked for forever and the other agreed, and in that bright day forever was real.

And when we are finished, the memory has vanished.

Now all the two-leg has is a notion that it once had happiness, but the light inside is gone. It cries out, one hand clutching the flower to its chest, the other digging fingers into the dirt and wrapping them around cool damp roots. Sharp grit digs under its nails, tearing at the soft flesh of its hand, leaking its red water against our roots.

We drink, the warm iron as sweet to us as honeysuckle to the two-legs.

It eats another petal, and we feed more on its past joy.

It is so desperate to forget the pain it eats another petal, and another, until the flower is gone, and all that remains is its grief.

Then it sinks into us and wraps its not-legs around us, and it weeps.

Eventually, we will devour this one's flesh as well.

Harebell, for grief.

The first to eat did not know what we could do. We did not know it ourselves. It stumbled into us, weeping, broken, mad with hunger, and it ate of us for the simple sake of having nothing else.

Its pain was deep, a cavern hollowed out inside. This one had seen too much, lost too much, and its soul curled into itself, a flower wilted from too much dark. Its sorrow came over us like an early frost. Our feeling was one of sympathy, of a desire to console. To take the pain away.

And so we did. We sucked it free from that one like the serpent's venom from flesh. It cried in anguish, a thing we only wished to spare it, and it tore at us. But once we had eaten our fill, that one's pain was gone. All that remained was a memory of pain, like a knotted scar in treeflesh, growing over what had been clawed away.

It pressed the blossoms and leaves to its mouth, holding the soft pink bud to our own buds, but not eating of us. Over and over it did this, water streaming down its face, and finally it whispered, thank you. Thank you.

Although that one's pain hurts us, although some of us had wilted from it, we were able to bring life to what was near-dead, and for that, we were happy.

Because the days were young, and full of chaos. And once, we were forgiving.

Peony, for happiness.

Many seasons passed before the second one came to us. It had a desperation like the first, and we saw the many times it tried to still the red sap under its flesh and return to the earth. Gladly, we took its pain.

Even for the third, we were glad. The fourth. The fifth. This was a good thing we were doing, though our bright blossoms were fading to dull brown and grey. This was good. We were helping.

But we were also growing tired. And the pain these two-legs came to us with was increasingly trivial.

Their grief and anguish fed our soil, until we were nothing but bitter weeds.

Anemone, for lost hope.

The first time we ate of joy felt as if we were bursting through soil into sunlight and rain.

For a time we were careless, and we gorged. We were like the two-legs, taking all and giving nothing. We devoured the joy and peace, leaving only rage and grief behind. The two-legs would tear at us, rip us free from the earth and scatter us to the air. But there were so many of us and so few of them, and their joy kept us alive.

We did not care that all they had was grief. They should find some gratitude, for at least they had something.

Because sometimes we would continue to eat long after happiness was gone. These husks were forever trapped among the flowers, knowing little else but how to breathe. With time they would grow thin and gnarled like dying weeds before dropping to the soil, lying still. They would feed us yet more.

And we were so hungry.

Like the two-legs, we gorged, and like the two-legs, our abused supply began to dwindle. Word of the misery spread, and fewer and fewer came, leaving only the desperate ones, who were so empty of joy that there was little for us to eat.

We tried to stop consuming memories altogether. Return to what we were before the first two-leg came. But that time had long passed and we could no less keep from eating of them than we could keep from turning to the sun and shunning the weak light of the stars. Soil and rain were not enough for us. Perhaps they never were.

Balance was needed. Feed enough to keep ourselves alive, release enough to keep their hope alive. And as we found, even their grief could feed us.

So we carry on, eating enough to survive, drawing strength from these beasts. The other animals have learned to stay far from our field, but not the two-legged ones. We do not care, so long as they continue to return, clutching their small blankets and necklaces and photographs, their metal sticks that fire stones to kill, so long as they come, we can survive.

When we dream, we dream of teeth of our own. We dream of drawing our roots from the earth, of stalking our prey as we have been stalked, of devouring the world until nothing remained but dead grasses.

These can only remain dreams. Because so long as we know moderation, we will survive.

Forget-Me-Not
But we are so very hungry.

— REEF —
K. C. Norton

Coral Reefs are a communal creation, made of many colonies that in turn are made of many individual, yet deeply connected, polyps. In the case of stony corals, thousands of polyps live side by side, nested in cups of calcium carbonite and connected by gastrovascular canals. These canals allow the polyps to exchange nutrients and some cellular material. The polyps in a single coral colony are genetically identical.

Most coral reefs that we enjoy today are about 5000-10,000 years old, although their ancestors began growing around 240 million years ago. Coral have a symbiotic relationship with algae. Each polyp houses a single-celled alga that produces oxygen and other nutrients. In return, the coral provides the algae with other nutrients and with carbon dioxide. There are dozens of other symbiotic relationships on the reef that don't involve the coral so directly. Clown fish, who are immune to anemone stings, hide from predators in the arms of the anemone, and in return the clownfish clean the anemone, provide food, and chase away the anemone's predators. Many species of fish make a living by cleaning the skins of other fish. They get food, and the other fish get relief from parasites and contaminants on their skin. The coral reef is a land in which nothing exists in isolation.

A coral reef is made of many organisms that are connected both physically (by means of connecting tissue) and mechanistically (the coral polyps need each other and the polyps and the algae need each other). For all practical purposes, they are essentially one giant organism. While the animals that make the reef their home are more obviously individual, they are singular in the sense that they all depend on the reef and on each other to live. A reef is a riot of millions of individuals and yet it is also a single, cohesive, interdependent ecosystem.

"The Reef", by K.C. Norton, pictures a reef as having a single mind that can unite and direct all of its inhabitants. Reefs are terribly threatened by global warming, invasive species, and pollutants. They are also threatened by over fishing—usually not from people seeking food but from people seeking to sell fish for private aquariums. Millions of reef dwellers are collected each year for the aquarium trade, and most do not survive. May all reefs be as ferociously defended as the reef in Norton's story.

There is no joy like the knowledge of your own infinity—there is no joy like the joy of coral.

I am my neighbor; we are the pillar and the breakwater and the wrecker's reef. Starfish kiss us, parrotfish eat us, paired seahorses hook their tails around us to avoid being eddied away into loneliness, and we love them. The whole of me loves them.

No single living creature has a heart as unified as the uncountable hearts of a reef.

There is a human girl who comes to visit us. By now we know her as well as the sharks and triggerfish. We call her Nei, because unlike coral, humans think of themselves as individual creatures.

She has long limbs that flash bream-brown in the filtered light. Sometimes her skin is all she wears. She fills her lungs with air and plugs her nostrils and dives down from her world to ours, where her quick clever fingers explore us until she finds what she is looking for. Usually she is after pearls. Perhaps it is their shine, or their layers, or their paradox—we don't know what she likes about them. When she is finished, she darts for the surface, chasing her own bubbles of used-up air.

Nei is not the only diver, though there are fewer these days. But she is our favorite, and so from time to time we yield up secret gifts for her: we coax her alongside an eagle ray, we lure the whale shark to her and the great white away. Once, we give her a tiny fraction of our own body, a shiny black shard of ourself.

The next time she appears, that part of us hangs around her neck from a goat-hide thong. We emit our own used-up bubbles in pleasure. We like to see ourselves there, our dark skin against her dark skin, although the part of us that hangs there has gone numb and dead.

In early summer, the sea becomes warm and gentle—we trust summer, before the storms roll in, uprooting trees and washing inland sand out through the rivers. Summer is the calm time between cold and chaos.

Or it should be.

This summer, the swells bring something new: not the carcasses of whales, or sharks on their parade across the Atlantic. This summer, the sea brings unfamiliar boats.

They are small boats, with small engines that cut the waves into slices. Nei stands along the shoreline to watch them come in. Like us, Nei is unused to polished boats with fresh paint and foreign names. She seems nervous, but she speaks to the boaters in a confident jumble of human words. We cannot tell what they want. On dry land, they are too far away to hear.

For a few days, the boaters motor through the gardens; they skim at us with nets, tearing up our weeds, netting fish that they do not toss back. But they do not seem happy.

We do not give them anything. We hide our gifts.

On the fourth day, it rains, and the boats leave us be. But on the fifth day that are back, and this time they bring Nei.

We know why they bring her: her limbs are tough, strong as shark fins, and she knows us almost as well as we know ourself. We have shown her our secrets. She wears the evidence about her neck.

When she dives from one of the new boats, we greet her reluctantly. She wears one of the strangers' black rubber suits and in it she does not look like Nei at all. We feel hesitation, distrust, and it is not a familiar feeling. She is reluctant, too. She dives a few times, never touching, only looking. She is a tourist here today, not our guest.

But every time she returns, our resolve weakens. This is Nei. Our Nei. We love her. We have known her since she was small, since the first time she visited. Air and sunlight linger in her hair and skin, as they always have—and when she surfaces, the sea salt clings to her fingernails and eyelashes. We do not want to hate her.

We love her.

When she finds a seahorse, she cries out with surprise, a wordless burst of bubbles. We know she loves them, because she has always been delighted at their alien bodies, their delicate proportions.

This time, she pinches the seahorse between her fingers and bobs to the surface. She knows this is not right. We do not understand; the seahorse does not understand. He is distressed to be taken from his mate. He is afraid of air and the faraway blue of the sky.

Nei shows the boaters her prize—they shout and clap their hands and pet her hair. They are happy. Nei is not sure whether to be happy with them.

Only minutes later, the first diver drops in.

Seahorses mate for life. They are bound together by an unseen thread. When one is taken, his mate searches for him until he is found or given up for dead. A seahorse's heart is not too small to break.

We are bound to our fellows by proximity. By our life force. We need every polyp; we are bound by every polyp; we are every polyp. We do not suffer when we are apart.

We simply die.

Cyanide spray, the strangers tell Nei, is only meant to stun. The divers, twelve altogether, point their spray bottles between my layers, targeting the smallest and most brilliant fish: purple grammas and gradated gobies, spiny puffers and striped clowns, angels and triggerfish and seahorses. Everything is hauled up to the boats in little nets and sorted. The plain fish, mackerel and butterfish and scowling john dories, are dumped back overboard. They sink dully through the water, unable to swim; the sea moves them in little eddies as they drift to the sea bed.

Whole sections of us, whole colonies, go silent, poisoned by the spray. Those of us on the edges of ruin reach out only to find neighborhoods gone necrotic.

Individuals—seahorses and girls—know how to hurt from loss. Nei curls over the side of the boat, her eyes wet with tears like seawater. One small hand clasps the branch of me that she wears. Her fingers polish the fragment smooth as sea glass. But one mind, one heart, cannot feel grief like the grief of coral.

Half of the fish on the boat are coming to, confused and groggy. The other half are already dead.

There was not always a reef here.

Once, aeons ago, there was only stone. The world was too young for sand then. There was no beach as it is now, only dead rock sloping into lifeless sea.

And then: we came.

We came in ones and twos, then clusters, then clouds. We floated and explored and finally settled: staghorn, brain, blue maomao and black cabbage, fire coral and elephant ear. One by one, branch upon branch, we built ourselves into the reef.

When something is dead, is cannot be revived. We know that. The fish that sift down to the bottom and lie there, glass-eyed, are lost. They mean nothing to the boaters.

But they mean something to Nei.

Love is not stagnant. It moves, like the arms of an anemone, and it grasp. It clings. We love Nei, and she loves the reef. Nei is not a polyp, is not a fish, is not at home in water.

Nei's eyes seek out the tanks of wriggling fish. Those that have survived dart back and forth behind the glass, their colors overlapping.

Nei is not a polyp, but she is part of the reef. She tucks the necklace into her damp shirt and rises on unsteady legs.

While Nei paces on the boat, we are taking our own action: subtle variations in current carry Irukandji and box jellies toward the divers; scorpionfish and blue ringed octopuses creep out from our cracks and crevices; stingrays shake the sand off their circular bodies; cone snails begin their slow suction-cup march toward the intruders. We may be living stone, but we have a hundred weapons at our disposal. Strike at us with poison, and we will strike back in kind.

Nei struggles with the weight of the glass tanks. She pours the first one over the side; the fish spill back into my realm like living jewels. One of the boaters cries out at the sound, grabbing at her, threatening her health. Her life.

She dodges, clutching at the second tank. The boater strikes at her with his fist—he's got strong arms. Nei lifts the tank to tilt it, spilling some of the fish into the deck. When she sees the seahorses and clownfish wriggling there against the boat's glass bottom, she chokes.

The boater clutches at her. His fingers leave bruises on her arms. But Nei is stronger than she seems, and slipperier than an eel. She tears herself out of his grasp and tilts her body in the old, familiar arc of the dive, takes a deep breath, and plunges.

The boater moves to follow her—but lionfish fins cut the water to ribbons, and the translucent white-blue bodies of jellyfish bar his way. He slips in the spilled tank water, clinging to the boat for dear life.

Through the glass bottom, he watches Nei descend. A dozen fatal species part before her, granting her safe passage as she dives.

Eleven divers return to the boats, many of them stung and bitten, their hands too swollen to hold their spray bottles. They wait for the twelfth as long as they dare; in the end, so many of them need care that they feel it more urgent to leave than to stay.

When the sun sets and gibbous moon hangs above the ocean like a flying fish, Nei returns to shore. Her skin is raw and rashy from salt, but she is otherwise unharmed.

The surviving boaters are all in hospitals or sleeping, bitten and stung, made weak. They are not there to see Nei drain the rest of the tanks into the surf, praying for fish who she knows are unlikely to survive.

She laces the boats' fuel tanks with coarse-grain sea salt and dead coral dust.

When this is done, she comes out to the ocean's edge, staring out across the black waves. There are people who only know the ocean from that angle, from the froth and boil of water.

Her fingers find her necklace. She knows better.

Nothing is certain on the reef. Storms batter ancient formations to pulp in half a day. Crown-of-thorns starfish digest us alive. A warm winter or a cold summer can leave us blanched and sickly.

But there are dangers everywhere.

And no single living creature has a heart as unified as the uncountable hearts of a reef. even when one of those hearts beats in a skinny human body on dry land.

— OUROBOROS IN ORBIT —
J. Daniel Batt

The image of the Ouroboros, the snake that eats its own tail, appears across many mythologies. While the details differ across mythologies and cultures, the symbol tends to represents eternity, the joining of opposites, and resurrection.

In Western mythology, the Ouroboros first appeared in a collection of Egyptian writing known as The Enigmatic Book of the Underworld, which was found in the tomb of Tutankhamen. In this text, the serpents represent the beginning and end of time. In ancient Greece, Plato described the Ouroboros as the first being in the universe: a completely self-sufficient creature.

The Gnostics took the image of a snake up a notch, by picturing the sun as a disc surrounded by a dragon with its tail in its mouth. In Norse mythology, Jorgamunder is a giant serpent, the progeny of Loki and Angrboda. Once Jorgamunder grew large enough to encircle the earth, he earned the name Midgard Serpent. He bites his own tail, and when he lets go, the world will end. In parts of South America, indigenous people believe that the world is a disc with water at the edges, and that a giant anaconda circles these waters. Ouroboros imagery is seen in Aztec and Mayan art, Yogic traditions, and Gnosticism. It's also found in nature. The armadillo girdled lizard protects itself by putting its tail into its mouth and rolling into a ball when threatened.

The Ouroboros has taken on new life in the modern era of chemistry. August Kekule used Ouroboros imagery to figure out the structure of Benzene. He dozed off while working and dreamed that atoms were forming twisting rows, like snakes. One of these atom snakes circled around and bit its own tail. Kekule woke up and used this image as the basis for his hypothesis regarding Benzene's structure.

The disparity first arose as they slipped into the elliptical of the solar system. All sensors were aimed at the oxygen-thick globe. There were no rings around this planet, and yet, as they viewed it from the safety of the asteroid belt, a shimmering silver belt encircled Earth. It defied all attempts at explanation. They could see it through their telescopes, but every other sensor confirmed the initial projection that this was an unguarded world.

So, they moved the armada, each ship several miles long and decorated with cascading cannons. Only when they crossed into Mars orbit did they see it fully. Even then, they did not understand. The silver ribbon writhed, a glimmer of green racing across its back.

The cluster of ships were within Mars' wake when they witnessed the serpent unwrap itself from around the Earth. Gliding between planet and moon, it slung its head to face the fleet, its eyes shining like small suns.

Aboard a hundred vessels armed for conquest, soldiers and strategists roared in alarm. The invaders had braved the dark quiet between stars to find this world. Earth had been chosen for its simple societies and lush world. Easy to win. Easy to hold. But the gigantic creature that was uncoiling itself was an unknown. Their robotic scouts, sent over decades before to monitor every pulse of the planet, had alerted them of no such thing. The analysts, under the shouts of their commanders, wrestled to reconcile what their eyes saw against what their data had promised.

With eyes not born of the soil of Earth, the invaders saw the serpent slink from its sleep and pass through the expanse of space to where the fleet stood. If anything was alien, this was alien. Hundreds of worlds had fallen to them. They had conquered a forgotten number of planets, from infant world with barbaric scavengers burrowing across their surfaces to civilizations exploring their planetary neighbors to empires with system-wide defenses. Yet, there had been nothing like this. A world guarded by a spirit. A world whose soul wrapped around itself in wait.

Named Jormungandr by the shivering, teeth-chattering berserkers, the serpent had nursed on the blood and milk of trickster gods. The dead grew it. It fed until it looked at planets and planetoids as peers. Invisible to the eyes of those born under its guard, it was still seen by the dreamers and inward-looking visionaries of the varied civilizations to skitter across Earth's surface. The pyramid-makers knew it and named it Ouroboros, the tail-devouring snake. The philosophers and the gnostics carved its image into stone. The forgotten son held its image up in the desert and healed his people.

Its scales glittered green and red, the galaxy's stars dancing disturbed through its skulking form. The serpent drifted ever outwards. Even if their sensors could not discern it, they still feared it. Ouroboros' dancing bright eyes first opened in the dawn state of

Earth. Its eyes blazed with every hope and dread of humanity. The serpent set its gaze on the largest of the ships.

From the deck of that capitol ship, his own heart racing in fear, the commander directed his squadrons apart to circle the creature. And the serpent waited. And pulsed. A spirit of a world, of an entire species, brushed against the cold minds of the invaders, minds of metal and engines, minds that had explored nebulae but never imagined the soul.

Maybe it was out of that spark of fear, maybe out of restlessness, but one of the ships, far from the capitol ship, launched its volley of concussive cannons.

The beast swung its head around. It struck swiftly, snapping far and slicing through the squadrons. Every ship responded with their entire salvos. But it was useless. The serpent was every where at once and at once, it was every serpent. At once an anaconda, thick and consuming. And to another ship, the cobra, furled back and striking with precision to cripple and then, to kill. To another ship, it was the python, clutching and choking until the ironed vessel split in two, spilling its crew like blood into space. The serpent launched itself against those arrayed around it.

As the bodies of millions of would-be conquerors floated into the empty, Ouroboros returned to its orbit, taking its tail up again between its fangs, slowly closing its continent-sized eyelids to sleep. It rested, circling the globe, waiting for the next threat to come from the stars.

And its future? As its humans reach into space, will it grow with them? As humanity colonizes its neighbors, will the serpent twist around the system, basking in the light of the Sun? As we move through this galaxy, will the serpent grow, will the soul of Earth travel with us?

Or will it still rest, spinning slowly, around a forgotten planet? Will it wait for us to remember our soul? To remember our serpent soul?

— IN THE WATER, UNDERNEATH —
Damien Angelica Walters

Holland Island is a low island in the Chesapeake Bay. It's basically a glorified mud pie, made of silt and clay instead of rock. The island was named for one of its first European residents, Daniel Holland, who settled there in the 1600's. There was a fishing boom in the late 1800's, and Holland Island became a busy place. Over 360 people lived on Holland Island in the early 1900's. By 1920, erosion was already taking a major toll on the island. Most of those islanders moved on, taking everything with them, even their houses. One house, which was built in 1888, remained through the years, as the sea came up closer and closer to its threshold.

Why are the Chesapeake Islands sinking? One reason is basic geology. The islands were created by Ice Age glaciers, which pushed up bulges of land. Over thousands of year, those bulges have been settling. Another reason is climate change. Ocean levels are rising, which means the death of small islands. Holland Island hasn't just sunk—it has eroded, because it's made of unstable materials.

The house became an obsession for Stephen White, a retired minister. He formed a non-profit organization to try to save the house and spent thousands of dollars of his own on the project. He tried to save it with rocks, with sandbags, with timbers, and by sinking a barge offshore to use as a seawall. The wind and waves destroyed them or ignored them. White fought the sea for fifteen years, but in 2010 the sea won. The house collapsed and now is completely underwater.

What remains of the island is marshy and during high tide the island completely disappears. During low tide, it's a useful resting spot for seabirds. For Stephen White, it's a reminder of failure. Along with the house, Holland Island was home to a graveyard. White was deeply moved by the message on a young girl's grave. "It said, 'Forget me not, is all I ask'," White said. "And I didn't. I still haven't."

———◄●►———

Touching the silt of my shore, he whispers, You are mine.

He wants me to believe that I have always belonged to him, but once I was my own. Holland Island, I say to myself. I say it to remember, I say it so I don't forget I had a history, had people who made of me their home. They loved, slept, dreamt, fished, lived.

And they left me because of him.

It would be easier for me to give in, to forget the laughter of children, to forget the warmth of footprints, the slide of a boat returning to my coast, but I can't forget the way the empty houses fell one by one. When the last finally tumbled to the ground, the boards creaking and crying out against the destruction, I did what I could. I opened myself, made a womb of silt and clay, and pulled it in. A desperate hiding place. I cradled it with lies: everything would be all right, they would come back, they would take care of us.

But there is no they anymore. There is only him.

He tongued open my center, slipped inside, swallowed the wood, the mortar, the walls. Slowly, so slowly, as if I wouldn't notice, but I heard him taking his meal, the sound like mirthless laughter, like cruelty.

Alone now, I think madness would be preferable. Then I could give of myself freely, not knowing or caring what I was losing.

I've beseeched the moon, begging her for respite against his tides, but she answers with nothing but the pale of her light. A silent betrayal, yet I should not be surprised, for she was ever his willing accomplice.

You are mine, he says, as he crashes against me. You have always been mine.

I know, I hope, he believes he loves me, believes he is returning me to his embrace, but it hurts. He's biting into my soul, gnawing my self into shreds. I struggle to hold what's left, but he is relentless and hungry, always hungry.

He devours me bit by bit. Undoing. Unmaking. With gentle susurrations and rage's force. For a long time, I told myself he was remaking me into another shape. I don't believe it anymore, for if he is taking my pieces to make another whole, that new creation is insensate and holds nothing of me inside.

Mine.

Once he was life and health, not diminution and gluttony; once he listened to the shape of my shore. I try to remember that he did not ask to play this part, only accepted his role. But when he has reduced me so, it's hard to believe such a thing is or was ever true.

I hate him.

By day I have the company of birds—terns, herons, pelicans—but every year, they are fewer in number. They chatter and squabble amongst themselves but ignore me when I speak to them. They care naught of my plight and will notice my passing as but a small annoyance and when I'm gone, they will seek a new place to roost. Still, their presence is a small comfort and better than solitude.

When I'm gone, will anyone search for me? Will anyone remember?

He brushes against me, retreats, brushes again. Teasing and taunting beneath the heat of a sun that brings no solace.

My lover, my enemy.

Should I hate the fishermen for abandoning me, for taking their boats, their children, and their wives away to land strong enough to withstand his brutality? They called him the Bay, the Chesapeake— they call him that still—but he cared little for their names.

When they first realized what he was capable of, what power he held, they tried to keep him back with walls of stone. He laughed at their efforts. Was he angry because they hooked his fish, dredged his oysters? He welcomed them once. I know he did. Is his nature so capricious? I've asked him time and time again, but he refuses to answer.

One afternoon, he caught a child unaware. I tried to hold her feet within me, to anchor her in place, but I wasn't strong enough to keep her safe. He pulled her into his depths too fast for anyone to do anything but scream.

They loved him, they respected him, and he repaid them by destroying their homes and their children.

No, I cannot blame them. The memory of their touch is the only thing that gives me the will to fight.

For fight I do. I will not release my name, for that is what he wants. He wants me to forget who I am, to become only a footnote in his existence, and I will not.

I will not.

Am I a fool to think my name something worth remembering, something worth holding onto? To want to stay here instead of surrendering and becoming merely something that was?

But I'm afraid. I'm afraid I'm not strong enough. I'm afraid one day there won't be enough of me left, and then, will my ghost join that of the little girl he took? Will he even allow a ghost of me to remain?

I think not.

He is far larger than I ever was, and far stronger. His strength is brute, callous; my heart is fragile and filled with too much fear. He demands submission, and I yield because I have no choice.

Always mine.

The birds fear him too and take to the sky as he creeps closer. Would that I had wings for escape, would that I had a place to hide. I gather my will. Hold myself together—each bit of clay holding my heartbeat, each grain of silt, my breath.

He comes.

Inch by inch, he takes me. Turns the warmth of my memories to helpless cold. Is this what the little girl felt when she knew she'd never break his surface? This inescapable futility? How long, how hard, did she fight?

He covers me completely, his touch deceptively soft.

Mine, he says as he bites and bites and bites.

Liar, I say. I belong to me.

As always, he laughs. I'm trapped until morning comes to pull him away and he knows it. Not even the glue of bird guano can hold me together against his onslaught. I'm drowning beneath the madness of his embrace, but I fight to hold on. I fight as hard as I can. I say my name as he tears another piece of me free. I say it so I won't forget, but every night, it gets harder and harder to remember.

So when I taste his salt, I choke it down; if this I must bear, then I will hold a small part of him captive and take it with me into the waiting dark.

— SCAB LANDS —
Wendy N. Wagner

The title of Wendy Wagner's story, "Scab Lands" holds multiple meanings. The family in the story bears many generations of emotional wounds that they struggle to conceal. The family is scarred by the legacy of WWII, and the family is shaped by the struggle of surviving in the Scablands of Eastern Washington.

Columbia Basin's "channeled scabland" was created during a series of ice age floods in which ice and water scoured the ground and washed topsoil as far south as the Willamette Valley in Oregon. During one such flood, water was released at a flow greater than ten times the combined flows of all the rivers on earth today. The flood would have moved anywhere from thirty to eighty miles an hour in a wave of water and debris from three hundred to a thousand feet high. The channeled scablands are the result of series of distinct cataclysms, unlike other badlands that are the product of slow but unrelenting erosion. The scablands are largely barren, but bits and pieces of the scablands themselves and much of the surrounding area is suitable for farming.

In 1943 the scablands became a pivotal site in the man-made cataclysms of WWII. The government needed a site close to water and far from towns and roads where plutonium for atomic bombs could be processed. Local farmers and ranchers were forced off their land, as were the Native American tribes who had fished and hunted in the area for centuries. An artificial town sprang up, filled with workers who knew that they were working on something for the war, but who did not know what, specifically, they were working on. In 1945, Hanford Construction Camp was the third largest city in Washington State. Plutonium production continued through the Cold War, ending in 1987. Through the years, radiation was released into the Columbia River, into the air, and into the food chain. It is now the site of the largest cleanup effort in the United States.

The government believed that any harm that came from the construction of atomic weapons could be hidden away, but the toxic wastes of that project continue to escape into the air we breathe, the food we eat, and the water we drink.

—◖●◗—

I came to work on the fences: so I tell my father. Life is hard out here; I often make the three-hour drive from Seattle to help with these kinds of repairs. I stuff my pockets with scissors and a skein of red yarn to mark the places that need patched, and set out to walk the farm's borders with the old man.

Our boots shush through the thin grasses as we move along the squared edge of our land. I find myself leading the way, the reverse of all our childhood hunting and fishing trips: the short girl who had always trudged behind her long-legged brothers and father, worried about dropping her tackle, her rifle, her pole. Now I have to wait for him and his big white dog to catch up. I unroll a length of yarn and re-roll it around my hand, the wool violently crimson against my skin, and wonder how I am going to explain that Alan, his oldest son, my favorite brother, the expert marksman, bull rider, and decorated veteran, killed himself a week ago. Or rather, I wonder how I'm going to explain all that without telling my father that I think it's his fault.

I have tried to find the right things to say, tried to find a way to tell just the facts of my brother's death without digging into the past, but my insides seem filled with a kind of barbed wire that tangles words and holds them tight. I cram the yarn back into my coat pocket and stare out at the gray land, stretching out in low hills like swells on a sorrowing sea. My family's land, going back generations.

But I am the first dirt witch in my family, far as I know—the land responds to my presence. It sends a whisper of wind into my ear and touches my heart with a finger of warmth, the same temperature as a summer-baked hunk of basalt. I'm not imagining it. Back in Seattle, I'm a landscape architect. I can grow things no one else can, because I can feel what the soil and the plants need. That's why I come back here—not for my father. The land, though, is a part of me.

I have to blink away sudden tears. If I didn't care so damn much about my connection to these dusty two hundred acres of channeled scabland, I could be back in my apartment instead of out here with my father. I'm tired of driving across the state just to be half-ignored or snapped at. Dad's not as bad as he was when I was a kid, but I can't love him. I can't even like him.

The ground shivers beneath my feet. My father doesn't seem to notice, but his dog runs up and licks my hand. When I was a girl, the land would sometimes throw me into the air with the exuberance of finally being heard. My brothers couldn't understand why I was so clumsy. They would laugh at me for talking to people they couldn't see and for hearing things they couldn't hear. By the time I was six or seven, I gave up explaining. If it hadn't been for my grandmother, I would have thought I was crazy. People in her family, she had explained, sometimes had gifts. She herself could work magic in the kitchen. Her cakes never failed to rise, and her biscuits were so flaky other women in town sometimes paid her to bake them a batch when their relatives came from out of town.

I don't understand how a soft-hearted woman like my grandmother had a son like my father. I can't even tell him that his bigotry killed his son.

The dirt twitches and gives a sharp buck. I stumble, but catch myself on a boulder. The stone is prickly with dry lichen. The smell of sagebrush is suddenly overpowering.

Then I am gone.

Or rather the winter view is gone. Down where the old farmhouse with the worn-out vinyl siding ought to be is its white-shingled twin. The air smells crisper, tangier, and while the hills are still gray, there are undertones of late autumn brown. I blink hard. I can see my father walking past me, but only faintly. It is as if a thin fog separates us. I put out my hand, but I don't touch my father or his dog. I feel someone else.

I know who it is immediately, even as my hand passes through her shoulder and I hear her inner voice. "Grandma?" I whisper. The fog flickers, and for a second I am back on the ridge with my father. The land's voice, its inhuman whisper of a wind, blows hard in my ear. Whatever is happening, the land wants me to see this. To hear this. It's not the first time it's shared a memory with me, but this feels more powerful than its messages when I was a child. My father vanishes again.

Elsie stood on the little crest of rock running behind the sheep barn. The dust and sagebrush stretched around her forever. It seemed impossible to her that anything lay beyond that immensity, that somewhere, thousands of miles beyond the gray line of the horizon, her own parents were probably sitting on their tidy white porch, watching the Atlantic Ocean slap against the shore. That part of the world was gone to her now, except for the letters that came once a week. When Elsie stood there, she saw only dirt stretching for mile after filthy mile.

She wiped her hands on her apron as she scanned the undulating fields, her lips tightening when she caught the finger of dust pointing up from the west quarter. After noon and he wasn't even halfway through the big wheat field. That tractor must be acting up again.

The apron twisted around her fingers. They owed over five hundred dollars on the tractor, and just thinking about the sum made her stomach hurt. They hadn't yet found the money to put a pump in the well or finish the house, but they did own the newest, most powerful tractor in all of Lincoln County. She couldn't have a washing machine, but they could have a new tractor that seemed to need repairs just as often as an old one.

Elsie smoothed the muslin apron out over her hips. Her fingers hurt. The dry air sucked the moisture out of everything, flesh and earth alike. Her skin split and bled and the tiny wheat plants sagged. About the only things that thrived in this country were hard-headed men and rattlesnakes. She eyed the finger of dust and turned her back on it.

At the bottom of the hill, beyond the short stretch of rocks and abandoned fence posts, beyond the sheep barn, the house and chicken coop sat side by side—the first hardly larger than the second. Dust storms had scoured the milk paint she'd laid on last spring, so that now the gray boards showed through like fingerprints beneath a layer of hand cream. The front door hung open.

Anger boiled behind her eyes even as fear whipped up behind it like a striking snake. That little brat. That stupid little brat. He knew he wasn't supposed to go outside by himself.

I push myself away from Grandma Elsie's angry voice. The virulence in it makes my gut roil. This isn't the grandma who wiped the tears off my face when my dad whipped me for crying over a dead rose bush. This woman is a stranger.

My legs wobble as I take few steps forward, blinking away the past. I don't want to go back into it. I try to focus my eyes on my father. Just ahead of me, he struggles up the rocky hill, his legs bowed into toddler shape again by time and knee injuries. His feet have to take small steps, their shape rounded by the black sneakers secured with Velcro tabs. Once he wore only cowboy boots, shiny ones for going out, worn ones for working.

He's not much like the great big man who raised my brothers and me. That man stood tall and straight and looked down at me with sharp black eyes. Now I am taller than him. I could hurt him without even trying.

This time the land doesn't just knock me down, it collapses beneath me, the stones shifting beneath me to form a shallow cup. Stone grinds into my knees and my palms. The land's voice is a roar in my ear. I can see Elsie's feet in their sturdy brogues beside me. Why does the land want me to see this so badly? Why do I need to know?

I push myself upright, thinking hard. At the time Elsie was looking for her son, the Japanese were still a threat. Planes were still bombing London. One hundred and fifty miles south of Elsie's homestead, engineers were finishing the nuclear production complex that would brew the bulk of the United States's plutonium, and power the bombs that would drop on Hiroshima and Nagasaki. Although her brother had joined the Army, her focus was on her home and her family. And while my grandfather's bad knee had kept him out of the war, that didn't mean Grandma had time to stand around listening to the news. She had her hands full running a household and keeping up with a mischievous boy like my father, who at this age was a good walker and a not-so-good user of the potty. He would refuse to wear shoes until he was eight years old.

The brogues pass by me and then I am in Elsie's head again. I can see and smell and taste the world of seventy years ago.

"Jack?" Grandmother Elsie called. Her voice is pure steel. "Come here this instant!"

But he didn't come. He never did. The anger tightened her eyelids. It had been coming faster these days, ready to leap into her forehead with the steady pulse of some primitive drum. The headache it inspired made her want to retch.

"Jack!"

Even the chickens went quiet.

The pressure on her eyeballs obscured her vision. Memory filled it instead, an image from her last bad wave of temper. Jack's hair, sleeked down around his face in dripping tendrils.

"What have you done this time, Jack?" She rushed forward, stumbling over the hummocks of bunch grass and pungent-smelling sagebrush, and forced herself to slow down. It seemed impossible that a little boy could be so quiet, not when he spent all his waking hours banging and crashing all over the house. His handprints clung tenaciously to every surface, resisting any combination of cleaners she tried.

She didn't want to get angry with him, but at some point he'd become defiant, almost gleefully intractable. Every day he was more of a little savage. If there was a dirty, disgusting, or rude activity, he found it. The more dangerous, the better. If he survived this stage, it would be from sheer luck.

Her eyes jumped to the wooden square of the well cover and the rusty water pump, standing out like a bright orange spoke of life in the gray expanse of yard. The enameled washtub sat placidly beneath it. Around the edges of the well cover, a few sprigs of green clung, bits of vegetation hungry for moisture. No boy.

"Jack?" Her voice rang out sharp and taut in the dry air. She broke into a jog and ran through her list of the boy's favorite playthings and hidey-holes. Maybe the dog house. He loved to play in the dog house.

My father's big white dog pushes her head into my side. I can't quite see her through the haze of the past, but I stroke her fur gratefully. There is something wrong with this memory. Elsie's memory of Jack's face, all wet and dripping—it frightens me. The dog licks my cheek.

I wrap my arm around her neck as the earth buffets me with another blast of the past.

Elsie stooped to peer inside the dog house. A cacophony of barking emerged and the border collies' black and white heads jammed in the doorway. Smelly things. She usually only paid attention to them to feed them. Surprised and pleased, they attacked her with their floppy tongues. One managed to squeeze out the door and rub itself against her leg.

"Where's Jack, dog?"

It pricked up its ears and pointed its nose toward the chicken coop. Elsie's lips tightened. She should have thought of the nesting boxes first. He liked to hold the eggs. Like to "help" gather them. And most of all, he liked pulling the chicken's tail feathers. His roughness could put them off laying a few days, and the family couldn't afford to miss out on those eggs. Who could afford meat when there was rationing?

"Jack Mueller, you get out of that chicken house this second!'

The chicken coop door burst open and he darted out, giggling. With a happy bark, the dog broke into a run. The anger-drumming started in Elsie's head, louder than it had been even the day he'd smeared peanut butter all over the green davenport her parents had sent her as a wedding present.

She remembered Oh god, I don't want to remember this—please stop—the bubbles rising up out of the wash tub, furious at first and then slower, the stink of wet peanut butter filling her nose. She'd had to wash him. Had to. The words repeated again, to the beat of the anger drum: had to. Had to. Had to.

The sight of Jack toddling around the corner of the chicken yard mercifully turns off Elsie's uglier memory. But I can feel her clench her jaw.

No child belonged in the no man's land between the chicken yard and the rock ridge, although it must have looked like paradise to a little boy. Small boulders and weeds vied for their share of sun and soil. During the summer, grasshoppers overran the place. Sometimes a pygmy bunny would race across the ground, headed from one patch of safe browsing to the next, hurrying to outrun the hawks and rattlesnakes. She felt like a bunny herself today. She had been running from one chore to another, stopping to clean up after Jack when she could, and then she'd taken one minute to check on her husband, one short minute, and the boy had gone and made a worse mess.

Thoughts of rabbit holes and black widow spiders and a dozen kinds of snakes (sweet, merciful Jesus, even rattlers) made her break into a run. "Jack, you just stop where you are!"

The black-and-white dog cut across the boy's path, stopping him in his tracks. "Good dog," Elsie called. She hopped over a pile of fence posts and laid her hand on the dog's back. "Good dog."

Beneath her palm, she felt the dog's heat and its steady breathing. It breathed faster than she did, nearly the same speed as a child did. She put her other hand on Jack's shoulder. A layer of grit coated both boy and dog.

The boy twisted away and broke into a trot. He giggled as he ran, an infuriatingly high-pitched chime that brought back the pulsing in her head.

"Come on, now," she snapped, but then the dog growled.

A thin dry rattle sounded in response. The boy stopped in his tracks.

"Jack," Elsie said. "Come here." She could see the snake now, curled on a slab of sandstone not a foot away from Jack.

The boy dropped into a squat and peered down at the snake. The snake rattled a second warning. Snarling, the dog launched itself forward. The snake arced upright, its bronze head flashing. The dog gave a startled yip and pulled its front paw close to its torso.

"Jack!" Elsie shrieked. She launched herself at the boy and grabbed him by the back of the overalls. They tumbled sideways.

The dog snarled again and leaped. It teeth closed just behind the snake's head and crunched down. The snake went limp. The dog dropped it and sat down. Its good front leg trembled, and its injured paw twitched.

"Good dog," Elsie whispered. The dog whimpered. It stretched out on its side and rubbed its muzzle in the dirt. She wasn't sure how much time it had left, but it was in terrible pain. She'd go back to the house for the shotgun, but they'd run out of shot three weeks ago and hadn't had the cash to buy more.

The dog cried out, a sound so human Elsie flinched. She thrust the boy behind the stack of fence posts and snatched one up.

"You poor dumb dog."

It spasmed in the dirt. She gave the post an experimental heft. She'd been killing chickens since she was a kid. Had shot plenty of coyotes. And this, well, this was mercy, wasn't it?

She swung the fencepost as hard as she could. The dog screamed. The fencepost came down again. The dog bucked and twisted. Dirt sprayed in every direction, covered her shoes. It didn't matter. She had to finish what she started.

"Doggy!" Jack screamed.

She slammed the fencepost down and something squelched beneath it. Elsie stumbled backward.

Last week, when she'd pulled Jack out of the washtub, his clothes had squelched like that. His clothes had made noise but he hadn't and that's when she'd realized that she'd done something wrong. His black hair clung to his forehead and ropes of water ran down from his bangs, his dark eyelashes. His lips looked blue. That's when the drumming slowed. Those little blue lips, no longer peanut buttery brown. She'd gotten lucky that time. So lucky.

Elsie dropped the fencepost. Behind her, Jack made a tiny whimper. A pinkish pulp clung to the end of the fencepost.

"He was sick," she explained. "The doggy was hurt real bad." The words sounded hollow in her aching head. "I had to do it, sweetie. I had to."

The boy popped his thumb into his mouth and stared up at her with flat ink-dark eyes.

"Oh, Jack," she whispered. She lifted him out of the sagebrush and gravel and hugged him to her chest. He kept his back straight, not even blinking at her.

The boy gripped her torso stiffly, not clinging but simply keeping his balance. He did not snuggle into her shoulder as he might have a few months ago. He did not kiss her cheek. He turned his head to look over her shoulder. His chubby finger pointed. "Airplane."

Elsie craned her neck and watched the big warbird pass overhead. A hot rage boiled up in her stomach. She dropped Jack to the ground.

"Goddamn Japs! Goddamn you slant-eyed sons of bitches!"

She snatched up a stone and threw it into the sky.

And I saw it then, the scrap of memory hidden beneath the peanut butter and water and the quiet, soaking wet toddler. A piece of paper sitting on that green davenport. A telegram.

I gasp for air, and the air is ordinary, dusty Eastern Washington air. The past is invisible again. I cover my eyes for a second, too overwhelmed to even cry. I feel heavy, as if I've swallowed a slab of stone. How many stories like this has this land witnessed? How much truth can this dust hold?

Grandmother Elsie's brother died in the war. Me, heartless grandchild that I was, I forgot that terrible fact, but I don't think she ever let go of it. Whenever anyone Asian came on tv, she would leave the room. She once told me we should have sent a hundred, a thousand more bombs. It was the only time I ever heard cruelty in my sweet grandmother's voice.

I pull myself to my feet and hurry to catch up with my father. The dog runs ahead of me, kicking up little mushroom clouds of dirt with her oversized paws.

"You all right?" he asks. He doesn't turn to look at me. His eyes are scanning the land.

I stroke the dog and study the fields beyond. They were once my granddad's fields, but now a big agricultural company owns them. They can afford to irrigate until the wheat is a slick, plump green. It's just about impossible for a family farm to stay in business these days. My father couldn't afford to live here if it weren't for his Social Security check.

"Dad?" I hesitate. "I've got bad news, Dad. Alan...Alan's dead. He shot himself a week ago." The words spill out, dry, dusty, just the unembroidered facts.

Dad's mouth opens. Closes. He stays silent a long time, and I wonder if he is thinking all the things I thought when I got the news. But of course he hasn't seen Alan in years. I am the only one of us who calls or visits my father.

He puts his hand on the dog's shoulder and stares out beyond those fence lines. His face hangs in heavy lines that look deeper than I've seen them. He blinks hard. "Was there a funeral?"

"Yesterday," I admit. Alan's husband had organized things very quickly.

He sighs, the air rattling in his throat. He still hasn't looked at me. It's as if the land out there is holding him up. "Those damn ragheads," he says. "He wasn't ever the same after they sent him into the desert."

I realize I'm taking shallow breaths, that my legs wobble. After all these years, my instincts are still waiting for my dad to hit me when I say the wrong thing. I dig my fingers into the dog's thick hair. But he doesn't see it, just like he never saw that Alan was broken long before he joined the Army.

"Looks good, don't it?" he asks. The green fields only stretch so far. Sagebrush encircles the green hungrily, lapping up the escaped moisture. Everything is thirsty in these scablands, where the soil is too thin to hold moisture and the endless wind drives away the clouds. Out here, every little thing has to fight to survive. "It's sure good-looking country."

His voice is so frail, so small. It is even—and I have to force myself to admit this—sweet. If I didn't know him, I would find him an enchanting little old man. And maybe he is. He's sure not the man I've been hating for the last thirty years. Haven't I seen that with my own eyes? And wasn't Elsie proof that people can change?

"It's beautiful," I agree. I let go of the dog's neck hair. The dog presses her head against my father's knee.

A jet streaks overhead, a black "v" slicing through the cloudless sky. My freed hand closes on my father's and we crane our necks. A little breeze whispers in my ear, soft and satisfied; not a real breeze, but the comforting voice of the land that only I can hear. My father smiles, almost like he can feel it, too.

The warbird heads west, toward the military base, toward the sea.

CACTUS FLOWERS
— AND BONE FLUTES —
Mercedes M. Yardley

Mercedes Yardley based her story "Cactus Flowers and Bone Flutes" on the San Rafael Swell. This desert area also appears in her novel Pretty Little Dead Girls: A Novel of Murder and Whimsy. "I spent many a night out there, staring into the dark to see what was staring back," says Yardley.

The San Rafael Swell is a desert area covering 2000 miles in Utah. The land has been sculpted by wind and water into sinuous canyons, unearthly rock formations called hoodoos, and massive gorges. The San Rafael Cactus (Pediocactus despainii) is an endangered cactus. It's estimated that there are only 6000 of these cacti on the planet, and they all exist in the Swell and nowhere else. The San Raphael Cactus, also known as Despain's Pincushion Cactus, bears gorgeous yellow or pink flowers, and guards them with small but ferocious white thorns.

People have always passed through the Swell, but no one lives there permanently now. The Fremont, Paiute, and Ute people left pictographs on the stone walls of the canyons. The Old Spanish Trade Route went through the canyon from the mid-1700s to the mid-1800s. Today people use the canyon for cattle grazing, uranium mining, and tourism. Because the terrain looks so alien, Hollywood comes to visit occasionally for filming, and the Mars Desert Research Station is located here. But no one lives permanently in the unearthly, barren, and beautiful realms of the Swell itself.

—◆—

The desert had devoured the parents of Lucas Marsh many moons ago. It hadn't come as a surprise, not really. It had been stalking them for months, leaving footprints outside the door of their house, pressing its face of sand and grit to their windows.

"You shan't have us!" his mother had shouted defiantly into the night sky. The universe was stapled with stars, and they gleamed and preened down at her, coating her black hair and the baby she held with the faintest of light. "We will outlast you!"

Baby Lucas cooed and waved tiny starfish hands. The desert laughed. Nobody outlasted it. It was created of dunes and bones and fur. It sharpened its teeth on rocks and scorpion stings.

The father disappeared first. Just a flurry of dunes and then he was gone. No sound. No screams.

"Dust to dust," the priest later intoned, and Lucas' mother winced at the choice of words, holding Baby Lucas far too tightly. Lucas squalled. So did the desert. A man is delicious and his skull polishes up nicely in underground caverns. But it still isn't as satiating when you wanted a man and his toothsome wife.

She survived two more years. Lucas learned to eat and crawl and walk and run. He played deep inside the nest of their home, never in the front yard, and certainly not in the back, where the desert left gifts for them. Slivers of birds. Shiny rocks. Flutes made from the bones of little girls (little girls are often forgotten and lost in the desert). The desert left its most precious possessions. It only wanted to share.

His mother took the last delicate bone flute, and her fingers tightened around it until she heard a sharp crack.

"Stay here, baby," she whispered to Lucas, and set him up in the womb of his playroom. "Mama will be right back after I discuss something with the universe."

She kissed him, turned on her heel, and strode out the front door, a shining apocalypse of fury.

Lucas played. He spun around in his playroom and hugged his favorite white tiger and pulled all of the books from the shelf. He looked at pictures of his daddy and rubbed his hungry tummy and eventually flopped over onto his side and fell asleep. He was still sleeping when his neighbor came and picked him up, cuddling the tiny boy to his chest. Tears disappear beautifully into a sleeping child's hair, and when the neighbor sniffled over Lucas's newly dead mother, the boy's hair was like magic, wicking the sorrow up and away.

Two days later a larger, longer bone flute showed up in the backyard. There was something familiar about it, something that would have made Lucas sob even though he wouldn't have understood why. But Lucas wasn't living there any longer, and didn't see it.

This distressed the desert, who played soft, mournful songs long into the cold nights. A man is lovely. A woman is charming. But a tasty little boy would be absolutely divine.

When Lucas was eighteen, he graduated school and moved back to his old home. College didn't attract him. Pretty girls and boys didn't interest him. He wanted to sleep in his old room, run his hand down the bannister that his parents' fingers had polished with use. He wanted to remember.

He sat on the front porch in his father's old rocker. The sun was going down behind the mountains, and the colors spilled across the sky and red sand like spattered blood.

Crickets. Cicadas. The sounds of lizards skittering across the sand, of coyotes stepping lightly through the sage, the smell of heat and sunbaked rock and eyeless fathers and dead mothers.

The desert prowled up to the front porch, eying Lucas Marsh with interest. Lucas eyed it back.

"I'm not scared of you, you know," he said. His voice was firm and clear and lacked the thick Spanish accent of his mother.

The desert wondered if he'd taste of limestone and tumbleweeds.

Lucas sighed, leaning his head back against the rocking chair, and for a second, the desert almost felt ashamed. This boy was too young to be so weary. He should be fighting and kicking and running across the dunes like a jackrabbit. He should be climbing the mesas and screaming at the sky when he made it to the top. All of the things that boys did, he should be doing. But he was not.

The desert's heart wrenched, briefly. It beat, and inside of that great, big, calcified heart beat the tiny hearts of night animals whose eyes shone in the dark, of unfortunates who were left to die under the bleaching sky, of Mr. and Mrs. Marsh, whose dark eyes alone made them irresistible to the oldest of the elements.

It beat, and then it stopped, and the desert shook its head to clear it. It sniffed at the boy, at this Lucas Marsh, and heard the blood running a bit too slowly through his veins, and smelled his apathy coating the irises of his eyes like desert honey, like nectar in the red cactus flowers, and then the desert smiled and opened its mouth.

— THE SOUTH CHINA SEA —
zm quỳnh

zm quỳnh's story "South China Sea" is both harrowing and healing. Her story follows the efforts of a family to escape from Vietnam by boat in the aftermath of the Vietnam War. Between 1975 and 1995, approximately 800,000 people fled Vietnam by boat. Many of them travelled in small fishing boats, without adequate food or water, easy prey for pirates. Some people drifted at sea for weeks. Women had a terribly high risk of rape and abduction at the hands of pirates. According to the United Nations High Commission for Refugees, between 200,000 and 400,000 refugees died at sea—drowned in storms, dead from dehydration, starvation, and disease, or murdered by pirates. Many people who survived found themselves spending years in refugee camps in Malaysia, Indonesia, and the Philippines. Those who fled to Hong Kong found themselves in internment centers awaiting resettlement. Others experienced forced "repatriation" to Vietnam. Despite the horrors of the journey, many families attempted to leave Vietnam again and again.

In Vietnamese culture, it is crucial to treat the dead with respect and ritual. The dead must be properly buried, ideally at their home village, and families pray for the safe journey of the dead to their next incarnation for up to a hundred days following their death. Moreover, the grave of the deceased must always be tended for generations afterwards. When this doesn't happen, the dead cannot find peace. They are trapped in the pain and terror of their death and they cannot move on to the next life.

zm quỳnh was inspired to write "South China Sea" by the struggles of her own family during the exodus from Vietnam:

Vietnamese culture has been through thousands of years of wars, colonization, enslavement, and massacre—and so there are many, many ghost stories. Vietnamese legends and myths are often tragic. They do not have the "happily ever after" of American fairy tales. They appear to prepare children for suffering, for death, for tragedy.

Thus my story is a hybrid of this experience—a clear reflection of the fact that I am a Vietnamese American—a person that has survived that flight from Việt Nam. One for whom the word "hope" has become a strong part of my cultural identity rather than "suffering." My story has a happy ending— it departs from the mythology and legends of Vietnamese ghost stories which all end in tragedy. I have yet to come across one that has a happy ending (in the American sense of a "happy ending").

It's not that I want to minimize the experience of boat people. Rather, it is a fantasy dream. A dream in which I am able to do what I can never do. Relieve the spirits that hang over the South China Seas, usher them into peace and tranquility (hopefully they have found their own way—but I have no power to do this or help them with this other than my own intentional thoughts) and…Can I say it? Bring back my cousin and his wife who fell prey to pirates in the South China Sea. He is dead, she is…? Through my story I erase or obliterate their tragic fates, bring them back from the dead into this country where they can join their parents and siblings, where they can celebrate their sacrifices so that their family can survive together in another land.

They are in the fragmentation of raindrops during monsoon season and the quivering of evaporating dew in the dawn of sea salt mornings. I am intimately familiar with them, for I have always been surrounded by spirits. Our village was built around a cemetery abandoned during the war. That was where we migrated to when our hamlet was massacred and over a thousand lives lost. Ghosts were seen as regularly as any villager, wandering through the tombstones in our gardens, passing the evening dinner table, and swirling in the incense in our temples. I often caught a glimpse of them in the air as if in shards of broken glass. With them always lingered a scent.

It was this same scent that permeated the air when we drifted into the crests of the South China Sea. It was intermingled with the smell of misery and remorse and the taste of sweetened rust, as if you plunged an abandoned nail into sugar cane and then sucked on it for days on end. I knew then that we had ventured into that ghostly stretch of sea in which the souls of people still lingered aimlessly, struggling against the powerful waves, gagging at the descent of salt water into their lungs, playing out their deaths over and over again as their hope for life somehow continued long after their demise.

As soon as her swells began to coil around the boat, I felt the mood on board shift. Elders grouped together above us on the deck to set up a small altar. Damp joss sticks were lit and inserted into nicks in the wood and muffled invocations whispered.

"Let us pass in peace dear sister, dear brother, dear mother, father."

From the darkness of the cabin below, I felt them pass through me, the victims of the sea, friends and family and strangers.

Twice she had beaten me. Swallowed my brother and sister, captured scores of people in my village, and betrayed my father.

"I hate you," I whispered to her.

"Mine…" I thought I heard her whisper back to me.

But it was only the sound of her salty tentacles rippling against the rotten wood of our fishing boat. My back was turned to her as I methodically dumped the mixture of bile, feces and urine that had been collected in the buckets kept at various corners of the small boat. She felt uncharacteristically calm, a quietness that made me nervous. I averted my eyes from her, focused on my task. The mere sight of her caused such anxiety to well in me that I had taken to severe bouts of vomiting.

She was nearly impossible to avoid though; her blue green eyes taunted me from all directions. Trying my best to shut her out, and preferring the familiarity of the contents of the buckets to her misleading beauty, I studied the mixture of bits of rice and undisturbed fish bones from the previous night's meal. They were the markers of our life. So long as we breathed, these buckets would be filled.

Leaning back, I dipped the first bucket into the warm waters, keeping my eyes on the deck in front of me, following the lines of the wood grain. Instantaneously, I felt her tongue brush against my fingers, lapping at the blistering salt seared there. I pulled back reflexively, causing the bucket to fall overboard. Swearing, I reached to retrieve the bucket. It was then that I caught it out of the corner of my eye—a smudge of blackness on the horizon, half dipped into the ocean, half set against the sky. I turned toward it, although it loomed over the sea.

Within seconds the vastness of the sea reached out and struck me flat across my face. A wave of nausea overwhelmed me as I was flooded with visions of my brother and sister devoured whole in our second attempt to escape Việt Nam and the faces of children, shallow and starving, in the arms of their mothers who held them above water as they themselves were slowly pulled down, their legs entangled in the seas' slimy tresses. Nausea buckled my knees, dry heaving the dehydrated contents of my stomach onto the deck.

"What use is this child of yours?" said the man near me. He gave me a disdainful look and then turned to seek out my mother, whom everyone had paid with their blood and treasure for passage on our family's small rickety fishing boat.

His scan of the deck was stopped short at the black mass that was once nothing more than a stain in the corner of the sky. It was gaining size as if it was absorbing the sky, the clouds and the ocean around it.

"Row—row the other way!" my mother yelled.

"But that will take us back!" But the oncoming blackness motivated all hands. People began to row back towards the country we had fled. Try as we might though, we could not travel as fast as the patch was growing. I felt paralyzed as I watched it swiftly consuming everything around it. With it came a deafening howl and the stench of sweetened rust filled my senses, pungent and sharp. But, here in the black void, I noticed a difference. Here there was also the distinct musk of human sweat perspired in desperation.

At one time I had loved the sea. Every waking morning was filled with rituals of welcoming her waters, which always stayed damp on my skin. Nearly ten years ago when our father first purchased this boat, we had all looked towards her as our savior, a means to carry us away from Việt Nam. Since we lost Khánh and Trúc though, she was nothing more to me than a cruel deceitful being that could never be trusted.

Our first attempt was foiled almost immediately by the police patrols along the shoreline. The patrol boat had forced us ashore and all those passengers that did not dive into the waters had been shot on land. Several dozen people decimated within seconds.

On our second attempt, we got as far as we are now, the South China Sea. On that trip the fear of police had passed into the fear of pirates. We had been six days at sea and our supplies were low. That was when she betrayed us. When we were at our weakest, when the human waste we threw overboard spoke of death and starvation, she let out her siren's call. And then they came, partners in treachery.

They invaded our boat, carried away our food and supplies, captured all the women and girls. The screaming was manic with people lunging, flesh and bones sacrificed to attempt to stop them. But they had strength and machetes. And we had nothing. It is a nightmare that keeps playing over and over in my head. My brother had charged at two men who had grabbed my sister. For this the sea clamored up and claimed him.

As they dragged us onto their ship, I grabbed my sister and dragged her overboard. The sea promptly pulled us down until we were both under our boat. I felt her hand loosen from me in the same instant that my consciousness slipped from me. When I awoke I was lying on the deck, the sound of sobs all around me. My mother hovered above me, her graying hair disarrayed about her face, the body of my father, his face bearing the sharp laceration of a machete, in her arms.

Despite all this, or in spite of it, three years after burying our father, we began anew, recruiting the same families that had once lost members with us. What else did we have to lose? Many thought we were cursed. All the more reason to flee. We had two choices. A country that had lost all respect for human rights or the sea with her unpredictable melodies. Which was more treacherous? We chose the sea.

On this third trip, only twenty-five people came with us. The boat felt oddly spacious, as if each individual had at least five extra inches of space in which to breath. In past attempts, we had crammed a hundred people into our tiny fishing boat. Every inch of space on the boat had been filled with a body, often sitting on top of each other, the hope of escape overriding the need for personal space. Two hundred total for both attempts. Fewer than seventy-five survived those, only to return to Việt Nam were they languished in prison for the treasonous act of attempting to escape. My mother and I were the last of our family of five. We had nothing left to lose but each other.

With no light, there are no markers of the days and time rolls into itself hour after hour, minute after minute, second after second until it becomes irrelevant. We had among us a single box of matches and a few candles. Though their wicks were long, we sought to conserve them, not knowing how long we'd wander in the dark void. It was on my watch that it first occurred to me that the candle, like my hunger, remained still as if frozen in time.

The wick seemed not to diminish nor the candle wax drip, and the spoonful of the salted rice I had eaten lay savored on my tongue and cooling in my belly as if I had just eaten it. And yet in the next instant, I was hungry again as if I had not eaten in a month and the candle had burnt down almost to the end of its wick. When I rose to blow it out, for fear of losing our only source of light, I was once again staring at a candle that seemed to have been burning for only a moment.

Like a story told in reverse, out of order and out of context, moments passed or were about to occur and occurred over and over again as if they just happened. I could not take the inconsistencies anymore. I retreated to the cabin underneath the deck, huddling among the children and elders where I sat numbly staring at blackness all around me.

Mother poked her head down into the cabin from the deck.

"Child!" she hissed.

I ignored her.

"My child!" She marched down the steps, trampling over people as she made her way to me. Peering right into my face, the flame of the candle in her hand burning my eyes, she pinched me. Hard. But still I refused to respond. What would be the purpose? The damn sea had won again. There was nothing that can explain the darkness above except our deaths.

"We are dead mother," I said, "Dead."

"Shut up and get up. I need your help!" She grabbed my arm and dragged me up to the deck. She was fierce, like a firefly, unwilling to be daunted. She attempted to lift me up but gravity helped me stay dumb and docile.

"No mother. There is nothing out there. No light, no life, no fish, no sound, nothing. We are on our journey to the next life. I want to see father. I want to see Khánh and Trúc again."

She slapped me then. Hard. It stung and I blinked.

"Father would be ashamed of you," she said.

The words struck at me harder than her slap. I shook her off and started up the stairway, into the impending darkness.

Reaching the deck, a wave of intense anxiety immediately overtook my senses. I could feel the sway of the water so much more strongly than below deck and the boat leaned, tremulously unbalanced on one side. I searched for something to grasp onto as the feeling of sinking came over me. I whimpered and my knees gave and I fell onto the deck.

On deck stood and squatted all of the adults on the fishing boat. I should have been with them. I had come of age last year and was by far the strongest and tallest among them. I could see all this in my mother's fierce eyes. But instead I had chosen to cower among the elderly and the children, welcoming death to my side. At least there my family members would outnumber the living.

"We need you to help us bring down the broken mast. Its weight is making the boat lean into the water. If it falls, it will bash a hole in the hull."

"No…ma…no…I can't…" Violent images began to flood me. Mother guided me to the mast that leaned to its side nearly cracked in half but not quite broken all the way through. It hung over the side of the boat, pulling it into the water. People were furiously bailing water. The sight of water immediately threw me into a fit.

I started wheezing, my eyes shut tight. I dropped to the ground again, pulling my arms around my head, blocking out the image of water pummeling me, water pulling Trúc and Khánh into the sea.

Mother shook me. "This is our boat, this is our responsibility. You know this boat better than anyone here and you are the right size. We are all too small, the children all too small, you are strong. You need to do this or else this boat will sink."

I began to inch backwards. I felt my mother's arms around me, trying to grab me, and I broke into a sprint until I reached the stairs. Before she could catch me, I had made my way back down to the corner of the cabin where I pressed myself against the children there.

Mother did not return. We listened as the adults began to speak quickly and excitedly, shouting commands and urgings. I clamped my hands over my ears shutting out their voices, shutting out my cowardice. Then there were yells and screams that I could not shut out and a heavy splash into the water.

The boat began to rock and shake as footsteps could be heard running back and forth, then more shouts and splashing before a sudden chilling silence. We all looked up towards the opening, though the darkness was so profound that we could see nothing.

Then I heard my mother's wail. A pang of guilt stabbed at me and I bolted up the stairs onto the deck, reckless of the wrenching in my belly. Immediately I was accosted by a frantic man.

"This is your boat, we paid you to take us on this hellish trip. Get up and do something or you'll see your mother die. What kind of ungrateful child are you?"

Pushing him aside, I ran onto the deck which was completely illuminated for the first time since the darkness had descended upon us. The strong smell of sweet iron filled my nostrils and a chill immediately entered my bones.

Before me, rising rapidly from the water, was a serpentine creature glowing silver, and massive in proportion. Around it the whipping lashes of the sea framed it on all sides. It roared as loud as thunder, echoing with tortured voices. The monster's ascent finally halted and at the very top of it was the face of a man, small and severely disproportionate, as thin as a skeleton, the hollow of his cheeks caving inward as his mouth distended unnaturally. He reached two long limbs towards mother, who was sitting stiff in fear on the broken mast, a butcher's knife in her hand, poised as if in mid-action at the edge of the mast.

"Mother!" I screamed, shock and guilt mingling violently on my tongue as I realized that she sat where I was supposed to be, doing what I had refused to. I began to scramble up the mast, attempting to reach her.

Several men and women grabbed oars and began hacking at the monstrosity only to find that it began to sprout limbs—arms, legs, and hands began to distend from the trunk. Mother stabbed her knife at the man reaching down towards her. I inched closer to her, but the sweat and slime of the sea and my own anxiety created a slippery coat on the mast, making me lose my grip and forcing me back down.

Then faces began emerging from its body, each grotesquely pulled back as if stretched too far. They peered at us, screaming words that were blended one into each other. Their voices dripped of grief and sorrow, speaking of the dream we all had, of escape, of freedom. Faces wavered in and out, faces I knew well.

Nghĩa

Thuy

Ngọc

Binh

Khánh

"Khánh! Mother, its Khánh!"

I caught mother's confused expression. In that moment a man directly in front of me pierced his oar deep into the creature, sinking it between the faces of two villagers that once lived side by side, both lost to the sea in our last attempt to escape. Their faces scrunched up in pain.

For an instant, their voices became clear, calling my mother by her name: "Hoa." Different tones, different dialects, different pitches, but all the same name. I lunged after her, attempting to climb the mast again but flailing miserably on the oil of my own fear. Mother threw herself onto the broken mast, wrapping herself around it. The limbs of the man at the top of the creature elongated, grabbing mother, tearing the broken mast from the boat. The boat immediately shook sending everyone on deck tumbling.

Mother's face twisted in pain as her torso and legs were swallowed by the mutilated human appendages, the trail of a tear etching a faint scar along her cheek. Within seconds she disappeared into the creature. Almost as suddenly as it appeared, it sank swiftly into the water taking its glow deep into the abyss, leaving us shrouded in total darkness.

Once again, I had been inches away when the sea stole someone from me. I stood and screamed out at her with all the rage in my being.

"Give her back to me!"

For durations I cannot remember, the instances of my mother's disappearance, of arriving on deck to see her perched on top of the mast, of staring at the tumble of arms and legs and tormented faces, replayed itself out of order.

Around me people began screaming as the spell broke, slipping in and out of what had happened, what was happening, and what will happen. Attempting to avoid insanity, we talked ourselves through each interval of time. We began to move through time collectively, no longer allowing separation to tear at our minds.

When I could grab cognizance of the now, it felt as if I was taking a seat within my own body. As soon as confusion came, someone would shout, "Now!" and immediately we busied ourselves; the various tasks of maintaining the deck became paramount to avoid losing our minds. We became more and more cognizant of when we were, of the instant moment and when we would fall out of it. I sharpened oars and created makeshift weapons. I darted back and forth from the deck to the cabin to check on the children who ran in circles, unable to cope with the ever-changing slippages in time, and the elders who sat holding their heads.

"What is happening to us?" they moaned to each other.

Excrement, urine and bile lay strewn haphazardly in the cabin. No one cared anymore to use the buckets, their minds a field of havoc. I packed the raw pieces of their innards into the buckets, feeling the familiar comfort of their stench relaxing me in between intervals of my own memory lapses.

It came again several times over. Each time we fought it off, our sharpened oars piercing through it and each time it claimed more members of our boat. The last time it came, the deck was full of children and elders. Our inattention to hygiene in wake of all that had happened had started to produce sores on the skin of the children. Three children were brought up at a time to stand in a large tub of salt water while water was poured over their bodies and a quick rag rubbed over them. The same was done for elders.

It was in this instance, when every child was on deck and running about naked glistening, salty and clean, and elders slowly being brought to the tub of water that the sweet stench of sweaty iron filled the air.

"It's coming!" I yelled.

The children were rushed downstairs and the elders were carried one by one into the cabin below. Those on deck grabbed their makeshift weapons and readied themselves. A roar broke from the waters of the sea and rising once again in a pitiful wail was the creature framed by a tidal wave of water. Voices screamed from within the wave. Arms reached out and faces pressed forward, changing between expressions of grief and happiness.

Each face cried the name of a person on board and random limbs and fingers reached out, brushing up against our skin, attempting to grab us. Then, a woman's face emerged, soft and flattened, beautiful almost. Staring down on the deck she wailed, "Grandmother!" and reached her arms out to an elder who had been left behind. The elder screamed up at the woman, sobs coming out of her chest in crests. "My child, my child!" she cried. Her arms reached out to the woman.

"No!" I yelled, running to block the girls' descent.

"I want to go with her!" sobbed the elder.

The girl's face flitted in and out of distortion until she looked just as she did when I last saw her. It was our second attempt. She had jumped, like me, like Khánh. The sea had grabbed her. I remember her face sinking below the water.

"Moi," I said, "Moi was your name."

She smiled then and it was neither unnatural nor terrifying. Before I could stop her, the elder jumped up and grabbed Moi, pulling her back onto the boat. Arms reached out to cling onto the elder. We pulled her back onto the deck but her hold on Moi was steadfast. She pulled until Moi fell onto the deck and behind her tumbled a line of people who had held on to Moi's legs, and behind those others that had held onto each other's limbs.

"Grab them! Grab them!" yelled the elder and she began reaching for the limbs that appeared from the creature, pulling at arms and hands. Her strength seemed amazing. One by one people tumbled, children, infants, adults, crying, smiling, relief thick in their voices.

I dropped my oar and began grabbing at arms and faces. Others starred at us in horror but when the bodies of people, naked and smiling, began to appear, we all began to pull. Oars were dropped. Knives were thrown into the sea and the boat became a clamoring of arms reaching out to grab at hands, fingers, toes, hair. I called out the names of my family.

Khánh!

Trúc!

Mother!

I heard myself echoed in the voices all around me as people began to yell out the names of loved ones they had lost. One by one they tumbled from the wave that hovered over our boat. Then a face emerged. A face I knew like the back of my hand. I grabbed her face. Khánh. My sister. She fell onto me, bursting into sobs, burying her face into my neck, her hair long and twining about her body.

From within the wave we had pulled out nearly a hundred people. We sat like sardines on the deck and in the cabin. In those moments, we forgot the void. We passed the candle back and forth identifying faces, calling out names. I sat staring at my brother and my sister as my mother held onto them both. Beyond them were the faces of people dear to me, faces I had passed every day in our village, faces I had convinced myself to forget because missing them was too painful. Voices continued forever into the darkness as people spoke, whispered, cried about a haven, the sea's safe harbor.

How did it happen? That in this place the sea suddenly became the only solace for lost souls. Going back and forth between trying to catch glimpses of my family and the wavering movement of the candle, I curled my fingers into the sea. In the sheath of the darkness, I made my peace with her.

When the darkness parted, fading into the soft blush of dawn, the fear left as suddenly as it came, as if our involuntary journey had passed through a gate, our purpose met. All around me screams and yelps broke out. I knew the sea must be opening all around me. Her music began playing, drowned only by the cacophony of the passengers. It was the lapping sound that I heard first. Instantly, I drew my attention to the deck, focusing on the ragged worn lines of the wood as it trailed old stories. I drew down closer to it, squatting until all I could see was feet. I watched the interplay of small feet with big feet, heavy feet, tiny feet all walking, running, jumping, dancing.

A familiar hand rested on my back. Then a head, grey hair falling into my face, tears soaking warm on my torn shirt. She came into full view and I remembered how beautiful my mother was. Is. I wrapped myself around her, becoming a child again. I let myself cry, darkened her shirt with sobs for all those faces I did not see, those that were not returned to us, those not taken into the protection of the sea, like father. Her arms curled about my body and we clutched each other. Khánh and Trúc joined us, tangling their limbs about us.

Then a familiar sound reached my ears, halting my tears. We all heard it. It was another boat. We looked at each other, our eyes wide with excitement, then fear. But no, the ships of pirates are loud splashing taunts thrown flat against the sea, not round and curling like the soft gurgling sound of the large vessel. Mother stood up and we joined her. I expected to be curled into myself within an instant, dry heaving into the deck. But instead, waves of calmness washed through me. The sea, blue and green, wavering calmly, was winking at me, her arms spread and inviting all around me. And I was not afraid anymore.

Khánh and Trúc ran to the edge of the boat where they joined others who were waving and yelling at the huge vessel. It hovered above the water, barely touching the surface of the waves. Did anyone even notice that?

On board we could see the shadowed face of a person gazing down at us. Việt cộng? The thought entered my mind and stabbed at my chest threatening to cave it. The vessel descended and glided to rest beside us. For the first time, everyone on our fishing boat caught a clear glimpse of the woman on the vessel. Before she was nothing more than a shadowed face. But now her features were clear. She was like no other woman I had ever seen. The sides of her head were cleanly shaven and in the middle of her head was a braided

"Where do you hail from? Are you in need of assistance?" Her words were Vietnamese, but they sounded as if her tongue had been taken, wrapped around a poem, and restrung in curves back to us.

"We are refugees from Việt Nam," mother stepped forward speaking words many had waited ten years to voice, "We request asylum."

"You are under the protection of the Waterlands of Lạc, we will grant you sanctuary." Cheers and sobs broke out at the welcoming words of the strange woman. Ropes were thrown down from their vessel and the woman descended along with two other people onto our fishing boat. Their eyes and their skin, the features of their faces, their voices clearly told us they were Vietnamese, but their clothes, their height…they were as tall as the tallest American soldiers, if not taller. Their hair was in motley cuts with wild colors. Their skin and faces were marked with black drawings like the ancient fisherman who had taken to carving sea monsters on their bodies. We backed up instinctively, alarmed at their strangeness. The blue-haired woman approached an elder, bowing deeply.

"Grandmother." Her voice undulated in reflections of the respect so endearing to our people. "The sea has brought you to us and we will care for you. Come and we will brew tea and cook rice for you." She reached out to the elder, whose face broke into a grimace of blackened teeth and relaxed sobs. She lifted the elder and passed her like a child to receiving arms on her vessel.

One after another, people allowed themselves to be lifted, carried and transferred away from our fishing boat, until I was the only one left.

"She is yours?"

I looked at the fishing boat, a glimmer of nostalgic remorse creeping into my heart. "No. She belongs to the sea now."

Then I asked her, "How far from Việt Nam are we?"

Her calm smile told me that she knew more than she was ready to share with me. "Far enough to be safe, close enough to be home."

Then she turned and leaped gracefully onto her vessel and extended an open hand to me. I accepted it.

— THE OTHER SHORE —
Rebecca Campbell

Rebecca Campbell, author of "The Other Shore", grew up in the village of Cowchican Bay on the coast of British Columbia. Originally home to First Nations People, it was settled by Europeans in the 1860s and for many years was a busy fishing and logging community. Today, the main industries are fishing and tourism. The lives of people, fish, birds, mammals, and all other life in the region are completely dependent on the health of the ocean, and the life cycle of the salmon that spawn and hatch in the area every year.

In 2011, a tsunami caused three nuclear reactors at the Fukushima Nuclear Power Plant in Japan to meltdown. As a result of the accident, tainted water flowed into the ocean, causing concerns about the impact to ocean life and, by extension, human beings. Campbell found this to be "enraging". It became the catalyst for her vision of an avenging genius loci who could protect the sea from the predations and pollutions of humans.

In this story, the archeologists incur the wrath of the Genius Loci because they refuse to comprehend the inter-connectedness of the people, animals, and other organisms that make the whole of the sea. Every small thing has some purpose, some story, some place in the story of the ocean. To ignore this, to exploit the sea for the need of the moment, is to invite disaster.

The shoreline is indefinite, having been closer to the village, or across the bay, or far out in what is now a channel. For a few hours on a day in 1700 it was a kilometer up the river valley. I know this because I remember the day in 1700, but if one is shorter-lived—or not so clever—one might know that temporary high-tide by the shattered stumps that still stand just short of where the ground rises, exactly as they did on the afternoon of the tsunami. It's a ghost forest now, and runs all along the river, so far inland that when one reaches its edge, one can no longer hear the waves.

Every summer for a decade now, Charlie brings a gang of them to town. They change year to year, students mostly. In other years I ignored them, maybe said hello Charlie when I passed him on the street or the restaurant.

This year, though, their dig takes in the midden. Do you see the grey heron poised above his supper, where the beach is the white of discarded molluscs? That is a human undertaking, and nearly as old as I am. Its history does not instantly reveal itself to shortlived creatures of Charlie's kind, and in ten thousand years there has been little change in the whorl of the periwinkle, or the abalone's deep and iridescent shell. Someone pried them open. Someone cut the muscly foot that anchored the hinge, and ate its body, and discarded its shell on the heap. If Charlie climbs up the hill from the midden, into town and the restaurant, I'll serve them a similar creature garnished with lemon wedges, or wrapped in a cone of irradiated nori.

Charlie's crew brings trowels and huge spools of high-visibility twine. They bring the laws of stratiography that fix time and its progressions in place by measuring the earth below their feet. They segment the ghost forest and dig up flat spangles cut from mother-of-pearl, chips of obsidian from a quarry eight hundred kilometers to the south and far inland; a dusting of volcanic ash, and the denser, blacker deposits of a forest fire.

They don't often know what they're looking at, though their work is meticulous. Even Charlie misses evidence of the other shore: ancient tree-roots sunk in the unforgiving salt. Palm fronds. They find but do not recognize the tooth-chip from a shipwrecked sailor who left a village outside of Quanzhou during the reign of Gegeen Khan. Filaments of rope from an outrigger canoe. A Tahitian pearl. They find a glass float—faintly bluegreen, as though constituted in the water from which it emerged after decades mid-Pacific, passenger on a March storm of 1930—that belonged to Susumu, a Meiji fisherman.

In the afternoon the sun throws long shadows toward the beach, and Charlie leads them up the hill from the dig to the restaurant, where they take one of the big tables on the sidewalk. I make sure they're in my section, so I can listen, and say, "Hey guys, I'm Lin. I'll be looking after you," and bring them pitchers of Sea Dog Amber Ale. One of the younger men talks—uninterruptable—about microbrews until I don't know how Charlie stands it.

I bring them calamari and the aforementioned sweet abalone (imported, having been fished to near-extinction twenty years ago). Chips, deep fried mac&cheese, sashimi (the salmon is farmed, the snapper is not), mercury-rich tuna tataki. Extra napkins. I know what they want before they do, in the manner of one who serves with great talent.

"So, what did you guys find today?"

The girl with the unwashed hair says, "Some rope fragments. A glass float."

"Those are so pretty!"

"Pretty. Okay." Corrected by the young man who cares so much about microbrews. He's the one who explained to me, the first day, that they are archaeologists. He is an MA Candidate. He works on pre-contact material culture of the Malahat Nation. I think of Susumu, and how he lost the five floats his uncle made when he was little, that he inherited from his father the season before. How four shattered while this one survived the Pacific gyre to alight here. Unlikely. "They're for collectors," he adds.

"They're nicer than Styrofoam, that looks so awful on the beach. We're doing a great oyster burger today."

"How's the halibut?" Charlie asks.

I look for my manager. She's distracted.

"I wouldn't, if I'm honest. But the chowder is awesome." I think about immigrant cattle from Jersey, and the long migrations of saffron. Their unlikely collision with bacon and scallops at this far western margin. They order the chowder.

From the sidewalk we can see most of town, hear the sharp, sweet echo of footsteps on concrete at the bottom of the street, where the kids are now emerging from the afternoon, caped in beach towels, their parents laden with coolers, laden also with radiation and its malignant gleam. On my way to Charlie's table with ketchup bottles and malt vinegar I stop to watch the kids climb toward the ice cream shop and wish I could tell them to fill their mouths with seawater and then order a double cone, so salt might render the ice cream sweeter than anything that has ever existed.

Their first opportunity came in the form of a button that unsettled their stratiography. I felt the frisson when they found it, spreading through the six as though through a single body and I knew they had touched the other shore. I thought maybe it's time. I was hopeful.

The button arrived on the waistcoat of a very young midship-man-and-water-colourist who leaned over the gunwale of the longboat in which he travelled from the HMS Encounter to an earlier iteration of this very village. Under the water he saw an even earlier village, drowned, though he could make out the fallen poles of a longhouse. He was contemplating its age when he realized that a face returned his gaze. It was a whale, perhaps, or a thunderbird carved in wood, with a few grains of paint still affixed, showing the eyes staring upward. An amnesiac ancient, he thinks, god or genius loci dozing among the dooryards of what was once a village, that had squatted on what was once the shoreline, before the glaciers melted, the waters rose, or the land fell.

The watercolourist is not a good sailor. His uniform is in bad repair, and one button of his waistcoat rests against the gunwale as he reaches down to the surface through which he looks—past his own eyes, which make anxious contact with their doubles, as though in warning—and down to the other shore, just out of reach. He leans, dirtying further his dirty cuffs, and the indifferent stitches of his last mend break and the button springs over the gunwale and into the water and clops like a stone that won't skip. The old creature, the amnesiac, reaches out one hand to catch the falling button to its bosom.

That's gone, then. Back onboard HMS Encounter he'll be admonished for his disgraceful appearance. Behind him the button remains, covered in silt, then in sand, then in a plastic baggie with a tag in Charlie's terrible handwriting. He keeps it in his pocket because it confuses him. It is a disobedient button. It undermines known laws regarding the deposition of strata, and the careful exhumation of the past. It is only the beginning.

But before that, and just this moment, the longboat surges toward the shore and the arboreal haunting stands knee deep in yellow grasses, the midden white at its feet. The Midshipman cannot imagine it, but there was once an enormous wave, rising through the shallows until it curled over the low bush of the shore, and rising through the villages it dragged the children out to sea, sending them all down to the other shore.

If Charlie's lot were the kind who had prophetic dreams, and if it were among my talents to provide them with prophetic dreams, I would send them this. I would have one—the girl who doesn't wash her hair, perhaps—awaken in a longboat, or a kayak, or a canoe. She would look down to find herself wearing a skirt of cedar bark.

She would lean where the watercolourist also leaned, and seeing the drowned world, the faintest, whitened outline of its foundations, a glimpse of stainless steel through the seaweed. Or—if I am ambitious, and trust her to understand—the gleam of something that does not yet exist from her perspective: an underwater bulb attached to a surviving solar panel that still works, sometimes, despite the microbial haze of seawater. In the manner of dreams she finds her eyes zooming in to see, beside the panel, a cellphone lying on the ocean bed, where no such thing should exist.

The next day my feet hurt before I'd even put on my black nurse's shoes, and the hot oil of the fryer had so penetrated my work skirt that it stunk—like fish, like fryer grease—even as I pulled it off the morning laundry line. And I thought, I will never not smell of fried fish, even if I live another ten millennia, even if the Kula plate rises again like Lost Atlantis. Even if the radioactive plume re-collects itself, and the glaciers return with the Thunderbirds and abalone. I remember smelling of smokehouses and doghair, and before that of mud and green things, but never so inescapably as I do now.

That is the day—when I cannot stand the humanish smell of my awful black polyester work-skirt—that they come into the restaurant carrying a yellow sony sport alkman, filthy, from 1986, and set it on the table.

"Oh, hey," I say pointedly, "do you guys want a towel for that?" And when they don't answer—rendered giddy and stupid by the object before them—I bring them bar towels anyway, with which they do nothing, preferring to stare at the alkman as it leaks ash onto my nice red plastic tablecloth. Though they found it under the deposits of a pre-industrial forest fire it is still brightly yellow. Inside there is a mixtape from 1987 whose second side is made up entirely of "Heaven Knows I'm Miserable Now" repeated six times.

"We've got some awesome specials—"

"—Charlie, it's a hoax—"

"I'll give you some time," I say, but Charlie calls out to me, over his shoulder, waving his hand as though I'm a taxicab. It would only be worse if he snapped his fingers.

"A couple pitchers of the Lager, eh?"

"Yeah yeah," I say, "on their way."

The next morning it rains. When I've finished with the ketchup bottles I go out back through the kitchen with bag after bag of trash—dirty napkins, and child-gnawed straws from lunch, the fragile shells of shrimp with their powerful stench. In the parking lot, which is puddled and oilslicked with rainbows, I think about them under their tent, washing the fragments that so obsess them. These tourists, who reach their hands for the other shore without knowing a damn thing. These temporary souls, trespassers, immigrants, how immune they remain to unlikelihood.

They will find or have found the anklet of a Tuamotuan woman who reached this blue-green shore by a series of tragedies and accidents I alone remember. She arrived in an outrigger, blown from the far western islands, four months pregnant, her skin caked with salt and her eyes fluttering in their sockets, but the little swimmer in her womb turning his somersaults, and kept safe in his own seabed of salt and blood. I brought her water, and fed her salmon and salal berries from a cedar bowl. She bore her child. She died twenty-five years later, left five children, and her anklet in the earth below a longhouse whose remains are now halfway across the bay. A black Tahitian pearl, a bead of polished lava, and another of island coral that shed a faint light—diffuse, atomic, tropical—from the atoll of its birth.

They'll find the pearl. They'll find the stone weight from five thousand years before, that a young man strung on a line of tendon and flung out across the bay, and promptly lost, the silly boy, though it was my gift to him, when he needed it.

That evening I brought them three pitchers, and then another three, and they drank under the awning while the rain fell. The first, prescient bronze on the maple leaves, hinting at autumn in high summer.

"So it's contaminated," Charlie says, his greasy grey hair hanging in elfknots to his beard. He is remarkable for the constant dirt beneath his fingernails, the nervous flutter of his eyes.

"But the sedimentation—"

"—Sure. Fine. But there's a coke bottle in a strata of archaic cedar ash."

Charlie has made it clear that he will not be taken in because Time's voyage is one-way—even in a Tsunami—and he is blind to the tangled logic of the high-tide line. When I ask if they want to try the banoffee pie we've got on for dessert, he ignores me, and that's just childish, Charlie, I thought you were better than that. You're just rude.

"Okay. You want coffee?"

Charlie snaps his no so sharply it might be a door slamming, and then I think back at him what do you take me for, little monkey? But he is impervious, so I lean on them with my own sharpness. They're too stupid to feel their minds ripple, to notice that the slammed no opens into yes. In the kitchen I collect mugs on a tray, and I breathe over them, and over the sugar packets, the cream, covering all with the faint and invisible film of my breath. Salt.

It will swamp you with the smack of saltwater, especially you, Charlie, in the instant your lips touch the lip of the cup that has upon it the salt of my mouth. You will find yourself unable to stop thinking of the moment your head goes under, how for an instant your scalp is dry under your hair, before water winkles through to the roots and your skin leaps to goosebumps, and then submerged you tilt your head and seawater is in to your eardrums, and your sinuses, and down your throat, and all the wrigglers, the drifters, the spunk, the free-floating ovum, combining into the drifting zygotes of a billion different creatures, the single-celled and the amoebic, microbial colonies and embryonic clusters. Charlie. The salt stings inside you, as the water carries all those creatures up into your skull, before you release them in a snort and a bloom of mucus. You're tumbling and buoyant in the cold and the salt, a bluegreen element constituted of bodies fucking, and dying, and being born, and growing, and leaving behind their recombined genetic matter to further recombine.

For an instant he is a drowned man. He rouses himself long enough to pay the bill and trail after the others up the hill to the guesthouse. He knows that somewhere there's a trigger, but he's too stupid to remember the taste of my breath in his coffee. That evening the setting sun glanced between the edge of cloud and the horizon. For a moment the air was cool-smelling and wet, as it will be in October, when the tourists are gone, and only newly-drunk teenagers will still go swimming.

That night some of Charlie's crew will creep into bedrooms not their own, carrying condoms and bottles of brandy. The tedious young man who so loves microbrews will smoke a cigarette in the gazebo at the bottom of the garden, the one that overlooks the wetlands at the head of the bay. And he will call his girlfriend, and plead with her to just talk to him please just talk to him.

At home, my feet out of their work-shoes will be swollen and bear the imprint of my socks, so I put them up on the coffee table and decide to skip laundry. I think about the girl from Tuamotu with her anklet of pearl, and try to name her—Afaitu? Poe?—but in ten thousand years there are more names than even I can remember.

Though it began last night when Charlie felt the wave close over his head, that—like the alkman, like the button—was only the harbinger. One of the youngest ones, just twenty, assigned to the meticulous work of the teaspoon and the whisk, finds a Starbucks mug showing the name and skyline of an unfamiliar city.

"I don't know," she says. For a moment she is stupid. She thinks the mistake is hers, and she'll get in trouble for digging into the wrong past. She looks through the earth to comfort herself with familiar things, the threads of a cedar apron, the abalone spangles. Instead she uncovers a flip phone with a pink sparkly butterfly sticker on the back. It's covered in ash. If they had a Geiger counter it would tick.

"What did you do?" Charlie asks the girl when she shows him the flip phone. He didn't sleep well last night, and when he did sleep he dreamed of deep water. His forehead is muddy where he scratched in the compulsive motion he makes when he is anxious, and his work goes poorly. When he's not working, he thinks—incessantly—about the moment of submersion.

Though he snaps at them, it doesn't stop. They find PDAs and tamagochis, a bottle of Spelman's Elixir ca. 1873. A single white tennis sock with a pale pink bobble folded as though to protect the delicate whale-bone hook from an antique carver of great art. Find greenstone from Aotearoa, and black argillite that traveled down the coast from the Gwaii in the foot of a canoe. Find a bladder of oolichan oil. Find Oribeware, up the coast from what is just now called "Oregon," the result of a shipwrecked Japanese fishing boat in an earlier millennium. Find a single page of that Rolling Stone from 1993, with Janet Jackson on the cover.

Charlie sweats through his khaki camp shirt. He stops the three who've uncovered the Rolling Stone and calls them all to the tent. It is summer again, after the previous day's unseasonable rain. They think he's going to reveal something to him, some plan, some theory.

"That's it for today," is all Charlie says, after a long moment in which he stares at their assembled feet. "Go on back to the house."

When they troop past, I see the beer-enthusiast text his silent girlfriend, thumbs jabbing his unnameable anxiety onto the screen, though he deletes the words before he can send them.

Charlie, left behind, stops his work to stare out into the bay. Despite my little gift of the previous night he is too stupid to know that he stands on time's faultline. The kids know better than to play there, and the teenagers don't go there at night to drink and fuck in secret, though it's far enough from town to be suitable for both activities.

But Charlie is not clever, so he keeps digging, alone, and finds a piece of gorilla glass and aluminum fused in an unfamiliar configuration, embedded deep in what must have been hot ash. A tetrapack of juice with a chip that raves in a thin, repetitive voice about the miraculous properties of its organic Jaboncilla.

It is not the noisy tetrapack, nor the evidence of ash that surrounds the unfamiliar hardware that stops him. It is the skull just visible beneath the most ancient layer at the bottom of the pit. A skull that— when it is disinterred—bears the irrefutable signs of an embedded electronic device, gold fused to the bone at the right temple beside a worn hole—trepanning of a still-to-come kind—where filaments once passed into the long-gone brain.

When he reaches the skull Charlie leaves without saying anything, and walks up to the restaurant, which is empty but for me at a table where I can watch the door, wrapping flatware in paper napkins.

"Charlie," I say, as he pushes the plastic ribbons aside and comes in. "Charlie?"

"Oh," he says. "Right, it's...?"

"Lin."

"Okay, Lynn." He says. "Can I get some coffee?" It looks like a question, but it doesn't sound like one.

I gather the cup and the coffee, and I think it's not easy to touch the other shore. He has been narrow-minded. He has ignored the evidence of time's instability, though it is before his eyes. But it is not easy.

"Maybe I can help," I say as I set out his coffee. "Maybe I can give you a hand."

I wait. An opportunity for repentance, I think. A chance to ask.

"Lynn, look, I'm kind of working here. I kind of need you to leave me alone."

You are insistent in your ignorance. I would like a little awe.

Lean hard. It's all there: earthquake, tsunami, subduction, meltwaters, gyres, currents, rising tides, reactors. There were prophetic dreams, and floods. Immigrants and refugees. Sasquatch and contrails and fallout shelters.

He's sweating now. He puts a hand up to his head where he sees sparks that swim—like sperm, like schools of bright-bellied fish—through his peripheral vision.

Under the silt, and hidden by the barnacles of an earlier tide-line, the bronze canon of a Spanish galleon. There was a giantess with a basket made of snakes, kidnapping children to eat for her supper. There were gold ingots in the woods, and a set of steps carved in the granite mountainside, descending to a corridor that, once found and left, is never found again. The epoch of the glacier and the epoch of its withdrawal, when breakneck meltwaters trip down the hillsides, and all the things taken up by its dragging underbelly are revealed again to the air. I remember when we found frozen mammoths in the till of withdrawing glaciers, how we'd search them out, and relish them for the tang of extinction.

Charlie makes a sound like gurgling.

Drones. Oil spills. The ticktick of the geigercounter. The goo of dormant nanobots. Charlie's breath bubbles in his chest. Thunderbirds—a family of them lived as humans, far to the northwest of here. And, Charlie, there will be thunderbirds again. The sea withdraws or advances daily, seasonally, on an epochal clock.

The other shore is indefinite: saltwater, and fresh, stone and liquid, invertebrate and mammal, spit and inlet, then and now shoved against one another by time's tectonics. If you were a wiser man, Charlie, water logic would not so disturb you. But you are stupid, and you are small.

I have often forgotten how fragile they are, thinly-armoured like spot prawns, their minds translucent like the grey-green shell they call Pododesmus macrochisma. The hightide line I make on the inside of his skull swells one side of his face, one eye rolls up, as though he is searching the ceiling.

I am always so sorry, and it is always too late. I should be punished for what I've done, but who can punish me? There's only exile, which I chose after Afaitu, with the Tahitian pearl on her ankle, or the silly boy who lost the bone hook I carved for him with great and original art.

As I have done before, I should walk into the island's interior valleys, and live with the mountain lion and the argumentative corvidae. I should walk until I can no longer hear the sea, and then walk further, and wait for the terminal wave that is, one day, coming, soon, yesterday, tomorrow, that will disorder time with its passage, or has already done so, that will leave nothing in its wake. Not even me.

— THE THREADBARE MAGICIAN —
Cat Rambo

Cat Rambo's story "The Threadbare Magician" involves a trailer park. Trailer parks are special places in America, places that endure despite social stigma. They are small cities with their own neighborhoods and traditions. Why should they not have their own guardian spirits?

Trailer parks are an American invention. The first trailers to be pulled by car were canvas tents that folded onto a wooden platform. The first patent for such an arrangement was issued in 1914, and by 1916 more elaborate versions, including the hard top trailer, were being mass-produced and sold. With the onslaught of the Great Depression, people started living in their trailers full time. Campgrounds that accepted the trailers were dubbed trailer courts. As trailer courts grew, so did backlash against them, with many cities passing zoning laws that banished the trailers to areas outside the city limits.

WWII brought a demand for temporary housing for defense plant workers and the trailer industry responded by creating the first house trailer. The government created 8,500 trailer parks to house their 35,000 trailers. During this time, trailers were constructed that could hook up to water, sewer, and electricity services. Trailers were popular with returning GI's at the end of the war, and the first true mobile home parks sprang up all over the country, with discriminatory zoning laws springing up in their wake.

In the 1960s mobile homes transformed into—well, homes. They were set on foundations. They were widened, often beyond the point where it would be legal to drive them out of the park. In 1974, Congress finally recognized mobile homes as housing. As of 2013, an estimated 20 million people live in mobile homes. While some fit the stereotype of the poverty-stricken trailer park resident, other trailer parks are inhabited by people who are reasonably well off, and who like the combination of freedom and community provided by the parks.

The American Dream involves two visions: bettering yourself by owning a home, and following the call of the open road. Trailer parks are mocked ruthlessly in the media and pop culture, but in a way they represent America's deepest visions of itself—small, intimate communities in which people both own a home and are never tied down.

——◄●►——

Old fabric holds smells better than the cloth of more recent decades. New stuff is all chemicals. It rubs the roof of your mouth like steel wool if you sniff too hard, bites like a spell's sting.

Older silks, wools, cottons—the organics—hold household odors. Cedar and cinnamon, turmeric and garlic. Perfumes you can no longer find, like L'Origan or Quelques Fleurs. Camphorated moth balls or talcum powder. More rarely the whiff of a person, a smell lingering long after every other scrap of their DNA has vanished from this earth.

Most often just the lilac assault left by a hasty dry-clean. But the other times make it worth it.

I pulled the green XL circle aside with my thumb and kept going widdershins, into the Ls. So far the Value Village's rack had yielded only two possibilities: an XXL black with a bamboo-patterned weave, cream-colored dragons curled and coiled amid sun-ridden clouds and an XL crimson rayon whose flame-pattern suited it to throw-away magic. A protective cloak perfect for next week's trip to Portland.

I fingered through the fabrics, searching for silk among the rayon and cotton. *Nope, nope, nope.*

A pretty day outside. One of the last days before summer slanted to the other side of the clock and the days began shrinking into the grey days of Seattle fall. A day for turning up the radio and blasting "Dani California" until the sound came up through your bones. A day for wishing you were in love. Or some reasonable facsimile.

My own shirt was printed with umbrellas. Parasols really, pinwheeled against a gray sky and white cumulus clouds. Protection, and even though it was newer and untested, I trusted it to ward off anything. Like wearing magic protective gloves, more supple than lead-lined canvas but surely at least that solid.

Shouldn't have trusted it.

The spell struck up from a black background, red serpents, scales lined with scallops as blue as the sky outside. Slashing bites along the outside of my left hand, locking on, tails sticking straight out as they attached themselves.

I lurched sideways.

The floor crashed up into my face, thunked against my forehead in painful collision.

Then I was gone.

—⟨●⟩—

When I awoke, I was in a car's back seat alone, my cheek pressed to sticky vinyl upholstery. I could not raise my head, couldn't move other than a slow blink. I found myself fighting for my breath, had to focus entirely on that activity, as though my life depended on it.

There was a good chance it did.

"Awake," a voice said from the front seat.

Someone else grunted. They weren't addressing me, just reporting my state.

Although my body was immobile, my mind raced.

They could only want one thing. What almost every magic attacker wanted: to strip away all the magic I'd accumulated and take it for their own. Lucky me, most of it was stored in my house. Unlucky me. If I'd had some of it with me, if I'd worn a more powerful shirt than this one, I might have been able to fight this off.

I tried to gather what clues I could. The beige vinyl smelled of itself and old tobacco. We were in traffic. Whoever was in front wasn't talking. The radio was on, but tuned to static, a whisper so faint I had to strain to be sure I was really hearing it.

We were on a busy highway. Perhaps I5? If so, I'd been unconscious a good quarter of an hour, probably longer.

"Just lie still and be," the first voice said, presumably to me. "There in an hour. You're full of poison, man. It'll kill you soon if you don't get the cure, so lie back, rest easy."

"Why the fuck are you explaining anything to him?"

"Make him lie quiet, knowing he gotta."

An annoyed grunt.

So perhaps I wouldn't be devoured. But it couldn't be anything good they were taking me to. Otherwise why bother preparing a trap?

I lay there, working on the parasols, understitching each rib, readying my spell. Whatever had paralyzed me was ebbing slowly. Too slowly.

The rumble underfoot changed quality, became higher-pitched. Time.

I gathered up my legs. Thumb and little finger of my left hand grinding together for leverage, I flipped up the door lock, fumbling with the handle's release mechanism.

"What's he..." the first voice said from the front seat. The handle popped over and I flung myself out.

Neon ghosts of parasols surrounded me, slender ribs of flickering magic barely visible, contrails of light and shadow. I used them to bounce myself up from the road. Cars swerved around me, one glancing off the railing in a crescendo of sparks.

Startled faces gaped at me through windshields. One locked eyes for a split second that seemed an age long. A dark-featured, handsome face not staring like the rest, but, bizarrely, smiling as his eyes met mine.

Then I sailed over the railing's metal curve towards the water.

The Aurora Bridge has seen a lot of suicides. There's even placards along its rails, directing the desperate to suicide hotlines and support.

I wasn't trying to kill myself, though. I was trying to live.

The parasols let me glide down to the water, let it carry me eastward towards the University. Now that I was away from whatever had deadened my abilities in the car, I could think more freely. I worked at my bonds, rubbed them away on a concrete outcropping as I clung to it.

I crawled out of the channel under an overpass. A gnarled homeless man had set up camp there, had a tent and an oil drum for his campfire. Two crows waited patiently for leftovers from the pan boiling in a makeshift sling over the drum.

He watched me warily, smoking a hand-rolled cigarette, as I shook myself free of the water. The startled crows flapped away.

He didn't speak, but he pointed me towards a trail up through the bank of English ivy to the Montlake station. I took the 545 back to Redmond, digging change out of my pocket and accepting a transfer. The bus driver eyed my dripping clothes unhappily but forbode from saying anything. Other people edged away.

Half the bus was reading their cell phones, and by the faces, it was unhappy news this late afternoon.

I didn't pay much attention. I swayed my way past the middle of the bus and the swivel benches there, went a few seats back to a deserted seat and took it.

I'd have to catch the bus back in tomorrow to go get my car. As we started over the bridge, I stared out the window at water lilies and assessed my body.

Something was wrong, terribly wrong, I could tell that. A slow acting magic, I could feel that by the way it had seeped into my bones.

Not painful. *So far, at any rate.* Poison, they'd said. Not ordinary poison but something magical. Something that acted slowly.

Slow, very slow. I had days rather than hours, but how many? Who was the guy they'd meant to take me to?

They'd try for me again, I knew that. They'd known my patterns well enough to plant a spell on an item calculated to lure me.

They might be waiting for me at home.

A crowd jostled onto the bus at Evergreen Station. Someone sat down beside me despite the water dripping from my clothing.

Middle-aged, dark-haired, muscles rippling under a plain black t-shirt, three silver rings in his left ear, was he selling something?

His white teeth flashed at me in a smile. Not a false, "I want something from you" smile but a genuine expression, the sort of smile you give someone you love, all the joy at seeing them again, showing in your eyes. It made my heart skip a beat.

He said, "Didn't you just move into Friendly Village?"

"A few months ago," I said.

I thought surely he was too young to be living in the same 55+ mobile home park, but he said, "I'm Al Lorca, from Coho Lane, Unit 42. How are you liking it so far?"

"Roy Macomber. It's not what I expected of a trailer park," I said. I wondered when he was going to acknowledge that I was sitting there dripping wet. The puddle I was sitting in was seeping into his jeans but he didn't seem to notice.

"Mobile homes," he said, and we both laughed, because that was one of the characteristics of the denizens of Friendly Village, that they eschewed the words "trailer park" at all costs.

"You're in that white Merlotte across from the unit with all the gnomes and flamingos? Nice trailer."

"The Cadillac of mobile homes," I said.

"I've been in there, visiting Ed. He put some time in it."

"Pergo, central air, and a tankless water heater. Lots of nice little amenities. I was lucky."

He nodded. A little smile hovered off and on his lips.

It made me uneasy. *Pretty lure. Pretty, pretty lure, but surely he's part of this.*

I pulled the cord for the next stop. Lorca looked surprised as I stood up. "Not headed home?"

"Got to visit a friend."

I felt him watching me as I got off.

I went to Kirkland to see Jason, though it was against my better judgment.

Still, what better to heal you than a magical spring, like the one he was the hereditary guardian of?

I could surreptitiously test the water against this poison. Who was to say it'd work?

I felt defensive about seeing him. I always did. He had a way of seeing through me, of rolling his eyes, that made me impatient and balky as a mule about asking for help. I'd rather beat my head against a wall trying to solve it, and the bloodier it was, the harder it became to make the request.

Where I can be downright bitchy, Jason was one of those golden folk who are always in a good mood, for whom the half-full glass is near spilling over. Beautiful and holding an advanced degree in anthropology from Princeton, which he'd somehow parlayed into a job as a buyer for a very small, extremely select, and obscenely lucrative gallery.

How did we meet? I'd like to say it was something significant, but it was a missed connection ad in on Craigslist that he placed. I mistakenly answered, thinking he'd been talking to me. I found out three months into the relationship, or rather I guessed that, and his silence confirmed it.

I don't know how long he would've let me go on believing he hadn't been talking to some other lanky blond man he once made eye contact with on the light rail. *Maybe all my life.*

But still, that was the linchpin of our meeting, founded on confusion and silent, tactful kindness. There are worse things, I know, or do know now, at least. But back then I was young and stupid and wanted to be cherished for myself, to have been chosen for something I and I alone could provide. Now I'm no longer young.

So—Jason. Gray chinos and a faded blue shirt surely purchased at that stage rather than being allowed to weather into it. It made his eyes Pacific blue, a blue that would have made the ocean itself jealous.

I'd screwed things up, but Jason kept trying and trying to make it work. He'd coax me into showing up, for a couple of weeks or months, we'd be all right. And then at some point I'd lose my cool and the fight, as familiar as a next-door neighbor, would appear again. Finally I just gave up.

Still, every time I saw him, it made me smile.

For a moment it felt as though he was blocking the doorway, denying me access. *Is he part of this too?* Then he fell back and I felt ashamed of my suspicion.

"The bad penny," he said. He stood aside as I entered, Mr. Fips bouncing on his shoulder and chirping greeting. "What do you need this time?"

I couldn't help it. The derision in his voice forced to lie out of my mouth, horrifying me even as it passed my lips. "Nothing. I just wanted to see you."

I glanced around the hallway. I loved Jason's house, its immaculate candy-colored interior walls, Mr. Fips the parakeet, the photos on the walls, all Jason's work, young men and women in black trenchcoats, ascending a large interior staircase, all black and white.

He said, eyes narrowing, "Why are you all wet?"

"Someone tried to kidnap me."

"Who?"

"I'd like to know that myself. He used a spell to knock me out and two goons to collect me."

"But you got away, clearly." He looked me over. "And your escape apparently involved a great deal of water. Go take a shower; I'll bring you in a change of clothes."

Everything in his bathroom that could be white was, all immaculately clean except the bathroom mirror, which had the usual black marks in Sharpie drawn on it. You don't want anything getting through, after all.

I changed into the t-shirt, jeans and tightie whites he'd left out for me and went downstairs.

He was in the kitchen, chopping fennel. He looked up as I paused in the doorway.

"Why here?" he said.

"Wanted to regroup before I get home to an ambush."

"Fair enough. Are you staying for dinner?"

I eyed the fennel. "What's on the menu?"

In answer to his repeated question over dinner (braised fennel, crispy tofu with almonds, an excellent Oregon Pinot Gris, consumed while Mr. Fips serenaded his reflection in the birdcage mirror) I shook my head and underscored the lie. "Wanted to see you, that's all."

His eyebrow quirked up but he smiled in a way that made me feel as though warm hands were cradling my heart.

While we were watching TV at seven, I learned what everyone on the bus had been so engrossed by. A sniper and a playground, down in Arizona. Eight kids dead, three wounded.

"Life doesn't make sense sometimes," Jason said. He cuddled into me and I put my arm around him.

Around ten, he stretched and said, "I can make the couch up for you."

He looked directly at me as he tucked a towel around the birdcage. "Or you can come to bed with me."

I hesitated just a moment too long. He flushed.

I leaned over and put my hand on the back of his neck, pulling him to me. I kissed him hard.

It had been a long time.

By the time I snuck from his bed at two in the morning and went down the back stairs to the fountain, I felt pretty miserable. The words "I love you" had been hovering in the air tonight. It was why I'd stayed away, to tell the truth.

I am a wizard. That's not an existence that facilitates family. We're always dealing with deadly creatures, ancient evils. The sort of things whose tentacles roil endlessly in the eternal darkness. Those creatures have a way of going after those near and dear—it's much worse than killing a wizard to cripple him or her with grief, just before killing them. Jason had more inkling of the Hidden World than most, it was true. But the world would be a lesser place without him.

And he was the last of the fountain's guardians. It was well past time for him to find or father his successor.

The thoughts weighed down my footsteps as I went through the herb garden, past pots of lemon and rose-scented geraniums, a patch of basils, Italian to Thai, and chives silver fuzzed with chilly moonlight.

The tiny fountain burbled and plashed near the path's end. Once it had been a spring, but Jason's ancestors had fetched flat white stones and built this round to contain it. Pickerel rush and blue flag throve in its basin, and two white and orange carp rose as my fingers broke the surface, goggly golden eyes watching the movement of my hand.

"No bread for you, fellows," I said.

I cupped my hand underwater and drew it up through the reflection of the moon. As I raised it, the reflection stayed in my hand. When I dipped my lips to drink, the water's coldness almost burned, and as I pulled my face away, my breath hung steaming over the few last drops pooled in my hand.

I swallowed, feeling the cold move down my throat, take up occupancy in my gut.

Any difference? I shook my head and vertigo assailed me. *No.* I was unhealed, the poison still there with me.

I would have to look elsewhere.

I turned. Jason stood on the kitchen steps, bare-chested, his skin smooth as silk in the moonlight. A frown smothered his face in disapproval.

"I should have known. What is it, curse, poison? Disease?"

"They gave me a magical poison."

"The water doesn't work for magical things," he said. His lips were thin and arrogant and quivered with emotion. "I could have told you that. If you'd trusted me enough to ask."

He took a step down till we stood on the same level. "You know, I thought for a long time we were destined. Hard enough to find someone who's gay, but a magical adept, someone who'd understand why I can't leave this place, that was rare enough that I figured the universe was stepping in." He eyed me. "Or punishing me. I don't know which, but either way it felt meaningful. Not random."

"Do you know what the opposite of paranoia is?" I asked.

He shook his head.

"Pronoia. It's the belief that the universe is secretly plotting to help you."

"Like the Truman Show?"

"They weren't out to help him, they were out to make television out of him. What I'm trying to say, is—the universe is random, Jason. Any meaning in it we see is something cobbled together out of our own blind spots and beliefs."

"A strange thing for a magician to say."

I shrugged. "I've seen demons and angels. I'm still not sure that means God exists."

"God exists," he said.

"Maybe. But if you think he—or she—is up there colluding with the fates to ensure you have a happy life, you are so far off the mark you're not even hitting the board. Children believe that sort of thing."

He cocked his head to one side. "So everything children believe in isn't true, is that what you're saying? But what I'm saying is that you've disappointed me for the last time. Don't bother coming around again."

He turned and went back inside.

Part of me was surprised it'd taken him so long. Another part was dumbstruck and hurt as a kicked puppy. I tried to keep either expression from showing in my eyes, kept my face impassive so I could pretend my heart was too.

Instead I just said, "All right," to the empty air and left.

This early in the morning the roads were deserted.

There's a particular feel to the morning's small hours, an insignificance in the midst of significance that I like. The taxi passed an empty double bus and the drivers, taxi and bus, nodded at each other as we did.

I could feel the poison eating at me.

Maybe it was my imagination. Either way, the sensation was unpleasant, clutching at my throat and drying my mouth out till I could hardly wet my lips, let alone spit. A hot feeling, as though my molars were being chewed on by electricity.

If I acted now, maybe my magic wouldn't be too screwed up. Sure, the poison would flip things around some, but surely I was focused enough I could shrug off any effects of the poison. Cast a spell.

But I was *tired*, so tired I felt as though I were physically propping myself up. I had a tendency to catch myself staring and then not know how long my mind had been vacant, chewing over something meaningless. I felt immobilized, heavy. Lethargic. Was that the effect of the poison or was it simply my mind imposing its own flutter over the picture? I could barely keep my eyes open. Muscles twitched in my cheeks, around my eyes, twitches of the same weariness.

Still, I managed to shrug off the way my eyes kept sliding closed. I had no time to lose, no magical energy to spare. I had to act or else face sliding into oblivion.

I went home to Friendly Village.

Yes, the place is perhaps as twee as the name might suggest. I moved in three months ago, when I finally hit their age requirement: 55. But it's a nice place, backing onto Bear Creek.

Nice, in that I had no one interfering with me, no one watching my spells or trying to snare my secrets. Bad, in that it was isolated. I used to think I wanted it that way. After all, how had Danny died? Back in Villa Encantada, he'd befriended a neighbor being attacked by another magician, and he'd been torn to pieces by a spell as a result.

Safer not to deal with people at all. You never know what's hiding behind someone's smile.

I took my time approaching it, but as far as I could tell, no one had been around. I stepped in through the front door and breathed easier. I was home.

I went into my workroom and browsed through the rack there. Rows of shirts, each more brightly colored than the last.

Everyone's magic is different. Sure, there are basic tenets, laws of contagion and similarity, the Rule of Three, karma, that sort of thing. But beyond that, it depends on your internal landscape, the metaphors that matter most to you, the ones that shape your dreams, your thoughts, your internal landscape.

For example, Danny, the guy who taught me, used thrift shops too. But he wasn't looking for shirts, the way I do. He was looking for what I call the Sad Orphans. You know them. The handmade plaque reading, "For Grandma Lolo from Susie." The personalized mug that says "Kitty C. Needs her caffeine." Peeling trophies and wooden boxes decoupaged with awkward puppies or pyrographed with western designs of bluebells and skulls in charred brown lines.

He could use those. He tapped into what might be unused, forgotten history—I don't know what you call it, but he could harvest it. Personalize an object and you're creating ties that a magician can use if he or she has the right handle on it.

Me, I use clothing. And a particular kind of clothing. The more fine-tuned you are, the more powerful. There are mages that can use anything, anything they pick up or are in proximity to—and I do mean anything—but they're low voltage, not much juice at all.

I use Hawaiian shirts. I'd been a vintage clothing dealer until an incident that I'm not going to go into at this time brought me, gasping and soaked with salt water, to Danny's feet. He took me as a student and I wouldn't be alive today if he hadn't.

But anyway. Hawaiian shirts.

You may not know anything about them other than they're usually gaudy and fat men seem to be drawn to them. But the Musa-Shiya the Shirtmaker shirt I'd been reaching for back when this whole passage began, was powerful for more than the design. Koichiro Miyamoto, Musa-Shiya himself, was one of the smart guys who put their heads together in the forties. They wanted to sell souvenirs to the servicemen clogging up their beaches. They noticed they bought postcards to send home. But a postcard—even a glossy color one—how much do you make off something like that?

So they came up with the wearable postcard, which they called the Aloha shirt. Nowadays, a Hawaiian shirt.

You can find anything on a Hawaiian shirt. Not just palm trees, angelfish, and lei'd hula girls. Dragons, tigers, scorpions. Robots, rockets, and Godzilla (not exactly, because of copyright issues, but close enough that you know what the designer was trying to get at).

That's what I use. The designs, and the older they are, the more potent they've become.

Unfortunately, few of them have anything to do with healing.

I flipped through my closet. The thing I needed was a dragon shirt, but all of mine were threadbare and worn. I'd used them unnecessarily, Danny would have told me, squandered the strength of their magic on frivolous things. If I'd faced up to things, I'd have some of their juju left.

Could I alter a shirt to save me? I did that sort of thing all the time. I sewed vintage bark cloth into linings, fashioned tiny pockets in hems that could hold a crystal or a gumball charm or lucky rabbit's foot. Often I changed buttons, particularly on newer shirts that used plastic instead of coconut fiber to create the fastenings.

I took out one of my early efforts. Danny had helped me with it, had insisted on including some bits of his magic. Now that he was gone, would they be of any help? I ran my fingers along the hem. He'd sewn some beads in there.

Taking out a pair of bird-headed scissors, I snipped each tiny, precise stitch away. The caution made me think of Danny. Tears came to my eyes.

The poison must be affecting me. I never cry.

And yet tears fell on the fabric, deadening the scarlet and amber cloth as I tugged away bits of thread to coax the little pouch open.

A tiny bead, unglazed, made of clay. An oval as long as my smallest fingernail, its sides ridged, and tiny markings between the ridges, like traces of cuneiform.

I squinted at it, then gave up and went to get my reading glasses. Aging sucks.

But even with the glasses, I couldn't read the bead.

Magic is semiotics, the art of reading the world, of knowing what each signifier has packed into it. Magicians love history and morphology and all the other soft sciences, even the most fragile, like the Kabbalah and Tarot and I Ching.

To use a bead whose meaning I couldn't read went against the grain. But it must be beneficent, or Danny wouldn't have used it.

I took the umbrella shirt I'd been wearing. It hadn't protected me before. Could I make it into something that could?

I studied it. The fabric's background was blue, studded with silver raindrops. I used pale grey thread, weaving a web between the umbrellas that was barely visible to the eye. I ran a line along the collar's topstitching, and sewed disks of mirrors under the collar's points. I picked out every bead that Danny had sewn into the other shirt. Each one got sewn into the underside of the shirt, centered beneath the umbrellas.

There were almost enough to do them all. I hummed under my breath as I did it, an old Disney tune. Drip drip drop, little April showers. It wasn't April, but I hoped that wouldn't matter.

Magic is about belief. It's about tricking yourself into believing it works because if you do, you can make it work. You have to think about it, but you can't think about it too hard, can't think in ways that will bring doubt into the spell.

Remember the joke about the centipede who, when asked how she managed to walk, thought about it too hard and then couldn't do it without falling over her own feet? That's a real danger for magicians, and sometimes if things go awry, they go awry in a big way, bringing about natural disasters or other chaos, things that could core a magician like an apple and leave him only a husk.

You have to learn to trust your intuition with your life. Or else you die. Or come so close to it you wish you had.

I shrugged on the shirt, buttoning it hastily. It felt comforting to have Danny's beads around me. Like Danny's arms. Some of the lethargy dropped away. Not all, not by a long shot, but this was better at least, let me blink away some effects of the poison.

Just in time. Someone was coming.

The thing about mobile homes is that they feel temporary. The skin that protects you from the outside world is thinner, more fragile. That's not entirely a bad thing because it keeps you from being ambushed, lulled into a sense of security by thick brick or stone or wood. Which is why I felt my visitor and put the shirt I was working on down long before his knuckles brushed the door, through the vibration of his footsteps on the front porch.

When I opened the door, it was Lorca.

He didn't feel like a magic worker, but something lurked under his surface. Not malignant, though, no hidden serpent or trap like the one that had caught me in Value Village. No, not like that at all, but a sense of some hidden wonder, like a lumpy gray geode hiding a cluster of amethysts at its core.

"I thought you might offer me a cup of coffee. Nice shirt."

I didn't step aside and let him in, though I almost started to do so. There was something complicated, frighteningly so, about Lorca. Something in the glitter of those long-lashed, dark eyes.

"Afraid I'm out of coffee."

"Here in Seattle? I believe that's a fine-able offense." He leaned in the doorway. "So what do you think of the place, now that you've been here a while?"

"It's good so far," I said diffidently. "Everyone lives up to the name. Very friendly."

He laughed. "They are! The tenant before you here, Ed, grew dahlias. Everyone will be over telling you what to plant."

I glanced toward the back. The three large flowerbeds edging my unit were a little daunting. I've never been good with herbal magic, other than the spells everyone knows. But I'd thought to grow some herbs out there, at least. Maybe a tomato plant or two. It was good, fluffy soil.

"There's plenty of activities," Lorca said. "Bingo in the winter." His eyes danced with some secret joke. "Very practical prizes."

"Practical?" I couldn't help but ask. "Practical how? Like a set of screwdrivers?"

"Cases of toilet paper and light bulbs," he said with a wry twist to his lips.

I laughed, we both did. I found myself charmed despite my suspicions.

"Plenty of women," he said. "You'd be surprised at the action some of these guys see."

Some of these guys, he'd said. Not himself. And there was an undercurrent there, enough to make me say, "I don't happen to swing that way, myself."

The sunlight caught his hair, which held a blue shine like the under-plumage of a Stellar's Jay, dark but unmistakable, as his smile swelled.

"Neither do I."

He's flirting with me. I wanted to flirt back. To banter, begin the dance that would lead us into bed.

This was not the time, with some unknown opponent laying traps for me. This was too probably part of that—at least my application of Occam's Razor argued that it did.

"Perhaps I'll come to a bingo game sometime," I said, reluctant to shut the door between us.

"That's in the winter only. Months away."

"Well," I said uncomfortably, "perhaps I'll see you somewhere else."

Disappointment flickered across his face. Again, the emotion seemed genuine. Perhaps I'd made the wrong decision.

I could feel the poison spell working in me. Solve that first. Otherwise I might be dead before we had any chance to go to bed.

"You're not a spontaneous person," he said. Not question, but statement. "You don't jump into things."

This was overly personal for someone I'd known less than five minutes, no matter how pretty he was.

"I have work to do," I said bluntly, resting the heel of my hand on the door.

He was graceful enough, I'd give him that. Inclining his head, he flashed me a smile that made promises: that he was not offended, that he was still interested, that what would eventually happen in bed would surprise me.

I closed the door. I rested my forehead against its cool hard surface and cursed things: the universe's odd sense of timing, my unseen and unknown opponent, the curse eating away at my blood.

And my own cowardice. No, I'm not a spontaneous person. I view the world with a caution and suspicion acquired through experience. Had I ever been spontaneous, had I ever had that easy grace of going with the flow, of being one of the people who skated easily through life?

Such things were foreign to my nature. My mother told me she hadn't seen me smile until I was over three, said she'd even worried about my development, taken me to a child psychiatrist (an event of which I have no recollection) who had pronounced me sullen but normal.

I made myself coffee, brewing it strong and dark and bitter as my thoughts. I had a long day ahead and I wanted to see the end of it. Right now, that was in doubt.

No time for distractions, no matter how dark their hair, how bright their eyes. No matter how charming the slight, unplaceable accent, the lilt to his voice. No matter what he had seemed to promise. Such things are never free, and the ones that claim to be often have the highest price.

What was it time for?

An Oracle, that was what.

I hadn't consulted an oracle in years. Never in this area.

I went to a closet and took down the usual sorts of accumulated boxes before finding a box of cedarwood holding a small red velvet pouch. I took out the contents and cast the runes.

And frowned at them. Had I been overly casual, insulted them?

I took the time to center myself and cast again.

The same result. Which couldn't be right.

An Oracle here in Friendly Village itself? Pleasant, unmagical Friendly Village?

Only a few trailers away?

The singlewide trailer was small, and dowdy, but a profusion of flowers surrounded it. Hummingbirds clouded the standing fuchsia spilling blooms across the compact-sized driveway. Beside the door, a silver witch ball reflected everything around it, inverted and in miniature.

Before I could knock on the door, it jerked open. A long-nosed, wrinkled face above a solid body in an "Embrace Your Inner Crone" t-shirt, said, "You don't need me. Go see the god."

"Beg pardon?" Behind her head, I glimpsed a living room decorated in white seashells and royal blue velvet.

"Go back to Osprey Lane. He's at the end there."

The door shut in my face.

I knocked again, but there was no answer. Very well. There's nothing obliging an Oracle to help everyone that stops by. Some keep odd hours; others have odder restrictions, though the runes should have warned me of either.

And, technically, she *had* given me direction. A street name, even. And an idea about who lived there.

A god? One of the beings discarded by our age, living a prayer to prayer life in a forgotten corner of the world? Usually they were hard to find. But there was no reason why one might not have taken up residence here.

Jason had steered me to Friendly Village. Had he known of its double nature? Surely not, when I'd had no inkling. On the other hand, he'd been born in this area. He knew the history.

When you grow up someplace, you learn many of its secrets.

Perhaps not all. But certainly most.

Friendly Village loops and winds, narrow lanes scattered among the trailers. Every patch of landscaping is different: cacti surrounded one mobile home, followed by a forest of rhododendrons, then dahlias that might have originated in my own garden.

Up along the creek a little road ran, unlined with homes. It led to a trailer of a peculiar pearly hue that might have been mistaken for grime at first. It was a Nordic style, almost, simulated white pine beams, rough wrought ironwork on the walls. Its landscaping was bare: a line of rocks, two tiny fir trees, one slightly larger than the other.

Outside, a massive rock crouched beside the mailbox.

In Greek mythology, such stones were sacred to Aphrodite. But I didn't think a Greek god lurked within.

A man stood on the front porch, watching me approach. His attitude was expectant, perhaps even impatient, as though my visit was overdue. His gray beard hung down to his belly, woolly as a blanket. His eyes were blue and a few golden strands showed among the silver on his scalp to attest to his Nordic heritage.

I stopped a few feet away, looking at him.

"You've come of your own accord," he said. "It would've been easier if you just let them bring you."

I acted unsurprised, and maybe I was. Occam's razor again. One) move to a new place. Two) be attacked by a powerful magical adversary. More than time connected that chain.

"I'm Forseti," he said.

I searched through crumbs of mythology. My knowledge might have only the depth of a Wikipedia article, but it was wide. You learn the names of all the gods, once you realized most still exist in our world, acting out their own plans, few of which are constructed to advance humanity. Or even take it into account, really.

"Justice, right?" I said.

He dropped a slow nod.

"What justice is there in killing me?" I asked.

He said, "Perhaps you should come inside for tea."

Inside the trailer, I could see its true aspect. Like many magical things, it was far larger on the inside than out. The ceiling glittered as though made of silver and pillars of red gold supported it. The walls were gone—or clear –as though we stood inside an open pavilion, able to see Friendly Village's trailers and hills all around, except at the back, where the home overlooked the low banks of Bear Creek.

A nifty trick. I would've liked to have known how to do it. But I didn't ask, just took the teacup my host summoned from thin air, and sniffed it. Gunpowder and lemon wafted on the moist steam.

I didn't drink, although I nodded in thanks. Everyone knows better than eat something conjured. You didn't know what the caster had been trying to create, or even if she or he was likely to get it right, without a single molecule twisted out of place.

He smiled at that.

I guess I might've too. I had the poison he'd already given me, permeating me. It was highly unlikely he needed to add something else to it.

The god addressed me, his tone formal. "Rahul Macomber. Mage."

I nodded this time.

Forseti said, "I must protect this place. I am the one who does so. You know as well as I that it's up to us."

The truth that none of us like to dance with, what I'd told Jason. At the heart of it, there is no balance of good or evil. It's all random. That sniper on the playground? No demon possessed him, no alien mind control set him off. It was all accident of chemicals and brain impulses.

We like to pretend, we gods and magicians, that we represent an order, but it's all hollow. There's nothing at the heart of it.

"You have a life, but you choose not to use it," he said. "Who would mourn you? You've shunned connections. You hide. You skulk. You never dare."

That seemed unfair to me. "I enjoy life, nonetheless," I protested.

He shook his head. "Do you?" He gestured all around us. "Here in Friendly Village are others like you. But they dance and quarrel and fuck and love each other. They live. You don't. You waste your life hiding from living it. Why is it not justice that I should take someone who has renounced life, and use them to protect those who have not?"

"How is it your decision?"

He drew himself up and suddenly was towering over me. "I am a god, one of the Aesir. And you question me?"

I squared my chin. "I do."

"Protest as you will, mortal," he declaimed. He could have made a fortune doing radio with that voice. It shivered down my spine and loosened my bowels almost to the point of accident.

He made a gesture and the beads sewn into my shirt exploded, one after another, striking me like blows. The air around me thinned with the magic's dissipation.

No one fights gods. No one sane, or long-lived, anyhow. I could see in his implacable gaze that his decision would not change. I set the teacup down on the ground between us.

"How long?" I asked.

He knew what I was asking. "One sunset more for you," he said. "If you are willing to come lay your life at my feet, I will use it to protect this place. Otherwise you will fall to my curse and no good will come to anyone from your death."

Less time than I'd thought. Not enough to escape to someone who might heal me, even if I knew anyone who might be inclined in that way. Not enough to research or dig out some solution, unless I was incredibly lucky. And I knew no way of binding luck: the forces of randomness are as implacable as any god.

I was tempted to try walking out through one of the transparent walls, but the thought of Forseti laughing at me after I'd broken my nose in an unsuccessful attempt prevented me.

Even in death, I'd retain my dignity.

For what little good it did me.

He said, as I left, "Will you be back?"

"I don't know," I said, and it was true.

Lorca was sitting on my doorstep. It should have alarmed me. The fact that it didn't alarm me should have alarmed me. But I found myself smiling at the sight of him, nonetheless.

What he said could have been a spell, but it was a love poem.

He said, "I will woo you with words like wine, like honey, like addictive smoke. I'll insinuate my name into things until you won't be able to look at a sunset, or the water, or even the smallest scrap of paper, without thinking of me. I will make you accustomed to me, till my absence becomes as marked as though your hand or foot were missing. I will make you drunk on me, will make you long for me. I will make you lonely without me, accustomed to me as though I were integral to your world."

I said, "Why?"

"Do you not know that I love you? Isn't that sufficient?"

Perhaps it should have been. I know it should have been. But as I said, I'm possessed of a suspicious nature and even here, with something that seemed too good to be true…well, as I said. Too good to be true.

I said again, "But why?"

"Who am I to decipher these things? I saw you and I knew you were mine."

"And how many men have you known were yours?"

His gaze was steady. "I love you as I have loved no other."

"You lust after me," I corrected. "And had you seen me before you came to my door?"

"Countless times."

His eyes glowed.

Now I knew who—or rather, what—I was facing.

Death.

No wonder Lorca had seemed so dark, so mysterious. So alluring. So unknowable in that way that every lover is unknowable, has unguessable depths that they will reveal.

I wasn't ready. Yes, my 55th birthday had hit me hard but not because I thought I was about to meet death. But because inside, like everyone else, I'm a teenager wondering what the hell this aging thing is all about.

When had I gotten old, when had gray crept into my hair, when had the spring in my step begun to ebb? I wasn't getting old—just more mature. Perhaps even distinguished.

I told Lorca, "I know who you are."

"Then we will dissemble no longer." He stretched out a hand, palm upward. Blue lines of veins throbbed there: a blood magician might have given way to that temptation. "Will you give yourself to me?"

Hope and sadness mingled in his tone.

This wasn't how I'd expected this to happen. Every mage's encounter was different, I knew that, but I've never heard of an amorous Death.

Perhaps no one had wanted to admit it, to set such a thing down.

"You can't wait for the poison to take me?" I said, a little bitterly.

He said, "Take my hand and I will heal you."

"That is not at all what I expected of Death," I admitted.

He laughed. "The main purpose of expectations is to be defeated."

Lore is carefully guarded among magicians. The ultimate currency, more precious than gold (you can always coax that from gnomes) or gems (you can only steal those from dragons) or any other object ever coveted by humans: tulips, spices, molybdenum, stamps, or other rarities like mummy amulets, or the bezoars taken from the heads of certain toads.

And within the categories of that lore, oneiromancy or speaking to trees, or anything else, knowledge of Death is among the most precious. Not what happens to the body after death: forces of decay and decomposition are easy enough to decipher, given how our bodies function. No, something more particular than that: the entity we know as Death, who doesn't turn up usually as a robed skeleton with the scythe. Instead he or she takes forms that seem unprepossessing: a little old lady in a purple hat, a flaxen-haired farmboy, a pregnant woman (though pregnant with what, no one knows).

So it was not unprecedented, this sexy form.

But the proposition, that was something else.

"Why me?" I asked.

For the first time he looked perplexed, as though he didn't know the answer either.

It was an unprecedented opportunity, though.

And, of course, it had presented itself at a time when I had nothing to spare for it.

Save myself first. Then talk to Death.

He said, slowly, "Something about the quality of your loneliness, I guess."

His eyes seemed very human.

Have you ever fallen in love over the course of seconds? At first, they are unremarkable and then, like a lens slipping into focus, they're entirely different and yet the same. They haven't changed it all, of course. Instead your position has changed: you're in a different alignment with the universe.

Magicians know love is petty and small, a thing built of pheromones and proximity. At least most of it. Fantasy books talk about love as though it were the most powerful force in the universe. But it's not. It's an entity as ineffectual as any of us. We can resist it. At least, in my experience. I'd never had a long-term relationship—Jason and I might have come close, but in truth a real relationship would have distracted me from my work. Would have made me a lesser magician.

I said, "You know I don't have time for this." And then, less harshly, "No matter how tempting."

That brought a flicker of a smile.

"Another sunset," he said.

His eyes searched mine.

"You have but to speak and I will hear you," he said, almost shyly. And was gone.

I unlocked my door and went inside to sit down on the couch.

I said there was one thing to keep in mind about magic, but really there are two. The first is that a magician's focus affects their power. But the second is that there are magic things that anyone can do.

They are not truly magic; they are the result of being able to read the Universe. A combination of semiotics and micro-expressions and maybe, just maybe a thin thread of fortune-telling, the vague and swimmy kind that you see in the I-Ching, changing to match the situation.

Magicians know things. They know that demons do not like the smell of rosemary but can force themselves to touch it, and that they can be caught in pocket mirrors at certain times, when the light is right.

We know how people's eyes tend to flicker when they lie and what words they will use to convince themselves that they are speaking truth. We know how to charm ourselves to sleep and that smiling makes you feel happier. We know all the practical little things, the shortcuts and tricks that let a magician navigate life more easily than most.

Death hadn't been lying to me. I would have known.

I took a shirt covered with white orchids, their throats scarlet, and sewed white barkcloth into it. I would try purification. I put every healing and cleansing charm I knew into it.

When I put the shirt on, I had a few moments of hope that it was working, that it was drawing out the poison. I saw the mouths of the orchids waver, grow cyanotic over the scarlet. But then they twisted, driven awry by the magic, and I felt it wrench at my bones again, as though in admonition.

I managed to stagger to the shower, ran it hot and stood in the steaming water, letting it run over me as though I had any hope of it cleaning the taint from my core, and retched, over and over again.

I was almost wretched enough to speak Lorca's name.

There was no reason not to, was there? Aren't we all a little in love with death?

I stumbled out of the shower and stared at the lines on my mirror, and the steam collected between each squiggle. I toweled off with a vast bath towel of the kind I like, savoring the softness of the Turkish cotton, the absorbent dryness, the smell of lavender clinging to it.

One more sunset.

Some people like to think about that sort of thing. Their bucket list. If you had twenty-four hours to live, what would you eat and see and do and all of that? What people would you make confessions to or tell off?

What was the joke about the magician who sees Death in the morning? As I heard it, he saw Death in the fish market in the early morning in Paris, and Death looked surprised to see him. So he fled immediately, by boat and carried in afreet arms and then by foot, high on the slopes of Mount Ararat and there he saw Death again. And Death said, There you are! I saw I was to meet you here tonight, however did you get here so quickly from Paris?

I contemplated my wardrobe. I took out an abstract orange on black floral, shot through with blue streaks of pistils, over jeans and sneakers.

I poured rum and vodka to my household gods and the three ancestors whose photographs I keep in the shrine beside my bed.

"If I don't come back," I said to them, pouring vodka. "Haunt the fuck out of whoever buys this place. I give you full permission."

What if Lorca was some trick of Forseti's? The old man was a god, after all, capable of all sorts of subtle illusions. Gods were a different kind of magic. They weren't limited in the way that magicians were. Although Forseti had a focus, just as I had my shirts. His was justice.

That seemed to be of little help under these circumstances. There is no cosmic justice that would ensure he had to play by the rules.

Lorca was too perfect not to be some trick.

But on the other hand, isn't that how one imagined death? The ultimate lover, the soft voice who'd draw you down into oblivion in a Bob Fosse montage dance number?

And Lorca had said he'd remove the poison, hadn't he? There had been no accompanying, And then carry you off to the underground, at least that I could remember, I thought about calling him to me, asking him for clarification. But what if I only got one chance to call him?

I went into Seattle to get my car.

Yes, for some people the car wouldn't have been a priority. But I like my car, and the thought of it just sitting there in the lot until it got towed away as abandoned bothered me.

I felt better once I was behind the wheel. At fifteen years old, the car has some quirks and creaks, but there's a Hawaiian dancing girl doll on the dash, a lei dangling from the rear view mirror, and some much less visible cantrips.

I swung onto I-5. The day was so dazzling bright that it lifted my spirits, as least for just as long as it took for me to think about it possibly, quite probably, being my last day, and then my spirits sank again.

The radio said there was a prayer vigil at Westlake Center tonight. For the playground victims.

Forseti wanted me to surrender to him. To die and have meaning brought from my life, a few years of protection for the inhabitants of Friendly Village. Did they know that a god watched over them? Or did they attribute the placid, untroubled nature of their lives to some other force?

I was still thinking about that after I left 520 and turned into the complex. Struck by some whimsy, I went widdershins rather than clockwise, began to circle the complex, examine the tiny streets, barely worthy of the name, named Steelhead and Pilchuck, Salish and Snoqualmie.

I'd done this once before, when I was first thinking about buying into the complex. But I hadn't looked hard enough then. I'd been complacent. Now I looked as deep as I could and found the clues I'd missed before: a swarm of leprechauns living in a lilac bush; a multitude of bird baths in a yard, shaped in a long curve to fetch fairies to the waters; orange and green witch-balls making a boundary between one trailer's demesne and another's.

What a fool I was, to have missed this.

But the supernatural isn't like it is in fantasy books. Bits of it are farther between, fewer than they're depicted. Most folks can go all their lives without seeing a ghost. I saw three as I circled this new Friendly Village: two suicides and a regret-filled natural death. Forseti had bound them to the place as watchers. Each trained its gaze on me, uncaring and cold as an ice-cube, but vigilant, as I passed.

It would not take long for the god to know I had returned. He wouldn't wait for me to come to him. He was too worried that the death he'd started growing in my bones would go wasted, that he wouldn't be able to pluck it, harvest it. Use it.

And to tell the truth, what good was my life doing anyone right now? I didn't defend the world from anything. I existed and observed. I didn't even have the excuse that most magicians did that, because most of them managed to live as well.

To do amazing things. And I, I lived in a trailer park and spent my days putting tiny, almost invisible stitches in Hawaiian shirts.

I left the keys in the Contessa when I parked her. I wasn't sure I'd be driving again.

As I was coming in the back, there was a knock on the front door. It sent a shock of adrenaline through me, even though I knew it had to be someone ordinary, a neighbor asking about something to do with lawn care, or the mail carrier with a package.

But Jason stood there when I answered it. He'd never been to this place. I wasn't sure how he'd found it. He must have asked around.

His eyes were so blue in the sunlight. I thought to myself that perhaps I should resign myself to dying from this and just grab what gusto I could in the time I had left. I should pull Jason into the bedroom and have one of those sessions of sex so good it almost became tantric. I've been with sex magicians and would swear he'd been trained by one.

Maybe that's just partiality talking. Not love. I was sure it wasn't love. He'd been good in bed but so bad elsewhere. He was arrogant about his beauty, felt he deserved the last cookie in the package, the best seat in the house, to have things set aside for him or given him.

If they weren't given, sometimes he'd take them, assuming you would have given them to him if you'd just thought of it. Yet another reason why we'd broken up. I felt taken for granted.

And sometimes, I thought, I deserved that last cookie. At least every once in a while.

All these thoughts flashed through my head, fast as the little barn swallows flickering through the air outside.

Still, I stepped aside and gestured him in.

He came in like a cautious cat, sniffing the air, looking around to inspect everything. When we had been together I'd been living in an apartment in an older building. It had a certain charm but I'd moved out because I could feel the press of people all around it, felt them pushing at my dreams when I was sleeping, trying to get in. They made things too random.

"Nice place," Jason said. "You've been here, what, a couple of months? I'd think it would look more lived in."

I tried to see it through his eyes. Yes, it was sparse. No decorations, no curtains, nothing to draw dust. My furniture was IKEA-simple, straight lines and no distractions. Uncluttered. The only place that wasn't was my workroom. I glanced towards its door and saw it was closed. Relief. I didn't need him snooping through there.

"What are you doing here?" I asked.

He spread his hands. "Look. I said some things I didn't need to say."

"You were being honest," I said. "I'd be irritated too if someone showed up to use my spring."

He shook his head. "It's not that. You could have asked me. Why didn't you tell me you needed help?"

"That's not how I work," I admitted.

His eyes were serious blue. "Why not? What would happen if you asked for help?"

I hesitated. Why indeed? Why had I chosen this solitary existence, why did everyone accuse me of keeping them at arm's length?

What was wrong with me?

Aside from the poison burning in my veins.

I would have answered, but a wave of dizziness swept me up and I fell forward. The last thing I saw was Jason's eyes, as blue as falling towards the sea.

There was chanting.

There was the smell of my own bed, and someone tucking me in it.

Then there were dreams, but why bother telling dreams?

When I awoke, I could hear voices in the other room. I was, indeed, in my own bed. By the look of the light it was heading towards my last sunset. Forseti hadn't said how long I'd linger after that.

I could feel the poison, like a lazy snake along my spine, heavy water pooled in the muscles of my back, my buttocks, and thighs. It didn't hurt, but it hovered there with a strong intimation that it could hurt, and could hurt very much indeed, under certain circumstances.

I focused on listening to the voices. Jason's and what I thought was Forseti's.

"No, back then it was very different," Forseti's voice said. "Just a few trailers. I nudged an old friend into buying the lot, setting up a perpetual trust."

"And the name?"

"Things become what they are called. You should know that, Guardian."

My eyelids were heavy. I blinked, and the sunlight bars crawled a good inch across the pale blue plaster of my bedroom wall in that momentary darkness. The snake writhed along my back once as I thought about stirring, and I discarded the thought.

"You knew what you were doing when you gave him the Friendly Village flyer. You knew he'd take a look."

Jason murmured, "It was up to him to examine things."

"He didn't because he trusted you."

Jason coughed out laughter. "Yeah? A momentary lapse on his part, no doubt. Not his practice." Then, as though startled at his own bitterness, he said, "But I didn't mean for it to come to this."

Silence, which was Forseti's way of saying Didn't you? At least that was how I read it.

"What now?" Jason asked.

A creak. Forseti was in the leather-covered armchair closest the bedroom door. Jason would surely be on the couch confronting him.

Jason, who had wished me ill enough to feed me to this ancient god. The thought hurt, hurt badly.

Forseti said, "He has a few hours. He'll wake soon. If he hasn't already."

Silence again. I imagined the two of them looking at the half-closed bedroom door.

Jason said, "Is there still time to heal him? If I willed the spring to do it?"

"No. You've delayed too long, waiting for him to ask you for help. You thought you'd win your lover to you forever, make him incur a debt to you he never could repay."

I inventoried the magic close at hand. But I was so tired, I couldn't imagine using the handful of charged marbles in the bottom drawer of the bedside fixture, or even going so far as to extract the thin silver blade, small enough that someone might think it a letter opener, that I'd slid between the two mattresses as one of my first acts of moving in.

I was dying. Was this what death was like, this heaviness, like bags of sand holding down my bones, as though everything, my flesh, the air in my lungs, the bedclothes heaped on me, were growing thicker and denser, more difficult to move? As though I were becoming frozen in a block of glass, unable to even change the direction of my helpless stare?

There was only one alternative.

But still I hesitated. I stretched out my consciousness, tried to extend it beyond the bounds of Friendly Village. But something deftly caught my thought tendrils, twisted them back around to this trailer, this room.

I could call Death.

Death, who claimed to love me.

Love, the same force Jason claimed motivated him.

What would happen if I abandoned myself to love?

Love was a rasping frustration, a teeth-grinding experience of shouting against the wind. Love was feeling small and misunderstood and feeble-minded and sad.

And yet a desire one came back to, again and again, because sometimes it wasn't that. Sometimes it pulsed in you, a song teeth-achingly sweet, a sound that hollowed out your heart, cored it like an apple, and replaced it with something else, fierce and hot as brandy and flame and drumming along my veins as though they were full of swallows, swallows battering themselves against me from the inside, soft insistent buffets like a toddler's blows.

Was that what would come about with Lorca? Was it possible? You can't force love, after all. And love traded for something else, whether money or some other commodity, like your life—what did that do to it?

Think of what Forseti could do with my death, after all. He'd use it to keep these lives serene, and who was to say they didn't deserve a little peace and spots of luck in their declining years? Particularly creatures of the supernatural, increasingly driven and hounded by forces of technology, disbelief fraying away at their existence? Imagine how much protection a magician's death could buy them.

But no one wants to die.

So I whispered, so soft that only I could hear it, "Lorca."

He was there.

He seemed so real somehow. Realer than real. Like something in a movie about to burn a hole in the film with its presence.

His breath cool on my cheek as he leaned over to whisper, "You want to be healed?"

There was a bargain being made here, I just didn't know its terms.

How do we read Death? You can begin with what signifies Death—a skeleton carrying a sickle, a grinning skull. A glimpse of the inside of things.

And the message of such things is to remind us of our own mortality. To tell us to live.

How odd, that we should say Death when the message is Live.

But when the thing itself, not the icon, stands before you with long-fingered elegant hands, and a mouth like a sunset's sigh, how do you read *that*?

Because surely, what it's saying is something entirely different.

My hand went up to touch his cheek. *Yes*, I said, without any words at all.

"Stop," Jason said from the doorway.

He stood there, Forseti just behind him. They both looked angry. I doubted that either had factored an appearance of this sort by Death into their plan. Jason had meant to drive me to asking him for help, thinking that it would change things between us.

Well, it certainly had changed things.

Lorca said, "Will you heal him, or shall I?"

"I will," Jason said. He stepped up. In his hand was one of my wine glasses, filled with a clear liquid.

Lorca looked at Forseti. "It is not the Guardian's decision, but yours. It will not work unless you allow it to."

"Which I will not permit," Forseti said. "A death was promised me."

All of this flew over my head, because I found another wave of lethargy washing over me, forcing my eyes closed. Each breath was long and labored; I could feel the room waver whenever I exhaled.

Jason's voice was small and subdued. "Will you take a substitute?"

No, I wanted to say, but the air pressed too tightly in my lungs. Lorca's hand was on mine, holding it. His fingers remained cool.

Forseti said, "That is not for me to decide."

I couldn't see who he indicated, but it must have been Lorca, for he spoke. "Rahul has chosen to live, or so he says. But he must agree to take on certain obligations if he is to exchange places."

How do we read Death, even in the flesh?

Always, he's that voice saying *live*. The message is unchanged. The signifier changes; the signified does not.

That's what the universe was telling me.

So I chose, and Jason chose.

Later, I woke. Lorca was sitting by the foot of the bed, drowsing in a chair that he must have brought in from the kitchen. It was fully dark outside, and there was no light on in the room. In the faint, faint light, he looked sinister, then childlike as a car passed outside and its headlights spilled over his face for a moment.

He said, without opening his eyes, "Go back to sleep. There is plenty to do in the morning. Forseti wishes to move the spring here."

"Why does the spring need a guardian?" I asked. The question had never occurred to me before.

"It doesn't. But it wishes one, and there is always someone willing to do it. Now it's your turn."

"What do I get out of it?"

"The same thing that comes with caring for anything. Irritation and petty annoyance, and the occasional flush of happiness."

He opened his eyes to regard me, underscoring his words.

"Why don't any Hawaiian shirts have pictures of Death on them?"

"Because no one wants a postcard that reminds them of mortality."

Why did he want my heart, as threadbare as an old shirt, too worn and tattered to keep out the wind?

But he did.

"Everyone wants a little happiness, now and again," he said. "Even Death."

"It occurs to me," I said, "that Jason's death benefits you a little. Removes a rival, in a sense."

He cocked his head and gave me a dazzling smile.

And I let that slide.

For now.

— IMPERATOR NOSTER —
Sonya Taaffe

The trade roads of ancient Rome are still legendary for their wealth, but it has never compared to that endless bounty beneath the sea, and the sea was the one realm which the Caesars were never able to tame.

He was the Emperor Retiarius and he never ruled from Rome, but they called him Caesar and Imperator nonetheless. Who else would rise from the Tiber-mouth with laurels dripping greener-grey than the waves of Tyrrhenum, a glistening rust-furl of cloak pinned at the shoulder with a whelk? He laughed at the name of Neptunus; he refused the Greek trappings of split-tailed Triton, his shins greaved in armor the pale gleam of an oyster's inner shell. His cuirass was of the same twisting pearl, ornamented with small snails and figures of murex-red algae that crawled so slowly, an observer could not mark the changes except by glancing back to see their stances had shifted: the riding figure was kneeling now, head bent before an edge of water that a moment ago had been crown-spiked rays of sun, and then a tree was a stream, and then the figure was rising, and then the waves had swallowed it. Caligula had claimed victory over him, he said, while Claudius had given him a tribute of land. His trident was bronze-barbed, taking his weight as if he stood on sand where ships of Egyptian grain rode low in the harbor. His eyes were blacker than mussels, than onyx or opal or the depth in the eyes of drowned men. None saw him come ashore; some said he could not. The sailors kept to Ostia's docks and prayed.

The Emperor at Rome treated with him: sent rings of jacinth and chalcedony mined in desert lands, wreaths and bowls of gold that would never perish beneath the sea, berry-bright still as silt settled on them in the endless twilight, perfumed oils in flasks of faience and honey-colored glass that would not melt in the warmest swells. The Emperor at Ostia left the chests on the wharfside, carelessly open to the swifts and the sun; returning at dawn, the Roman envoys found them filled with slippery weed and glittering scales, stinking like low tide and fishmongers. Dumped out on the planks in disgust, they clattered with lumps of wet amber, pearls in strange colors, cut with letters even the grammarians could not read. The Emperor at Rome sent a cup in silver, chased like a coin of old Sicily with Skylla at her sea-hunt. The Emperor Retiarius left a necklace carved in day-pink coral, the leaves and waving stems of some sea-plant out of which emerged women's faces and hands, water-streaming, mouths open as if in song. (The elder of the two envoys held it and said it was wet cold to touch, chilling as a tunny's skin. The younger said it hummed in his hands and he dropped it. He sat all night at the foot of the lighthouse, peering out over the silver-darkened sea; he saw nothing in the water but the reflections of fire above him, its devouring roar louder than any nereid could sing.) The Emperor of Rome was no fool and sent a toga of Tyrian purple, embroidered with gold as heavily as a sunset. The Emperor at Ostia was no fool and left it glinting in the morning sun, the embroidery replaced with fingernail rainbows of mother-of-pearl.

The Emperor sent no more gifts. The Emperor returned none. The boats began to go out from Ostia again, the trade-ships to come in from Alexandria and Rutupiae and Carthago Nova. There were no more sightings of a man as pale as washed ivory, standing where water should bear no one's weight, no more rumors of eyes open beneath the clear salt swirl, hands catching at poles or slapping the sides of skiffs, hawsers tangling in cormorant-black hair. Pearls and amber, necklaces and nacre were filed away in the coffers of Rome, where perhaps the Emperor thought of them sometimes and perhaps not. He was not a philosopher, this Emperor; he looked out on the sea from his marble balconies at Baiae and called it *ours*.

The younger envoy called the sea nothing; he was drowned in a storm off Corcyra, taking passage among a mixed cargo of garum and glassware. He might have gone down singing; none of the sailors heard him. The survivors clung to their splinters and prayed to the gods of sea-swell, of seventh waves, of fisherman's mercy for the catch too small to keep. Days away on the sea-roads, a man who had once kicked over seaweed on Ostia's docks woke in tears, imagining a colleague he had not seen in years stood before him like Hector to Aeneas, dressed in garments as wet and shining as sheets of sea-wrack. His eyes had blackened, his fingers were cold as fish-skin as he put a coin in the older man's hand, folding his palm closed around the crusted thing. It was stamped with the face of an Emperor, proud as a wolf, the crown in his hair slick-leaved, brine running from it. On the reverse, a trident, circled by small fish and snails. He woke with a palmful of water, no colder or more salt than crying. When he whispered the name of Caesar, he was not thinking of Rome.

— LONG WAY DOWN —
Seanan McGuire

In "A Long Way Down", a young woman has a complicated relationship with the creek that runs through her town. River spirits are common in folklore and mythology, and like the one in Seanan McGuire's story, they are not always benign.

Stories all over the world tell of river spirits. In Mexico and in the United States, children are taught to beware of La Llorona, the ghost of a woman who drowned her children and who wanders the night near creeks and rivers searching for their bones, wracked with grief and remorse. In some versions, she's harmless, in others, anyone who hears her cry will die within a week, and in others she will snatch up any children who are playing by the river and drown them, a twist which has presumably kept a lot of kids from falling into creeks.

In locations as diverse as Scotland, Gemany, and Japan, legends of river spirits remind the traveller to be wary and the child to keep away from the riverbank. The Kelpie of Scotland can appear as a human or a horse, and if a greedy traveller tries to ride the kelpie, the kelpie runs into the water and drowns the rider. Lorelei, a beautiful mermaid, guards the Rhine River in Germany and lures sailors to her death with her song. In Japan, the kappa are river tricksters, who are sometimes annoying, sometimes helpful, and sometimes dangerous, dragging children into the river to drown.

Rivers give and they take. Towns and cities are built around rivers and depend on them for sustenance and for recreation. But anyone who has lived near even the merest trickle of a creek knows that water can be treacherous. Life came from water, and according to legends all around the world, sometimes water takes us back.

C ome to me.
Oh, sweet child, come to me. Come to me, and be at peace. Come.

Janie stole another glance at the top of her test. The scarlet "F" blazed there like a mark of shame, forever branding her as a failure and a fool. She looked away, cheeks burning as red as the ink. She should have known better. She shouldn't have allowed her boyfriend to convince her that there was nothing wrong with lowering her guard and letting him use her notes during the test. He was so busy with his extra-curricular activities that he didn't have time to study. It wasn't fair for the school to expect that from him! He was paying for an education, and anyone who looked could see how smart he was, how much he understood the material. Why couldn't he just pay a little bit more and get his degree without tests that measured his ability to regurgitate pointless facts like some sort of trained monkey?

If anyone had ever needed proof of how smart he was, all they had to do was look at the grade at the top of her paper. How could a dumb man have talked her—a certified genius, a scholarship girl—into helping him cheat, even knowing what the consequences might be?

"I can still change your grade, you know," said the professor, dragging Janie's eyes back to his face. He was watching her, holding the crib sheet she'd written out for Danny, a disappointed look on his long face. It was the same look he'd had when he found the crib sheet on the floor during the test period, so clearly in her handwriting. She hated being the one who'd put that expression there. She wanted to impress her teachers, to shine, and instead, all she was doing was betraying their trust. "If you'd just tell me who you made this for, I can let it go. Just this once. Please."

Janie bowed her head, looking down at her desk. "I didn't write it for anyone. I don't know how someone got a copy of my study notes. I don't know."

"Janie…"

"I'll do what I can to make up the damage to my grade. I'm sure I can bring it back up to a C by the end of the semester." The damage to her GPA would be harder to undo. If it was bad enough, if she slipped far enough, she could wind up losing her scholarship.

It was almost more than she could stand to think about. But Danny would find a way to keep that from happening; Danny loved her, and he would figure something out. That was the way things worked between them. She helped him pass his classes, and he helped her pass her life.

"If you're sure." Professor Tillman sounded more disappointed than she had ever heard him. Tears burning in her eyes, Janie grabbed her things and bolted for the door. She was moving too fast, she knew that; she was running away. She couldn't think of anything else to do. In this moment, as in every other moment in her life that had burned behind her breastbone like this, she needed to get to someplace where she could think, where she could see the shape of things more clearly.

She needed to go to the river.

Poverty was not just a state of being: Janie was sure of that, had been sure of it since she'd started Kindergarten in her thrift store shoes, with her chewed-up pencils dug from the bottom of the kitchen junk drawer. All the years of school since then, elementary to university, had done nothing to shake her conviction. Poverty was a place, one that no one moved to voluntarily, but that crept in the cracks and the crevices until it had transformed the world into its own image. Poverty was a religion that claimed its converts from low-rent apartments and neighborhoods on the edge of falling off the map forever. It changed a person. Poverty was a kind of witchcraft. Maybe that was the truest comparison of all. Poverty transformed you, like a witch turning a prince into a frog. There were ways out, but no matter how hard you worked, you would never be anything but "that kid from the poor part of town," with poverty still clinging like a shroud.

Unless you could find someone so bright and clean that they scrubbed that stain away by their mere presence, turning poverty's frog into a princess with true love's kiss and true love's bank account. Janie had been a frog for most of her life. Never mind that she hadn't chosen to be born into poverty, that she had never done anything to justify or deserve a life of dumpster diving and government cheese; that was what the world had given her, and that was what she'd done her best to live with. She had always worked hard and gotten good grades, fully aware that if she was going to get out of the pit, she was going to have to be better than anyone around her would ever have to be. She would have to be smarter, faster, and more ethical.

And she was throwing that all away because she'd finally found a prince, and maybe he was the one who could kiss her into princesshood, who could press his lips against her skin until it turned soft and perfumed and perfect, not green with envy for the girls who had everything so easy, not scented with vegetable oil and fried potatoes by her hours at her cafeteria work/study job. Wasn't a prince like that worth risking everything for?

Wasn't it?

But for all the downsides of growing up poor and alone and scared of the future, there were a few small consolations. One of them was her river. She had been a local kid with a stellar GPA, and the local college was expensive but exceptional: it had looked good for them, publicity-wise, to be able to talk about the little girl who'd grown up in the shadow of their clock tower, who could now walk the campus as one of their own. She still lived at home, which meant she saved the cost of room and board...and better yet, she could walk the half mile to her favorite place in the world, the one place where she had never been poor, or different, or anything other than totally at peace.

Her mother was still at work when Janie let herself in, creeping through the apartment to her room, where she stripped out of her school clothes and wriggled into her swimsuit. It was two sizes too small and five seasons out of date, but that was almost better than having something new and fashionable. This suit knew her body like she knew her river, hugging every curve and forgiving every imperfection. It wasn't safe to go down to the river naked—not even for a skinny poor girl from the bad part of town, where most people looked out for their own—but it was safe in her swimsuit, which was skin-tight and yet still somehow no more sexual than a burlap sack.

(She had a different suit for school, of course, for the frat parties that spilled over into the pool and the campus mixers that smelled like fruit juice and chlorine and next-day regrets. It had been a gift from Danny, and it touched her like a stranger's hands, and she never wore it any longer than she had to.)

She left her clothes scattered on the floor, took her patched old inner tube down from its place on the wall, and turned and walked out of the room. Her flip-flops made no sound on the threadbare carpet, and the front door closed behind her.

Come child, come. It's been too long and it's all been shallow time, hasn't it, shallow time that skitters like a creek-bug on the surface of the water, too much tension to break down into the depths where peace lies dreaming. Come, child. It's been too long and I've been waiting as patient as I can, but you know I'm not made for waiting. Never was, never will be, not even for you. Oh, I can try, but I'll fail. We both will, if you don't come.

Come, child. Oh sweet child, come to me, and be at peace. You know you want to be at peace.

Come.

—⟨●⟩—

People in the neighborhood were so accustomed to the sight of Janie walking by with her inner tube over her arm and her legs bare to the world that she barely registered with them anymore. A few teenage boys whistled at the sight of her, only to find themselves smacked upside the head by their older friends. "That's Janie," said the older teens, the ones who had reached the cusp of adulthood, with all its trials and responsibilities, and chosen to hang back for just a little longer. "She's local. You don't look." And none of those younger boys questioned them, because they'd all heard her name, invoked by their mothers like some sort of talisman. Be smart, be diligent, and most of all, be lucky, and you could grow up to be Janie: you could grow up to see the way out opening in front of you like the very road to Heaven. You didn't catcall a talisman. You stood quietly by as it passed, and you hoped that one day, you might be that lucky.

Janie walked along the cracked sidewalk, eyes tracing patterns of cracks that had been there since she had been a little girl in pigtails, drawing her hopscotch grids around the broken places. There were smudges of chalk on the gray concrete, marking the spots where the neighborhood kids had kept up the tradition. No matter how poor the neighborhood got, there would always be children, and chalk, and games that required nothing more than the bodies that your parents gave you. Janie found that sad and hopeful at the same time, which was really the definition of her life to that point. Everything had its purpose. Everything had its cost.

Clutching her inner tube to her side in an effort to keep it from catching on the scrubby, untrimmed bushes, Janie walked between two apartment buildings and into the rough stretch of scrub that came after the half-dead, weedy strip of lawn. The apartment management claimed no responsibility for the scrub, which grew outside the reach of the sprinklers and despite the best efforts of every brand of over-the-counter weed killer. Periodically, a new family would move into the buildings that faced the scrub, one that still harbored thoughts of getting out, of moving into a house with three bedrooms and a big green yard, and then there would be a short-lived, highly focused war against the scrub, usually waged by a single man, his face flushed red in the summer heat. But those people always got beaten down like everyone else, and the scrub grew on, unchallenged ruler of its domain.

Sticker bushes snatched at Janie's ankles as she walked, hearing their dry stalks crunch under her flip-flops like the sound of coming home. She had always been grateful for the scrub. It was a barrier of sorts, a passageway between the world of kitchens that smelt like boiled cabbage and classrooms packed with rich kids who stared down their nose at you (starting in first grade, first grade, and how did they even learn to look down on other people in first grade? Who was standing by to make sure their kids knew that rich was rich and poor was poor, and never the twain shall meet?), and the world of green and brown and the smell of mud and water. That second world was a better world, always had been, always would be.

Janie reached the place where the scrub gave way to the trees, and slipped inside, out of the present, into the never-ending past.

Ah, child, there you are. There you are, with your toes like stones and your teeth like pearls and your hands like crawfish scuttling quick as ripples over the bones of my bed. I have been calling, child. I have been calling, and you have not heard me. What made you stay away so long?

No matter, child; no matter.

You will not stay away again. You are coming home to me at last, and home is where you'll stay from here until the tide rolls out. Here is where you belong.

Come, child, come home. Come home to me.

Even on the hottest days of summer, the temperature under the trees was bearable, easily ten degrees cooler than the blistering heat that bounced off the cracked asphalt and filled the air with blacktop phantoms, the visible shadows of the summer. It wasn't that hot by the middle of fall, but it was still a relief to slip through the loosely clustered trunks and down into the dark, green world that surrounded the creek.

The weeds down in the dark were different, species that never made it past the treeline, never cropped up among the prickly bushes and robust weeds of the scrub. These were more delicate plants, creepers that slithered like snakes around tree roots, patches of moss that squished between the toes, and tiny white flowers the color of fish bellies, so pale that they seemed to glow in the artificial twilight.

Janie kicked off her flip-flops and waded into the moss, heedless of the possibility of snails, enjoying the way the spongy green groundcover felt under her feet. Sometimes she thought that the whole point of shoes was to make moments like this one better: to make it more obvious that humans were designed to be barefoot, and needed to feel the ground beneath them if they wanted to understand the world.

As always, she kept her eyes downcast as she approached the water, counting the little white flowers and marking the jittery progress of the cabbage moths that sometimes got confused about where the food was and wandered down into the dark beneath the trees, where they would never be seen again by their forgotten cabbage moth families. Lotus eaters, every one of them, courting flowers that couldn't feed them and laying eggs where they would never be nurtured.

Bit by bit, the green beneath her feet gave way to smooth and earthy brown. The sound of the creek, which had been in her ears since she stepped into the trees, became too loud to ignore, as did the good, clean smells of mud and water. Janie had nearly wept the first time she set foot in a ceramics class. It had smelled, so amazingly, like coming home.

Finally, she lifted her eyes, and there it was: her second mother, the reason she had wanted to go to a college close to home, even knowing that the threat of princes would be great there for a frog like her, who should have chosen a college that could bring her into princesshood without anyone's lips touching hers.

The creek was five feet across at its widest point—an infinity once, when she was smaller and the world was larger. Now she could span the whole thing with her outstretched hands when she floated in the exact center, placing the fingertips of her right and the fingertips of her left on opposite banks. It was still wide enough to let her place her inner tube in the cool water, and deep enough that her butt didn't quite brush the bottom when her weight pushed the inflatable circle down.

"Hello, ma'am," she said to the creek, with the same ritual politeness she'd been using since she was a very little girl. The creek glittered silver in the light that filtered through the branches overhead, seeming to appreciate her manners. She stepped forward just a little more, letting her toes slide into the cool water. A crawfish went skittering off, vanishing under a big flat rock and leaving only a runnel of silt behind.

"I had a bad day, and I thought I'd come to see you," Janie continued, after tracking the progress of the crawfish. She set her inner tube down on the surface of the water. "You always know what to say."

The creek, glittering silver and bright and perfect, said nothing.

Oh, child.

You were always going to come to me.

Janie floated in the exact center of the creek, her hands trailing in the water for curious fish to nibble, her toes just barely touching the bottom. It had seemed like such a long way down when she was little, and now it seemed like no distance at all. Her mother's long-ago warnings that one day she'd be a drowned girl if she didn't learn to play on dry land held no strength, not here, not now. Not with the scarlet "F" blazoned bright across her mind, not with Danny's kiss aching on her lips.

"I don't know what to do," she murmured. The sun was warm where it touched her face, and the water was cool where it held her. "It all got so...so complicated, somewhere along the line. It shouldn't be so complicated." Life had been simpler when she'd spent all her days down at the creek, either with homework in tow, to be completed on the hard-packed mud of the bank, or floating in her inner tube. The future had seemed so big, and so untouchably grand.

But bit by bit, the future had gotten smaller, just like the creek had. Unthinkingly, Janie reached out to touch the opposing banks, expecting her fingertips to find resistance. They found only empty air. Janie frowned, fumbling a little, and still found nothing.

Janie opened her eyes.

She was still floating at the dead center of the creek, still with her head turned upstream and her feet turned downstream and her shoulders to either bank. But the banks themselves had moved, somehow: the creek's span was at least seven feet, putting even the nearest bit of land at least six inches outside of her reach. Janie sat up in her inner tube, briefly, bemusedly convinced that she was dreaming. Her mind had taken her back to an earlier, easier time, and she would find herself looking at her own childhood self, sitting on the bank, filling out a math worksheet.

But the bank was empty, save for her abandoned flip-flops, and she was still in an adult's body, and the water around her seemed suddenly so very cold. It had never been that cold before.

Janie pushed her feet down, seeking the bottom. She would wade to shore if she had to. Creeks didn't change their dimensions, not like this. Maybe there had been an earthquake? Maybe she had fallen asleep and it had jolted her awake, and this was a consequence, land erosion and decay. Never mind that the water was as clear as crystal, with none of the mud or cloudiness that would have accompanied that sort of shift.

Never mind that her feet didn't find the bottom, but kicked, seemingly suspended in space, above the depth that had no end.

"Ma'am?" whispered Janie.

Something wrapped around her left wrist.

Dully, with a sort of inevitability, she turned and looked at the thing that was holding her. It was something like an octopus's tentacle, but smooth, like glass, like crystal…like water. She could see tiny bubbles suspended inside it, and an infant crawdad, almost as clear as the tentacle around it, its little legs paddling as it looked for a rock to hide under.

hello child hello child hello child hello, chortled the water as it ran across the rocks upstream, and everything made sense, and nothing made sense, and it didn't really matter, because Janie was never going to be a princess. She was always going to be a frog.

Maybe it was better to be a frog with someone to love you than a princess with nothing but a crown. Maybe this had been the only way out that had ever been really open to her. And maybe it was past the time for thinking those thoughts, because the inevitable was upon her, and Janie was going home.

"Hello, ma'am," said Janie, recognition and longing and yes, quiet, beaten joy in her tone.

She didn't scream when the water reached up and closed over her face, pulling her down, pulling her a long way down. It was a mother's embrace, after all, for all that it was cold and formless and filled with little silver glimmers of light. It was love, of a kind…

And more, she would have needed air to scream.

Hello, child.
Hello, ma'am.
Welcome home.

—◖●◗—

They found her inner tube washed up against a bank; they didn't find a body. Some people in the neighborhood said they weren't surprised, that Janie had always been a drowning waiting to happen, but most of them didn't say anything at all. They just looked toward the creek, remembering voices bubbling over the rocks when they were children, remembering how they had always felt safe there... until the day they didn't. Until the day they'd grown up and left such things behind. Janie, for all that she'd been an old soul in a young body since she was born...Janie had never grown up. Not like that.

There was no body at the funeral. Danny didn't attend. None of her friends from college did. What would have been the point?

Time moves differently, for water. It's slow when the freeze comes and fast during the melt; it's never still, and hard to keep track of. It was nearly six months before a hand broke the surface, clear as glass and filled with tiny eddies.

The creek watched approvingly as Janie pulled herself together. The girl used none of her original body; the bones were buried deep, the flesh long gone to feed the fish and crawdads a good meal. But she drew on the water and the weeds, and there was a big green bullfrog where her heart should have been, swimming lazy circles and occasionally rising to the surface of Janie's rippling breast to steal another breath.

yes child go child I will be waiting, bubbled the water over the rocks, approving mother to the end.

Janie stood on tributary legs and waded toward the surface. It would be a long walk to the school, but she thought she could hold herself together that long, before her surface tension broke and she flowed downhill, back into her mother's arms. There was a boy there who had broken her faith in the world, and she was grateful; he had been the one to drive her home. He had tried so hard to kiss her until she became a princess, even if he had never really loved her.

It was time for her to kiss him back, and see if she could turn a prince into a frog.

The creek laughed, and Janie walked on.

SECOND VERSE,
— SAME AS THE FIRST —
Stina Leicht

C ome on, Em," Nathan said. "Rob said he'll close."
Emma rammed the key into The Liberty Lounge's front
door lock, muttering a long string of curses. "I know you're
operating under the delusion he's your best friend, but you haven't
been in Austin that long. So, let me tell you something straight. Rob
always says that. Rob is a dickhole. Rob always disappears before Last
Call. I always end up working a double. Don't tell me Rob is sorry. Rob
doesn't give a fuck."

Looking uncomfortable, Nathan said, "You don't really mean that."

"Oh, yes, I do," Em said, suppressing an urge to kick open the door.
She'd planned on sleeping late and then spending a few hours at her
easel. Instead, Rob had woken her up at noon with his latest weak-ass
excuse. *He's probably fucking that redhead. And if he put as much energy
into his DJ mixing as he does all those one-night stands, he might move to
New York and solve all our problems.* "Patterns repeat themselves, if
you're not mindful," she said. "And that's what Rob is, one six foot
tall repeating pattern with an addiction to manipulative redheads."

She was so pissed-off she could spit. Her best friend and roommate,
Blue, often accused her of having an over-active sense of responsibility. Even if that weren't true Em needed the extra money. Rob
damned well knew it, and he took advantage of that fact every chance
he got.

"Where's Blue?" Nathan asked.

"She and Javier stopped at Mrs. Johnson's Donuts after work. Didn't
get home until eight this morning. I told her to sleep in." Blue was
going through a rough break-up. Em wanted to make things as easy
for her as possible.

"Oh?" Nathan arched a dark brown eyebrow.

"Do you know what Blue is like when she doesn't sleep? Trust me.
I'm doing the world's drunks a favor."

Nathan had the intimidating build of every bouncer depicted in
film. Bulk in a bouncer was both asset and liability. There was a

particular type of asshole drunk that took one look at Nathan and decided to test themselves. That was what made Blue such a great bouncer. Blue was attractive, with big brown eyes so dark they might as well have been black. She had dark skin and hip-length blue-dyed dreads. At five-foot tall in two-inch heels, she didn't look dangerous. However, any drunk that took her for a push-over was in for a surprise of the emergency room variety.

Em met Blue several years before at a free self-defense class given by Blue's Aikido instructor. Blue was fiercely loyal to those she loved. She was also tough. Em admired that, but Blue could also be meaner than a wet alley cat in February when crossed. She saw nothing wrong with breaking a guy's legs because of a stolen tip jar. As Em saw it, everyone had potential for violence—that is, everyone but Nathan.

He'll show his true colors. Men always do. Em inwardly winced, knowing full well that that thought wasn't fair. *Dre isn't like that, is he?*

"Hang on," Em said, turning to face Nathan. "Isn't Twiggy supposed to be opening? What are you doing here? You're closing tonight."

Nathan's broad shoulders moved up once and dropped. "She closed last night. I didn't think it was fair she'd have to open today. Particularly so soon after surgery."

"It's been a couple of days."

"Back to back closing and opening shifts are tough even when you aren't recovering from having your wisdom teeth removed."

The tension in Em's jaw loosened. *Maybe Nathan is what he seems?* "Did you tell Dre you were switching with Twiggy?"

"Nah," Nathan said. "The shift is covered. That's what's important. Isn't it?"

"But if Dre doesn't know you're the one who worked, you don't get paid. Twiggy will."

"Twiggy will return the favor one day."

"Sucker."

"Takes one to know one." Nathan managed a boyish expression in spite of the tattoos on both muscular arms. It was spring, and he'd rolled up both sleeves of his white t-shirt--the left one even had the obligatory pack of cigarettes tucked inside. The graceful red, yellow, and orange koi decorating his biceps were on full display.

Dear Hormones, shut the fuck up, Em thought to herself. She'd tended bar at The Liberty Lounge for the last six years, longer than anyone but Andre "Dre" Martinez, the manager. She'd started working the door when she was seventeen—-the year that her mother had thrown her out. That was when she'd met Blue, and Blue had introduced her to Dre and Leigh. In turn, Dre and Leigh had taken Em in and helped get her on her feet. And when Dre got sick, Em had returned the favor by taking care of Dre when Leigh couldn't. They were family—her, Blue, Leigh, Dre, and Jules. At the bar, Em had worked hard and had been promoted to bartender a year later.

Em knew she was damned lucky.

Dre saw the Lounge as more than a nightclub. Every employee had a creative vocation. Em was a painter. Blue wrote fiction and had even sold a couple of science fiction stories to well known magazines. Nathan played drums for The Pictsies, a local Celtic punk band. Twiggy was lead guitar for the same group and doubled as the photographer. Rob wanted to be a professional DJ in NYC. Javier was an artist who specialized in pen and ink. Even though he didn't own it, Dre loved The Liberty Lounge more than anything but his family. He pictured it as an oasis where everyone's creative energies melded and reinforced one another.

Still, the Lounge had its issues. Most bar employees came and went fast, but for some reason employees at the Lounge came and went faster. Blue said it was because nightclubs attracted mostly musicians, and musicians were flakes. Em wondered if the place just spooked some people more than others. Everyone had their obvious reasons for leaving—-everything from the lure of dull, high-paying jobs like accounting to unplanned pregnancies, despair, and even suicide. Nonetheless, there were a few who stuck. Those that did, stuck hard.

"So," Em said with a small smile. "You're lying to your boss."

Nathan raised an eyebrow. "I may be new around here, but I'm not blind. Somebody gets a little hurt, no one talks to Dre. Something breaks, you fix it and don't tell Dre. There's a lot of that going on around here."

"Dre has done the same for the rest of us." She looked away and shrugged. "He's got enough going on."

"The leukemia. I heard," Nathan said. "But he told me it was in remission."

"Sure, but..."

"I get it. I just want you to know I'm with the rest of you, okay?"

Em forced her gaze from Nathan. She'd been nursing a crush on him since he'd walked in the door. Normally, she would've slept with him and gotten it out of her system, but he had a girlfriend, and Em had strict rules about that. *He's so not yours to play with.*

She took out her frustration on the filthy steel door, shoving it open. The blow made a dull drumbeat beneath her stinging palms, and the silver rings on her fingers chimed, metal against metal. She propped open the door with one Doc Marten boot. Giving him a sideways nod, she said, "Get inside. I doubt Twiggy put the bar towels in the washer last night, let alone ran it."

Nathan eased past. "I'm sorry you couldn't paint today."

Once again, Em wished the direst of dire fates upon poor innocent Jeannine, Nathan's girlfriend. *That's not nice.* "Not your fault," Em said out loud and let the door fall against her hip. She yanked the key free. "Sorry you aren't home practicing drums."

He shrugged. Blinking, she followed Nathan through and then locked the bright Texas sun away behind her.

The inside of The Lounge felt like a convection oven. Blind in the dark, she slapped the thermostat on before hunting the light-switches. The 1930s-era windows had been blacked-out and barred long ago. Feeling along the sticky-cool cinderblock wall, her nose filled with the same old over-cooked funky bar smell that had been with her through the tail-end of her teens and now, into her twenties— stale beer, vomit, urine, and unknowable bar-munge. Something darker lurked beneath it all. Something she tried hard not to notice. Something that smelled like rotten meat.

Every old building has its quirks.

Not like this place. Something evil lives here, and you know it.

It isn't always like that.

Built sometime in the 1920s, each occupant had left their mark on The Liberty Lounge like a series of failed relationships on a divorcee. Affectionately known as "The Lounge" to locals, it'd been around for twenty-three years—an eternity for an Austin music venue. Before it'd become a nightclub it had been home to a successful comedy troupe named after a 1940s era movie star who'd been famous for her swimming routines. Before that, it was supposed to have been a brothel—-complete with underground access for those too rich, moral, or well-known to be seen entering from the street. In its earliest incarnation, it'd been a lumberyard. Abandoned railroad tracks still ran behind the property. The latest owners had cobbled together a new roof from the bones of the much more illustrious Armadillo World Headquarters.

If she closed her eyes and concentrated, Em could feel The Lounge's low-slung heartbeat vibrate against her skin. It was powerful and electric like a Stooges bass guitar dreaming in a heroin daze. She loved that. But when the place was empty it could be downright terrifying. The bad feeling wasn't always decernable. If it had been, she wouldn't have remained, and she suspected, neither would the others. She used to wonder if it was the full moon like a movie werewolf.

Some nights The Lounge seemed more aware, more awake. Those were the bad nights--nights when the mosh pit went mean for no discernible reason, when the lead singer would lose her voice and the crowd would throw bottles at the stage, when accidents happened, fights started, and the blood flowed.

The light switches flipped beneath her hand with a hollow, finger-numbing snap. The club's mercury arc lamps let out a cranky mosquito buzz as they warmed up. She sensed the bitter echo of loneliness in the big empty room. It was easy to imagine The Lounge was a late sleeper nursing a perpetual hangover.

Em blinked back a memory of her stepfather. Fighting down a jolt of anxiety, she clenched a fist. There was a bad energy in The Lounge today. If she were honest with herself, it'd been building up for a while.

Don't be silly.

With a start, she realized it was exactly the phrase her mother had used when she'd gone to her for help years before. *Don't be silly. He's your father.*

Dumping the weighty key-ring in her jacket pocket, the keys rattled as they knocked against the handle of the switchblade she kept there. "Do me a favor," Em said. "Check on the Men's and the Lady's first. Then meet me in the office. I don't want any nasty surprises at the last minute."

Nathan didn't complain, but his trepidation surfaced in the tiny worry line sketched between his brows.

He feels it too. Everyone does, if they're smart. She swallowed her guilt said, "I'll go with you."

"It's cool." He squared his shoulders and left.

As senior bartender, Em didn't have to deal with the restrooms. She used to take it on anyway, but after last winter, she'd been granted a free pass forever. Everyone knew why. Briefly, she wondered who'd told Nathan. She hadn't. She didn't talk about that.

The afternoon she'd found the dead guy.

A homeless man had pried his way in under one of the garage doors that opened up to the outdoor seating area. He hadn't vandalized or stolen anything, but had passed out on the floor in the men's bathroom and then died. Em didn't know what had possessed him to do such a thing. There were streets in the worst parts of post-Mardi Gras New Orleans that were more sanitary and comfortable than the concrete floor in the Liberty Lounge's men's room. It was the single most disgusting surface she'd seen in her life. The soles of her Doc's adhered to the gritty concrete no matter how many times the floor was mopped with bleach. It didn't help that the urinal consisted of a sewer hole with an iron grate over it, a long ridge in the floor to keep the urine stream confined to the area closest to the wall, and a few beleaguered urinal cakes. The graffiti-scarred stalls had no doors. They barely had walls.

She'd found the dead man curled up on his side near the sinks, dressed in a baggy black business suit and a filthy white t-shirt. His once-red power tie had been twisted around to the back of his neck and drawn tight as if it'd been used to strangle him. The body had reminded her of the images of bog men she'd seen in Twiggy's anthropology textbook. He'd even had a braid knotted around the upper part of his left arm--secured on top of the sleeve of his worn suit jacket. Em had checked his vitals and shouted for help.

When Dre ran into the restroom the first thing he'd said was, "I thought we were done with this. We had a deal."

"What do you mean?" Em had asked.

Dre had frowned and turned away. "It happens once a year. I keep telling the owners they need to invest in better security, but they refuse to listen."

"But this-this looks staged," Em had said.

Nodding, Dre had said, "That's what I told the police. And they said I had an overactive imagination, and to leave the investigation to the experts. Like they give a shit about homeless people."

"Maybe they'll listen to me," she'd said.

"Don't get involved," Dre had said. "I don't want you to get the attention of the owners. I'll handle it."

Dre had ignored her questions after that, muttering that he needed to call emergency services. Alone with the body, she'd forced herself to search for identification. The nice leather wallet was empty of everything but a much-folded letter and some business cards. She assumed they were his. The man's name was printed in refined text and underneath that were the letters "CEO." She didn't recognize the company name. Some sort of real estate investment group. It was the folded note that disturbed her most, however. The letterhead was from a prestigious art gallery located downtown. It was a rejection letter.

That was when she saw what he'd scrawled on the floor.

Not good enough. Never good enough.

The police arrived, and eventually the body was taken away. Dre never did explain what he'd meant about the owners. That wasn't that notable, given that they rarely, if ever, interfered in how the bar was run, and no one but Dre had ever met them. Em went back to her regular duties with the exception of the restrooms.

The months afterward had been quiet ones at The Lounge. Still, the homeless man haunted her thoughts. What kind of a person had he been? How did he come to be homeless? Why did he give up on his dreams? In nightmare after nightmare, she'd walk into that restroom and find him dead on the floor. The failed artist-businessman would sit up, and his limp jaw would fall upon his sternum like Marley's ghost in Dickens's *A Christmas Carol*. She could count each perfectly capped and bleached tooth in his dark, dead gums. His eyelids would snap wide, and the cloudy irises beneath would stare. Then, in an American accent that hinted of Wall Street, he would say, *Stop playing at being an artist. Grow up. Be responsible. The real world is too harsh for childish dreams, Emma Jean.* Then he'd reach for her. And something in that hungry reaching reflected her stepfather's pursuit of her sister, Karen.

Em shuddered. Waiting at the office door, she listened to the massive air conditioner battle the heat. She laid a hand on her switchblade and the anxiety faded.

She felt ashamed for having sent Nathan alone. *You shouldn't have. Not today. And you know it.* She told herself no one needed to be afraid of an empty restroom.

However, if she were honest, she'd admit that she'd had her switch blade blessed. Such a thing was completely illogical. She'd discarded her Catholic upbringing along with her copy of her parents' house key, but the blessing had made her feel safe. And like Blue was fond of saying--ultimately, Em was for whatever worked.

Right about the time she was ready to go in after him, Nathan re-emerged and signaled all was well with a nod. She lost her fears in the recounting of the night's cash drawer and in running the bar towels Twiggy had forgotten to wash. When the time came, Em answered the sound engineer's knock. Blue arrived, and everyone got down to the business of opening the bar for the night.

"Nice shirt," Nathan said, a friendly smile disguising his intent. The drunk kid wearing a vintage Bowie t-shirt returned a blurry smile. Big black Xs sketched on the backs of the eighteen-year-old's hands--easily spotted from across the dance floor—indicated the reason Nathan had stopped by.

The kid looked down to check the front of his shirt and then resumed leaning on the end of the bar. "Thanks." The single word came out in a slurry of self-satisfied shout.

"Say, do I know you?" Nathan asked. "What's your name?"

"Pete Fowler."

"And how old are you, Pete?" Nathan glanced meaningfully at the backs of Pete's hands.

Pete's woozy smile tripped and fell off his face. Em's years of practice translating Texas Drunk into Sober English provided understanding in spite of the thumping stereo speakers. "Fuck you! I can vote! I can serve in the military! But I can't drink?"

"Not here, you can't. Just walk away, dude," Nathan said in his best Disappointed Father Voice. Again, Em couldn't help noticing the tattoo-koi peacefully circling his muscled arms. "Don't make me throw you out. Have some dignity. You're wasted. And you know why that's a problem."

The Industrial band Dre had booked for the night had wrapped up their first set. Rob's pre-recorded songs for the break were spooling off their countdown. At that moment, Front 242's *Headhunter* began ramming the speakers. Most of the patrons rushed to the dance floor. No one was waiting for a drink order at Em's end of the bar, or Em would've been too busy to watch. She'd emptied two bottles of top shelf booze so far. Wiping slimy, sticky hands on a towel, she then fished her bar key out of her back jeans pocket and went through the motions of defacing the tax stamp on the first empty.

"Fuck you!" Pete showed Nathan both middle fingers—because apparently one wasn't enough. "My dad is a famous lawyer!"

"Don't make me call the police," Nathan said with a sigh. "From then on everyone just has a bad night."

Em didn't know how the kid had managed to get so drunk. She certainly hadn't served him and neither had Javier nor Twiggy.

"I fucking paid for the fucking show. I'm going to fucking see it," Pete said.

"You should've thought about that before you got wasted," Nathan said.

The club's speakers shut off mid-boom. The crowd let out an annoyed groan. Nathan's words, pitched to be heard over the now dead speakers, echoed. "—make me call your dad." He caught himself and lowered his voice. "You'll never be allowed in here again. Just let your friends take you home. Sleep it off. Everything will be cool. Okay?"

Em knew that last part was a lie. Drinking while underage was the fastest ticket to The Lounge's ban list. No exceptions. Nathan had the kid's name. The End. Texas law was harsh regarding the drinking age. It didn't matter who was responsible. The bar almost always took the hit. Dre wasn't about to cross swords with the TABC—not to the tune of $20,000 and the threat of a revoked liquor license. The kid had to go.

A thoughtful expression eased onto Pete's face. He seemed to be giving Nathan's suggestion serious consideration. Em didn't know how Nathan did it. This was the fifth time she'd watched him talk down someone that Blue would've stomped, dragged outside and then stomped some more. It was like some sort of crazy Jedi Mind Trick.

Em relaxed and returned her attention to the tax stamp. The heavy steel key hit the bottle at just the wrong angle and whiskey-soaked glass exploded in her hand. Her reflexes kicked in. She dumped everything into the sink, but she wasn't quick enough. Sharp pain sliced through the meat of her left palm.

"Damn it!" Warm blood oozed down her wrist. Her hands were filthy with the night's drink spills and citrus slices. It stung something terrible. Tears sprang up in her eyes.

Across the room, the club's speakers let out an ear-piercing squeal. Everyone flinched and moaned. *Headhunter* cranked back up where it left off with catching the man. The crowd whooped and threw themselves into dancing again.

Twiggy snatched up a clean bar towel and charged in to the rescue. She'd bleached her hair blonde and streaked it in a riot of purple and pink that matched her outfit. She looked better than she had the night before, but she still spoke with pain-laced care. "Get some water on it."

"Doing it," Em said. It came out in an annoyed hiss.

"Let me see," Twiggy examined the wound with practiced hands and frowned. Her low voice dipped into that gap between male and female. She'd been Stefan when Emma had first met her. Twiggy started transitioning seven months ago, and sometimes stress affected her that way. "Won't need stitches. Nowhere near the tendons. Not deep." She smiled, and her voice returned to its earlier pitch. "That was lucky."

"Except I fucking have to go home," Em said, tucking her bar key in her back pocket with her good hand. The Health Department wasn't much for bleeding bartenders serving drinks. The cut hurt, but not as much as losing the evening's tip money or the missing shifts it would take for the cut to heal. "I hate when this shit happens! Can't I bandage it? Or wrap it in a surgical glove?"

"Yo, Javi," Twiggy said. "Grab the first-aid kit when you get a sec and bring it over. Will you?"

"I'm in the weeds!" Javi glanced up from the rum and coke he was mixing and spied the blood. "Shit. Be there in a sec!"

"Clock out. But stick around," Twiggy said, turning back to her. "You can keep your share of tonight's tip jar. Have a shot or two. On Rob. You got hurt because you took his extra shift, after all. He owes you that much."

Em glared at the dj booth. "I hope his latest conquest was worth it."

Twiggy shrugged. "She was hot."

Em pointed to Twiggy's hair. "You have to teach me how to do that one of these days. I can't be the only woman in this place without technicolor hair."

"Can't Blue show you?"

The pain was fading, and Em's head started to clear. She caught the hint of emotion in Twiggy's expression. *Twiggy has a crush on Blue? Does Blue know?* "Blue doesn't have the patience for that. But if you come over, we can make it into a girl's night thing. Our bathroom is bigger than yours, anyway."

"Deal," Twiggy said.

Setting the finished drink on the bar, Javi arrived with the first aid kit and returned to take on the bulk of the bar traffic. Twiggy bandaged her hand. Wincing, Em watched Nathan and Blue escort Pete and his friends to the front exit.

Em knew she should go home but understood that she wouldn't. She struggled with whether her urge to stay was protective or just plain needy. *We'll just hang out. That's okay, isn't it?* she thought. Ignoring her conscience, she clocked out and then perched on a barstool to observe Nathan in action. Sometime around one in the morning, Jeannine showed up. She didn't look happy. It was at that moment that Em stopped watching and started sucking back the free drinks Twiggy was supplying.

Last Call arrived before Em knew it.

Nathan and Blue shoved the last rideless loser out the door along with the kind-hearted sucker stuck driving them home. That's when Em spied the hurt in Nathan's face, and her thoughts leapt to Jeannine. That had been odd. What was even more unusual was that Jeannine wasn't still hanging around.

They had an argument. So what? You're just hoping for something that'll never happen, Em thought. *Stop it, already. Move on to someone else, will you?*

Twiggy and Javi drifted toward the office, beginning the ritual of shutting down for the night. They'd be another hour, counting cash and credit card receipts. Em had settled her drawer long before she'd finished her first Jack and Coke. So, she decided to pick up trash and wipe down tables. Rob dropped Em's Cocteau Twins disc into the club's stereo to appease her. She hollered her thanks above the speakers before he vanished with the others into the office. Rob claimed to hate 4AD bands. For her part, Em did her best not to see that as yet another character flaw.

When she'd finished cleaning, she perched on a barstool while Nathan and Blue swept the dance floor. It'd been almost an hour since her last drink. *Almost.* Teetering on her barstool, she sang along with Elizabeth Fraser's clear, breathy soprano. On a whim, Em hopped down and threw her arms wide. Then she spun round and round in a tight circle until she staggered. A steadying hand caught her by the arm. She swung around and landed face first into solid, muscular torso.

"Hold on there, Skippy," Nathan said.

With her nose planted in the front of his shirt, Em breathed in. *Oh, God, he smells nice.* "I'm fine."

"I know you are, but what am I?" Nathan said, distracted. Something was, in fact, wrong. His question didn't hold its usual playful timbre.

The Cocteau Twins stopped singing about frou-frou foxes in mid-summer fires in the middle of his question. Again, his voice bounced off The Lounge's grubby walls. Drunk, Em slapped both hands over a giggle-burst.

"You're laughing at something *that* weak?" Nathan asked, sounding more like his usual self. "Good thing I'm driving you home."

"What about what's-her-name?" The question had popped out before she could stop herself.

He winced and looked away. "I—I don't want you to drive. And I don't know if I can take any more bad news tonight."

"Bad news? You got bad news?"

He shook his head. "Not tonight. We'll talk about it later, okay?"

Right, none of my business. "Blue can get me home."

He glanced over at Blue who was changing the last of the trashcan liners. The Cocteau Twins cd finished. Without Rob in the DJ booth, dead air took over. Blue started singing that stupid song about King Henry the Eighth from the movie *Ghost*. Em frowned. That was a bad sign. Blue only did that when she was upset. Blue was full of odd shit like that.

"Blue isn't much better off than you are," he whispered. "She's taking the break-up with Rose pretty hard."

"They were together for a year. That's an eternity for Blue," Em said and shrugged. "I'll call a cab. You don't need to get involved. You've got your own problems."

"After tonight?" He motioned to her wounded hand. "You can't afford a cab. And it's too late for the bus."

Em didn't mention that Blue's parents were rich and Blue would be paying. In fact, Blue's parents owned the condo in which Em and Blue lived. And while Blue wasn't exactly on easy speaking terms with her family, they certainly hadn't cut her off—quite the opposite, but Blue preferred not to rely upon their money, and neither did Em.

"Focusing on someone else's troubles tonight might be a good thing, you know?" Nathan headed for the supply closet. He deposited the broom behind the door and exchanged it for the mop and the yellow wheeled mop bucket. "Your turn to do the bathroom floors, Blue."

Anyone who didn't know Blue would've missed the sudden unease that slipped into her posture—the way her shoulders rounded themselves in as if protecting her chest. She straightened and the fear was gone. "No way."

Nathan nodded. "I did it last night. And I just did the towels." He let the mop fall.

Blue stopped its slow arc with a precise one-handed grace that denied her drunkenness. "Shit." She gave the restrooms an aprehensive glance and sighed. Again, she covered her discomfort. "This just isn't my night."

"Tell you what," Nathan said, reconsidering. "I'll do the men's. You do the women's. After that, we'll head out. I declare a horror movie fest."

"Yay! My favorite!" Blue smiled.

Nathan said, "At your place."

"Oh, hell," Blue said. "You're determined to make me do housework, aren't you?"

"Who says you do it?" Em winked.

"Very funny," Blue said and stuck out her tongue.

Em took a chance. "Can Twiggy come too? She enjoys horror." She knew if Nathan said yes that would mean Rob wouldn't be invited. That was tricky, because if Rob weren't invited, and he found out, there could be drama.

Nathan glanced at the closed office door as if he were calculating similar social equations. "Why not?"

Now, to invite Twiggy without Rob noticing. If Rob spotted Twiggy's crush before Blue did, he'd mock Twiggy, and if he did that, Em wasn't sure she could keep from kicking him in the balls. Alas, Dre frowned on that sort of thing.

"How about a tub of Amy's Mexican Vanilla ice cream? My treat," Nathan said. "Ever ate it with bourbon and caramel sauce?"

"You're trying to buy your way into my good graces," Blue said and squinted up at him. She poked him in the stomach twice, emphasizing her last two words with each touch. "It's working."

Em glanced to the restrooms, and her anxiety worsened. "It'll go faster if I help."

Striking a John Wayne pose, Nathan tipped an imaginary ten-gallon hat off his forehead. "That's all right, little lady. This here bleach is guaranteed against germs, scum, and villainy." He dropped the hokey cowboy act. "Don't you go anywhere, now."

Smiling, Em crossed her heart and then leaned back to watch him go. *Oh my,* she thought. *He's got a nice butt.*

Blue sidled closer. "I have to ask if your intentions are honorable, young lady."

"Oh, hell, no."

"That's my girl." Blue leaned on her mop. "Does he know how you feel?"

"Who?"

"John Wayne, who else?"

"Isn't he dead?"

"As dead as Elvis."

"I'm not into that necromancy shit," Em said, knowing perfectly well she meant necrophilia, but Blue loved giving her crap about her vocabulary. Em hoped Blue wouldn't notice she was offering up an easy target. It would make her cranky.

"If the tabloids are to be believed, he's already resurrected," Blue said. "In that case, I'm not sure it counts as *necrophilia*."

"That's good news. Because I left my black magic kit at home."

"Hets these days," Blue said, rolling her eyes.

Rob poked his head out of the office. "Javi and I are headed to Troy's. His deadbeat cousin moved out. He's celebrating. Y'all want to come along?"

"You go ahead. We've got a date with Freddy Krueger and a gallon of ice cream," Blue said.

Em flinched.

Rob turned and called into the office. "You mind if we go now, Dre? Stacey said she'd be at Troy's. I don't want to miss her."

Dre's muffled response could be heard across the quiet dance floor. "Stacey is the goth girl that was hanging around the DJ booth all night, isn't she? Didn't you say you were done with goths?"

Rob ducked back inside to plead his case. Em decided it was a good opportunity. Venturing into the office, Em whispered the invitation into Twiggy's ear while Rob argued with Dre. Twiggy paused mid recipe-sort and gave a quick nod. A touch of pink darkened her cheeks. Luckily, Rob was too focused on wheedling a favor out of Dre to notice. Then Em returned to the dance floor, mission complete.

Blue was still there. Em assumed Nathan was cleaning the men's restroom.

"Stalling won't help, you know," Em said and waved at the Women's.

"Fuck that. You think anyone will notice if I move the grime around or not?" Blue asked, "I've got more important things to work over. You going to answer my question?"

"What question?"

"Nathan. It's obvious you're driving one another crazy. He's not your usual brand of asshole. He'd be good for you."

"I don't steal other people's boyfriends."

"Can't you just borrow him for a while, clean him up, and then put him back where you found him?"

"Fuck him behind her back? No!"

"Then ask Jeannine for permission."

"Somehow, I suspect Jeannine might find that jealous bone she supposedly doesn't own. Neither of them deserve the drama.

They've got enough of that right now. Anyway, I'm not into open relationships."

"Just because you aren't doesn't mean they aren't."

Em gave her a hard stare.

Blue put up a hand as if in defense. "I can't help it. You finding a nice guy attractive is a step in the right direction."

"Weren't you the one that told me not to sleep with anyone from The Lounge?"

"This is *you* we're talking about, right? The girl that fell for... what was his name?"

"Ralf."

"Ah, Randolph Scott. What's with you and the cowboys?"

"We live in Texas. Goat-ropers are ubiquitous. When did you become Dear Abby?"

"Daddy paid for ten long years of therapy in addition to my degree. I might have learned a few things against my will."

"Like channelling your aggression into a more positive outlet?" Em asked. "I'm not sure I'd say a job where you beat the crap out of people counts."

"I'm getting *paid* to beat the crap out of people," Blue said. "That's positive. Right?"

The phone rang. After a moment, someone inside the office screamed a curse. There was a loud bang as Dre forgot to catch the office door before it slammed into the wall. "¡Eso es todo! ¡Le dije a ese hijo de puta que no iba a tolerar que nadie lastimara a mi familia! ¡Te vas a arrepentir!"

"Dre? I didn't catch all that. Who's fucking with your family?" Blue asked.

Dre closed his eyes and took a deep breath before he continued. "Can you take over, Em? Baby Jules is sick. It's bad. I need Twiggy to drive my ass over to Brackenridge. Now. I promised Rob and Javi they could go to that party."

Twiggy yelled from inside the office. "I'm a better driver than either of you assholes, anyway."

Javi shouted. "You are not!"

"Leave the cash in the safe," Dre said. "I'll deal with it in the morning. I don't want you going to the bank alone. I'm serious."

Em wanted to point out that Nathan and Blue were still there and that three people didn't equate to being alone but decided this was no time to argue. "Cash stays in the safe. Got it. Just go, already."

Dre grabbed his jacket and bolted for the door with more energy than Em had seen him exhibit in some time. Javi and Rob were right on his heels. Em went to lock up. Last in line, Twiggy whispered that she'd meet them as soon as she could. Em nodded. Watching everyone walk to their respective cars, she whispered a quick *Hail Mary* for little Jules's sake. *Some habits die hard.*

Outside, the pre-dawn was a brand of stale and sticky that only a Texas spring could acquire. Twiggy's 1990 white Mustang Interceptor roared into the dark grey morning. The parking lot was empty. Em let the door slam shut, pocketed the keys after locking up, and returned to the now deserted dance floor. Feeling like a party guest who'd stayed too long, Em leaned against the locked door and listened to the lights hum their sleepy electric-insect song. It wasn't a peaceful sound. It was the buzz of a vicious killer hive, at rest but vigilant. *Set to spring upon the unwary with stinging death.* Her heart sped up with dread. *I'm alone.*

No, I'm not.

Just the same, the patrons were gone. The rules had changed, and the bad vibe was much worse than usual. She retreated to Dre's office. Somehow, it'd always seemed safer. There, she focused on getting things organized for the opening shift. It wasn't until she'd stacked the cash drawers and spun the dial on the safe that she realized she hadn't seen or heard from Nathan or Blue since they'd gone to mop.

The safe's heavy dial glided under her fingertips, making a series of quiet but authoritative clicks as it whirled. Her watch read a quarter to six. *They should be finished. Where are they?* She left the office. The dance floor was empty and silent. "Nathan? Blue? You done yet?"

A pipe groaned and shuddered in a throaty growl.

Em shivered, and the hairs on the backs of her arms and neck prickled. Wrapping her arms around herself, she whispered, "Don't be silly. Old buildings make noises." Her words—quiet as they were—seemed an intrusion.

Something fell. She started. The muffled clatter drew her attention to the men's room. A surge of cool relief poured through her. "Stop horsing around. Are y'all ready to go?"

Her question was met with oppressive silence. Her sense of danger sharpened, and terror pinned her feet to the cement floor. Her breath felt trapped in her lungs. *It's waiting for me to step closer to the shadows.*

An overwhelming urge to bolt to the office or out the door slammed into her. She staggered beneath the weight of it.

Stop it. You're being ridiculous, she argued with herself.

Debating entering the men's room, she paused. An image of the dead businessman drifted to the surface of her mind. Cowed, she turned on her heel and entered the Women's instead.

You're such a coward. "Blue? Where are you?"

The women's restroom was clean—or the Liberty Lounge facsimile there of—but empty.

She stood there for a few moments, dreading her next action when a muffled reply came from the next room. She rushed into the Men's before she could chicken out again. "This better not be a prank, y'all!"

The light from the overhead fluorescents was harsh. Blinking, she took in subtle cues. Bleach stunted the room's habitual urine stench. Everything was tidy--or as tidy as was possible, given the decades old munge. The wheeled bucket with its accompanying mop slouched partnerless against the far wall, beyond the stalls. It occurred to Em to wonder what had made that clattering sound earlier, and as she ventured farther into the men's room, she searched for the source--a fallen paper towel dispenser lid, or a toilet paper holder. There was nothing, until she reached the end of the row of broken stalls. Her stomach contracted into a freezing knot of terror.

An open passage to the far left.

"What the fuck?"

She edged closer. Inside the five-and-a-half foot tall opening, dirt, dust, and ragged cobwebs drifted on a breeze that reeked of mold, time, and discarded passion. A dim blue-tinted light illuminated the far end.

Blue and Nathan are down there. And they're in trouble. A sense of urgency squeezed her chest and kicked her heart. *Think, damn it. Don't rush in. Don't do something stupid. Not like before.*

Em examined the entrance for a hint of how to proceed. A part of the wall had swung back on a hidden hinge. Turning, she grabbed the mop and wedged its sturdy wooden handle into the doorjamb. Once she was sure it wasn't going to move, she checked her pockets for her lighter. She didn't smoke, but kept one nonetheless. Smokers tipped well if you did. The lighter's smooth, rectangular shape felt warm and reassuring beneath her fingertips. She also fished out the blessed switchblade. Exposed steel glinted in the weak blue-white light. Its weight in her palm gave her the courage to step inside the passage.

The floor felt gritty under the soles of her boots. Her breath and the quiet sound of broken-glass-laced sand abrading thick British rubber and ancient Texas concrete sounded huge in the quiet. Here and there pieces of forgotten trash hinted at the passage's history. The ceiling was made of old timber like a mine shaft.

Who do you think you are, Em? This never works out well, she thought. Em knew her fear was selfish, but she told herself it wasn't in her to leave someone alone and suffering.

It was once, though. Wasn't it?

Do not think about that. Not now. Not ever. None of what happened was your fault. You were a child! Her lips pressed into a thin line, and she wished the terror away. Often, when she knew she should feel happy or in love those emotions would evade her. Yet, anger and fear were always close to hand. Sometimes it felt as though they were only two feelings she knew. *Why is that, damn it?*

The lighter trembled in her hand, and she hated herself a little more.

"Grow up, Emma Jean. Be responsible. Stop your childish dreams. Art is only for people with real talent." The raspy voice ghosting up the tunnel triggered goosebumps up and down Em's arms and legs. "Picasso, Rembrandt, Monet. Real artists are men. You're just a little girl. A failed one at that. Why aren't you married yet?"

Recognition slammed her like a two-ton doully truck. She felt dizzy. Without thinking, she placed a hand against the sharp-edged, filthy wall to steady herself. A many-legged insect wriggled from beneath her palm. She squeaked, jerking away in revulsion with so much force that she staggered. The half-light flickered. A shadowy figure had moved to obstruct the way, blocking a good portion of the available light in the process.

Em thought, *Little girls don't marry. But sometimes* women *do, you asshole.*

"Go right back where you came from, Emma Jean," her stepfather's voice said. "This isn't any of your fucking business."

And just like that, she was back in that long-ago hallway. She blinked. Everything was a confusing mix of immediate dread and distant cold. She watched her far-away-self reprise an old performance. Standing straighter in spite of the terror that stole her breath and sent her heart into a panicked slam dance, her hand tightened around the handle of her switchblade. "Fuck off."

"Is that any way to talk to your father?"

"You're not our father." The knife grew slippery. "You're just an asshole our mother married."

"Put that away. You'll cut yourself."

"Get away from her."

"I'll call the police."

"Go ahead."

"It'll be your word against mine. You'll be arrested," the shadow-stepfather said. "Do you know what happens to little girls who go to juvie?"

Em swallowed. *I'm not little anymore.* And then a memory of what had happened surfaced. She'd cut him bad enough to need stitches. He'd almost died of the blood loss, but he hadn't told anyone that she'd attacked him. That is, no one but her mother, and even then he didn't tell the whole truth.

"You won't call," Em said. "Because you'll have to explain to my mother what you were doing." *Wait.* She paused. *It's 1998, not 1988. I'm twenty-two. This isn't real.* Something snapped. Once more, she was back in her body and in control. "You're dead. You had a heart-attack last year."

The shadow-stepfather tilted his head in confusion. She took advantage of the moment and lunged, aiming for the gut this time. He moved. *Fast.* His right arm swung in a graceful arc, hitting her forearm, deflecting the blow. He almost disarmed her with the same motion. She attacked again before he could, and again he deflected the blow with a foreign grace. This time with his left. But he wasn't quite quick enough the second time. Her blade sank into his left forearm. Too late, she understood she'd overextended her reach, leaving herself open. Cursing, she anticipated his final attack. Furious, he'd launch himself at her, throw her down, and choke her.

This is it, she thought. *I'm dead.*

Instead, he stepped back and put both hands in the air. It was so out of character that it gave her pause. *What am I doing? This can't be my stepfather.* And that's when she remembered Blue's advice.

Allow for the possibility that all men aren't like your stepfather. You don't have to agree, but you do need allow for the possibility. Without that, you limit your choices. There's no space for any other interaction.

Allow for the possibility. Em's heart was thudding in her ears and her hands were shaking. With a deep breath, she used conscious effort to release fear and anger. And that was when something about the shadow-stepfather's arms made her think of peaceful koi, circling.

"Em! Don't! Please! It's me!"

An overwhelming cold enveloped her and then was gone. Her vision cleared—strangely, it hadn't been until then that she understood that her sight had been hampered.

That's Nathan, not my stepfather. I've stabbed Nathan. "Oh, shit. Oh, fuck. Oh, no." She dropped the knife as if it'd burned her. "Oh, God. I'm sorry. I—It was an accident. I thought you were—"

Nathan clutched his bleeding arm against the front of his white t-shirt. "It's okay. I didn't see you either. I saw—"

"You're bleeding!" She hated herself for stating the obvious. "We have to get you upstairs. Call 911."

"No! Not yet. I can't get Blue out by myself. You have to help me. She's trapped. We can't leave her. I—" He stopped himself. His voice regained its steadiness. "We have to help Blue."

At the mention of Blue, Em's guilt and terror shut down. Her emotionless, practical side kicked in. "Where is she?"

"Down there." He pointed behind him.

Em got out her lighter and fired it up. "First, I have to know you're not going to bleed to death."

"Okay." He held his arm up to the flame.

The front of his shirt was dark with blood. He'd need stitches, but it was nothing like the wound she'd inflicted on her stepfather. She didn't know if she had luck to thank or Nathan's reflexes.

"Oh, God. I'm so sorry," Em said. "I didn't know it was you."

"Forget it. Things are weird down here. I didn't see you either. Not at first." His face was pale and eyes looked wide and haunted. "We have to hurry. I left her alone. I didn't want to."

In the distance, Em could hear Blue singing that stupid song off-key. Em made a bandage from a strip of cloth cut from Nathan's t-shirt sleeve. *She can't be hurt too bad, if she's singing.*

"Ouch!"

"Sorry," Em said. "Got distracted."

"It's okay. Here, let me knot it."

Once that was done, Nathan led Em to Blue. The tunnel branched in two directions. To the right, she got the impression of a dozen or so alcoves, and at the end, a t-intersection. They took a left and then another left when it divided again. On the right was a small cavern. Someone had stacked six-foot-long pieces of old wood into a primitive campfire tent. Around the base were bottles of what Em knew at a glance to be high proof alcohol. In addition, someone had tacked old religious medals, Catholic holy cards, and a wooden rosary on the splintered lumber.

Something is very wrong with that room. I don't want to go in there at all. The skin along her arms prickled, and the feeling she got on the Lounge's bad nights grew even more powerful. *Not that anything could be considered right about this place.*

"Are you coming, Em?"

Em nodded.

They'd gone a few more paces when the passage ended abruptly, and if Nathan hadn't been there to grab her, Em would've fallen into a pit.

Em yelped.

"Em? Nathan? Is that you?" Blue's questions floated up from out of the darkness. She sounded strange, and it took Em a second to understand what was off.

Blue was scared.

More like terrified. "It's us, Blue," Em said. Once more the flint wheel of her lighter sparked with a raspy click. Leaning forward with care, she spied Blue at the bottom of the hole. She was resting on a rocky floor, and the ground was scattered with what looked like small animal bones. *Gross.*

Wait a minute. That was when Em registered the tiny skull at Blue's elbow. Em's stomach turned, and she fought an urge to vomit. *Someone threw them down there to die. A lot of them.* Once again, she thought of how The Lounge had once been a brothel. Then she remembered Blue had had an abortion once. At that moment the lighter grew too hot to hold, and she flipped the cap closed with a flick of her wrist.

Blue does not *need to know what she's lying in the middle of.* "Sorry. I have to save lighter fluid," Em said. "Are you hurt?"

Blue sniffed. "Are you real?"

She's crying. Blue never cries, not when she thinks I'll see her. Em blinked. "I am."

"My ankle is borked," Blue said. "Hurts like a fucking bastard. I can't even stand up."

"We need a rope," Nathan said. "I was going back for one when I ran into Em."

Em frowned. "We should call 911."

"Don't leave me alone down here in the dark, y'all. I—I keep seeing things. Don't leave. Not again. I don't think I can do it," Blue said. "Please?"

"I've got your back. Don't you worry." Em turned to Nathan. "You go ahead. I'll stay here."

He swallowed, nodded, gave her the knife that she'd left behind, and then ran.

"Talk to me, Em," Blue said. "It doesn't matter what you say. Just talk. Okay?"

"Don't you worry. We'll have you out in a jiffy."

"A jiffy?" Blue laughed. Its echo carried a worrying edge of hysteria. "If you want me to believe that shit, the least you could do is not sound like a cartoon character. What's the matter with you?"

"You had me worried for a minute," Em said. "But now that you're your same old bitchy self--"

"Just fucking get me out of here. Okay?" The panicked edge in her voice was back.

"We will. I promise. What's got you so spooked?"

Blue paused. "I could ask you the same, you know."

Em let the unspoken question stand for a minute before she ventured, "Old ghosts." It seemed appropriate in more ways than one. "You?"

"The same. This is some seriously fucked up shit."

Em bit her lip and looked back down the way she'd come. *What if it attacks Nathan? He's alone. Would he be too afraid to come back? He won't leave us here, will he?* "D-did you know this place was here?"

"Nope. Did you? You've worked here longer than me."

"No. I wonder if Dre knows?" For some reason, Em's mind flashed to the conversation about the owners.

"He knows. Who else could've set up that thing in the other room?" Blue said.

"It could've been there from before," Em said. "It looks like it's been there a long time."

"Not that long. The tunnels are filthy," Blue said. "Anything stored here would be covered in dust."

"True."

Blue said, "Grandma Esther would say this place is haunted or possessed with a demon. Yesterday, I'd have laughed at the idea. Right now? Grandma Esther is sounding downright logical."

Em had some ideas in that department. However, discussing those thoughts meant bringing up the small bones, and she wasn't about to do that until Blue was miles away from The Lounge. "Whatever it is, we aren't the only ones. It has its hooks in Nathan too."

"Is that what all the screaming was about?"

Em swallowed. Her mouth was dry, but her eyes stung. She gazed down at the knife in her hand. The stain was the color of mud in the dim blue light. She could almost pretend it wasn't blood. *Almost.* "I didn't know it was him. I-I almost killed him. Just like my stepfather."

"It was an accident."

"How do you know? You weren't there!"

"I know you," Blue said, her voice suddenly rock-stable. "And anyway, your scumbag stepfather lived."

The backs of Em's eyes started to burn with real enthusiasm now. She blinked. "I never wanted to hurt anyone again. I shouldn't have kept the stupid knife." She closed the blade. "I'm getting rid of it." *As soon as we're out of here.*

"Don't you dare. We might need it. That knife saved your ass. It saved your sister too."

"No, it didn't."

"Is she living with your folks now?"

"No."

"Then how do you know it didn't? Maybe you introduced her to the idea that she didn't have to put up with him. It just took a while for her to save herself. I get you're Catholic and all, but you can't be responsible for everyone."

"I'm not Catholic. Not anymore."

"Right."

Footsteps echoed down the tunnel. Em turned and tensed up, readying herself for another attack. She let out a sigh of relief when Nathan appeared.

"Sorry that took so long." He knelt down and dropped two heavy duty extension cords on big plastic spools.

His face seemed to glow in the weird light the tunnel gave off. He didn't offer any explanations for his tardiness. However, Em thought she could read some of his reasons in his face.

"We're on our own," Nathan said. "Phone isn't working."

"You've got to be kidding," Em said.

He started unspooling the first extension cord and then the second. He lined them up. "Help me tie a knot in them every foot or so."

"Why?" Em asked.

"Blue doesn't weigh that much, and it's not that far down, but I don't want to risk using only one. She could get hurt worse," Nathan said. "I think this will do."

Em grabbed the heavy electrical cords and got to work.

"Don't worry. I rappelled in scouts. It should be the same principle."

"I knew it!" Blue called up from the pit. "You're a fucking Boy Scout!"

"Eagle Scout," Nathan said, not bothering to look up from his work.

Em rolled her eyes. "Like that makes it any better."

Blue shouted from the pit. "I could so kiss you right now! On the lips even!"

He finished making the knots and made a loop in the bottom of the cord. When it was ready, he fed the end to Blue. "Got it?"

"Yeah," Blue said.

"Use the rope to stand. I can help, if you need it. Once you're up, put your good foot in the loop. Try stepping on the cord," Nathan said. "Then we'll pull you up. Okay? That doesn't work, we'll try something else. Take your time."

"Don't drop me."

"We won't," he said. "Don't let go."

It took some doing—along with a large amount of cursing, but eventually Blue was ready. Nathan sat down on the floor closest to the pit's edge. Em grasped the farthest end of the cord and positioned the heavy reels so she was between them and the pit. Then she anchored herself against a wall. Nathan waited until she was in place and began pulling Blue up out of the pit. Between the two of them, they made smooth, laborious progress. The slick cords bit into Em's palms, and she quickly discovered why Nathan had bothered to tie the knots. Without them, the cords would've slipped through her grip.

"Oh, my God," Em said. "How many fucking donuts did you eat with Javi last night?"

Blue's breathless retort drifted up from the hole. "Cow."

"Bitch," Em said.

"Slut," Blue said.

Blue's laughter gave Em the extra energy to continue. The process seemed to take forever. Eventually, Blue crawled over the ledge, and all three of them lay on the filthy cavern floor, gasping for breath. Em's hands throbbed, and she could feel blisters rising in her throbbing palms and fingers.

"Thank you," Blue said. Her face was streaked with tears and grime.

Em scooted closer and gave Blue a tight hug. "Don't ever do that again. You hear me?"

Blue mumbled into Em's shoulder. "I won't."

"Maybe we should save the celebrations for when we're far away from here," Nathan said.

"The Boy Scout has a point," Em said.

"Yeah, yeah," Blue said and sat up.

"I don't think I can carry you yet," Nathan said. "My arms feel like jelly."

"It's okay. We can do this together," Em said.

She ducked under Blue's left shoulder, and Nathan took Blue's right. The awkward struggle to get to their feet without hurting Blue was more difficult than Em hoped, but eventually they worked out a method that didn't cause Blue too much pain. They paused every few paces when hopping became too much. Em fought the need to rush by focusing on Blue.

The breeze flowing through the tunnel strengthened and a susurrus whispered the hairs on the backs of Em's arms and neck to attention. At first, she couldn't quite make out words, but then she caught phrases she recognized. Shadows writhed within shadows at the edges of Em's vision. Shades of her stepfather materialized and faded, hissing a litany of her many failures. Sometimes the darkness suggested she cut her own throat or perhaps that she might be better off jumping into the pit.

"I didn't know Nick was in danger," Nathan said with an audible wince. "I was only ten."

"What did you say?" Em asked.

Nathan paused, shaking his head as if to clear it. "It's nothing. It's—," he said. "Let's just get out of here."

"Wait," Blue said. "Someone is crying. Can't you hear it? There are little kids trapped down here." She stopped and began to turn around.

"I don't hear crying," Nathan said.

"It's not real," Em said. "Whatever it is, it's fucking with you, Blue."

"No! We have to go back." Blue's struggles to return the way they came became more frantic.

"Nathan," Em said. "We have to get out of here. Now. This is going to go very bad, very fast."

Once again, they urged Blue to the exit, but it was hard going. The whole while, the voices in the tunnel ground down upon Em's resistance. *You'll never make it. You never do anything right. Why even try?* It made thinking difficult and navigating to the exit even harder.

"So much talent. Two lives in exchange for the happiness of so many," the voices in the passage whispered. "Leave them, Em. You will be successful. We will live. You and the others will flourish. All we ask is for a little blood. It's a small sacrifice in exchange for so much."

A little blood? Em lunged at the phantom. The point of the blessed switchblade pierced the shadow's chest. For a moment, it felt solid, and Em remembered what it'd been like to stab her stepfather—to cut Nathan. She shuddered. The thing let out a terrible, desperate howl and vanished.

Em put away the knife. She tried not to think about the shadow's offer. Nathan put his good hand against the rough wall to steady himself.

Blue began sobbing. "I'm so sorry."

Em said, "We don't have time for this. We have to leave."

Blue nodded.

Em said, "Nathan, I can't do this by myself. I need you. We need you."

He shoved his hair out of his eyes. Then he asked Blue, "May I touch you again?"

"Yes. Please," Blue said, not looking him in the eye.

Supporting one another, they stumbled onward. Em's feet felt heavy. She stared at the ground and concentrated on each labored step toward freedom. The effort of doing so required more and more energy. Whispering shadows grew more intense until she could feel them brush past with the breeze. She was shoved by unseen forces that alternately berated and cajoled her. *You could be one of the greats. Leave them behind. It'd be so simple. No one would blame you.*

Don't listen. Don't listen. Don't—

You aren't good enough on your own. You need us. It's the only way.

Em paused. "Are we walking uphill? I don't remember this. Do you?"

"Hold on," Nathan said.

"What the—?" Blue asked.

The tunnel had changed. Instead of the straight forward passage that Em remembered, the way in front of them was a rocky, twisted incline that became so steep that she didn't think they could walk it. *Not together. Not while carrying Blue.* Em asked, "Where are we? Did we take a wrong turn?"

Nathan frowned and then glanced over his shoulder. "I don't think so. It's not as if there were that many options—"

"It's fucking with us again," Em said. Tears burned behind her eyes.

Nathan stopped. "What do we do?"

"I don't know," Blue said. "If it's whatever it is that's haunting The Lounge then it can transform whenever it wants. We'll never get out of here."

"I have to think," Em said. "Blue, we have to sit you down for a minute."

"Do we have time?" Blue asked.

Nathan said, "Going farther will only make us more lost. We should stop and get our bearings."

Blue screamed her frustration at the ceiling. "Fuck you, asshole! We're staying together! We're not giving up!"

They all sat on the gritty floor. Em heard a faint tink of glass as her boot hit something. She looked but didn't see what it was and so, focused on getting Blue comfortable.

"We retrace our steps," Nathan said. "And try again. This time we can mark our way as we go along."

"I don't suppose either of you brought any breadcrumbs?" Blue asked.

"There are rocks," Nathan said. "We can line them up into arrows."

"I don't like the idea of going backward," Blue said. "It's what the fucker wants."

Hang on, Em thought. "This place lies." She reached out for a pebble. To her disappointment, it felt solid enough. She tossed it down the tunnel in disgust. "That's not it." Still, she had a hunch she was onto something, if only she could think it through.

"What's not it?" Nathan asked.

"Shhh," Blue said. "Em's thinking."

It's worth a try. Em said, "Everyone close your eyes." She did so, and she felt the ground beneath her change. She moved her palm in the dirt until she accidentally hit something hard and was greeted with the sound of breaking glass. A sharp pain forced her to jerk back her hand with a hiss. Her eyes snapped open at once. She spied the cut fingertip. Using her t-shirt to wipe away the blood, she scanned the area. "Where's the broken glass?"

"What broken glass?" Nathan asked.

Oh. An image of the three of them blindly stumbling up the tunnel and plunging to their deaths by way of another pit sprang to mind. *Shit.* "With your eyes closed, feel around you. What do you sense?"

"We're not sitting on the side of a steep hill, for one thing," Blue said. She opened her eyes and stared back at Em.

Em and Blue said it at the same time. "Allow for the possibility."

"What's so funny?" Nathan asked.

"That therapist was a hell of lot smarter than I give her credit for," Blue said.

Em spoke to Nathan. "It can lie to us. We're not seeing the truth. We never have in here."

Nathan swallowed and then murmured, "We have to walk out, blind."

Blue nodded. "And have faith in what we feel."

"I don't like it," Nathan said.

"Neither do I," Em said, not putting her real concerns into words for fear of the spirits or whatever they were would use it against them.

"How are we going to do this while carrying Blue?" Nathan asked.

"Do you have a better idea?" Em asked.

He shook his head and paused. "Piggyback. I'll take Blue. It's the only way."

"It wants to separate us," Em said. "I'll have to hold onto you, but that's going to make things even more awkward."

"Tell me about it," Blue said.

"Got it." Nathan began tugging at his belt buckle.

"Look," Blue said. "I understand that a thousand horror movies insist that this is the perfect time for the hets to inexplicably fuck, but—"

"We'll use my belt," Nathan said. He threaded the strong black leather strap through the two front loops on his jeans. "I'll have to trust you to lead me." He stopped, looked up, and blinked. "Oh. That's why—" He stopped mid-sentence.

"What's why?" Em asked.

Nathan shook his head once. "I'll tell you later."

Blue was faster on the uptake. "Jeanine dumped you, didn't she?"

Nathan focused on securing his belt. "Yeah. She did."

"Wow," Blue said. "I'm sorry."

"It's probably for the best. I shouldn't have waived the Joe Strummer rule," Nathan said.

"What Joe Strummer rule?" Em asked.

"The one where I don't date anyone who doesn't own a copy of *London Calling*," Nathan said.

Em blinked. *I love that album.* She glanced to Blue.

Blue said, "Say, Em, don't you—" She rubbed her arm. "Ouch. That hurt."

Glaring, Em attempted to give Blue the message via telepathy that her life could get very difficult if she continued speaking.

Blue stuck out her tongue and then asked, "*London Calling?* That's a little arbitrary."

"Says the woman who won't date women who wear orange," Em said.

"Fine," Blue said. "We'll talk about it later. Over ice cream and bourbon. Good bourbon. Assuming we ever get the fuck out of here."

Nathan nodded. "Em, the belt is for you. I have to trust you can lead me out of this."

"Just what Em always wanted, a hunky boy scout on the end of a leash."

"And a mouthy lesbian on his back." Em glared at Blue.

"*Hot* mouthy lesbian," Blue said. "Don't forget the 'hot.'"

"Yes. Yes. Let's get started." Em got to her feet.

Nathan stooped. "All right. Ready."

"Shit," Blue said. "Why couldn't you be Grace Jones?"

"I'll tell you what," Nathan said. "When you tell the others, you can say I was. I'll even back you up on it."

"You're a sweetheart," Blue said. "You have my blessing if you decide to fuck my roommate."

"Blue!" Em felt her face heat.

"One thing first," Blue said. "Will you trust Em enough to keep from peeking? I need to know. I'll be riding on your back, after all."

Nathan paused and an uneasy expression crossed his face. "I want to."

"There is no try," Blue said in her silliest Yoda voice. She reached into a pocket and pulled out a blue bandanna. "Only do."

"This deal is getting worse all the time," Nathan said.

"Pray I alter it no farther," Blue said, tying the blindfold in place.

"Are you two done geeking out?" Em asked.

Blue jumped one-footed onto Nathan's back with graceful ease, and Em took the end of Nathan's belt. She closed her eyes and silently prayed that she wouldn't lead them into a pit.

"From what I remember, we just follow the tunnel straight ahead and keep turning right," Em said.

"That's what I remember," Nathan said.

"All right. Let's go," Em said. Taking a deep breath, she scooted her right foot forward. She took her time and made sure of every inch of ground before stepping. It was taking forever, but too much weighed on her being careful. "How are you doing back there?"

"I'm good," Nathan said, although his tone indicated otherwise.

Blue said, "Me too."

They made it another twenty paces before whatever it was that haunted the Lounge decided to switch tactics. A low rumble vibrated beneath the soles of Em's Docs and worked its way up through the bones of her shins. Somewhere a lot of glass shattered and then was followed by a whoosh sound.

"Do you smell something burning?" Em's toe jammed square into something. It was very difficult to keep her eyes closed.

"It's s fire. Please hurry," Nathan said. "It's getting warm in here."

Blue began to cough.

"The smoke will be worst near the ceiling," Nathan said. "We need to get low. Now. Blue? Can you crawl?"

"I'm damned well going to try," Blue said.

Getting down on her hands and knees, Em felt around until her fingers touched the edge of the doorway. It was already easier to breathe. Taking a chance, she opened one eye and spied the paper towel dispenser hanging on the graffiti-scared men's room wall. Clouds of dark smoke crawled along the ceiling. Her eyes began to sting. "I've good news and bad news."

"Just tell us already," Blue said, squatting in the dirt where Nathan had deposited her.

"We made it," Em said. She helped Nathan with the blindfold. "You can open your eyes, but you won't like what you see."

Nathan said, "Because the club's going to burn down with us in it, if we don't hurry."

"Got it in one," Em said, coughing.

"Stay on the ground, everyone," Nathan said.

They crawled into the men's bathroom and as soon as everyone was out, Nathan yanked the mop free of the secret door's hinge. It snapped shut, cutting off the source of most of the smoke.

"Think that'll slow it?" Em asked.

"I'm not sticking around to find out," Nathan said.

"Follow me," Em said.

"Wait," Nathan said when they got to the men's room door. He laid a hand against it and then felt the doorknob. "It's cool. Thank god."

Then he held it open as she and Blue made their way through. He kicked it shut behind them. "Over to you, Em."

Thick, dark smoke curled along the ceiling as they made their way across the dance floor on hands and knees. Every once in a while, Em saw small patches of flames burst through the dense haze and then vanish. She tried not to think of molten lava. *Closing the doors behind us isn't buying us much time.*

Her eyes were stinging and watering so bad that she almost couldn't see as she led the way. The stench of burning bar made breathing difficult. She knew the others were close because she could hear them coughing.

Follow along the bar and the door is to the left, she thought. It would be shorter to take a more direct route across the dance floor, but she didn't want to risk getting lost in the smoke. They only had one chance at this.

At last, they made it to the front door.

Fumbling in her pocket for her keys, she got up on her knees. The acrid-smelling smoke was thick and had become black. They were all coughing now—nonstop. There was a terrible sooty and bitter taste in the back of Em's mouth, and the inside of her nose felt clogged with horrible, sticky ash. A series of bottles exploded in the storage room with muffled thumps and shattering glass.

Kneeling, she felt around the keyhole in order to get the front door key in. Tears were streaming down her face and sweat soaked her clothes from the heat. It took three tries to discover she had the wrong key.

"Shit-shit-shit-fuck!"

"Come on, Em," Blue said. "Hurry."

"I am." Em felt the ridges and labels on the various keys until she had the square one with 'FD' taped to it. She tried again, this time the heavy iron door swung open to the muggy Austin early morning. She knew it was hot and humid and awful out there, but compared to the inside of the Lounge, it was heaven. As they scrambled out onto the broken pavement in front of the club, Twiggy drove up. Her tires squealed when she braked.

"What the fuck?" Twiggy shouted out of her open window.

Em was too busy concentrating on breathing to respond.

Dre jumped out of Twiggy's Intercepter and sprinted to where Em, Blue, and Nathan were laying. Twiggy roared off in her vehicle—Em assumed to get help. As for Dre, Em was certain he was angry with her for letting the bar burn down. She hadn't even attempted to save the money in the safe. Nor had she retrieved her jacket or her purse. None of them had thought to get their things.

Everything inside the Lounge was burning. Dre's face was clenched in fierce lines of hate and rage. Em had never seen him that way before. She braced herself as he drew near, but Dre ran past, stopping in front of the burning building.

He screamed against the roaring flames. "Burn you mother fucker! You broke the pact! I fucking told you not to fuck with my people! I fucking told you! Me! Asshole! You could have me in exchange for their success! Me! But that wasn't enough for you, was it?! You had to go at them anyway. You fucking went for my kid! Now you're going to fucking pay! You fucked with the wrong man, asshole! You're going to burn! And I'm going to fucking watch! And then I'm going to pour holy water on your ashes!"

Blue wiped soot from her face and sat up. "So much for the question of whether or not Dre knew about that thing."

Nathan rolled over on his back. "Thanks, Em. I mean it. You're—you're amazing."

"You are too, Boy Scout," Em said.

"You now officially have my permission to fuck my roommate," Blue said. "Just do me a favor and wait until you get a room."

"Blue!"

"I know. I know," Blue said. "But he's good for you."

"Bitch!" Em said.

Blue gathered her into a tight hug. "Cow!"

Em spoke into her shoulder. "Slut!"

Twiggy's Interceptor roared up once again, doing a half donut as she parked. Leaving the door hanging, she ran to Blue's side. "I called 911 from the payphone down the street. The Fire Department will be here soon. Are y'all okay?"

"Blue," Em said, releasing her roommate. "Help Blue."

Twiggy nodded. "We have to move y'all farther away from the fire."

"I can't. My ankle is messed up," Blue said.

Blue accepted Twiggy's offer of help, and Em was happy to see Blue smile up at Twiggy with real affection. Em got the impression Blue would've kissed Twiggy by now, if it hadn't been for the circumstances. The mutual attraction was almost as thick in the air as the smoke.

"I thought you abandoned us," Blue said.

"No way," Twiggy said. "Someone had to call for help. Can I take more of your weight? How do you feel? Sit on the hood until help gets here. You'll be more comfortable."

Em got to her feet and then gave Nathan a hand up. Glancing back to Blue and Twiggy, she couldn't help thinking they looked cute together. "Hey, Twiggy!"

Twiggy looked back. "Yeah?"

"Do you wear orange?" Em asked.

— TWILIGHT STATE —
Gemma Files

*In "Twilight State", by Gemma Files, a person undergoes experimental
therapy that involves deep sedation—a twilight state. It's a story in which
neither the protagonist nor the reader knows who to trust or what is real,
and it's a story in which many relationships and locations seem trapped in
an in-between space.*

*The term "twilight state" in medicine refers to a state that can be achieved
through drugs, hypnosis, or some medical conditions. In surgery, this term
refers to a state in which a patient is anesthetized to the point of being heavily
sedated but not fully unconscious. The patient is deeply relaxed but is able
to answer questions and perform actions at the surgeon's request. "Twilight
state" usually results in amnesia—the patient can't remember the operation.
The advantage of this kind of anesthesia is that it doesn't require breathing
tubes and the recovery time is quicker than that of general anesthesia.*

*In nature, twilight is the time when the sun is below the horizon but its
rays continue to illuminate the sky. It's an in-between time, neither night nor
day. Similarly, the person in a twilight state is neither awake nor asleep. In
mythology, twilight is a particularly magical time, when the border between
the mortal and magical world is porous. In either sense, a person in a twilight
state is "betwixt and between". This is a time when great truths can be
revealed, if not recalled or understood.*

You don't have to look directly into the light," Dr Karr tells me.
"In fact, it'd be better if you didn't."

I nod. "How long will it take?"

"Today? Eight hours, tomorrow six, the day after that four—the
whole idea is to start high, then move down by increments. One way
or the other, if we see good results at the end of this session or the
effects aren't quite up to plan, we'll adjust accordingly."

"Just lie here, all that time? I'm not sure I can hold still that long."

"Oh, we'll secure your head, prop the chair up, and then there's
this—" She raises a thing like a cone, white and stiff, a human-sized
version of the sort of collar dogs wear after surgery, to keep them

from biting at their own sutures. "It'll diffuse the light, somewhat, but also direct it. And better yet, it keeps you from seeing the restraints."

I swallow. "I've…never been good with confinement."

"Well, that's what the anesthesia's for, Mrs. Courbet."

They call it twilight sleep, she says, a twilight state. Level Two on the descending scale of sedation. Just enough drugs, in just the right combination, to keep me from forming new memories. It nips the fear in the bud, supposedly, by not allowing me to notice exactly how long my "momentary" discomfort has already gone on, or speculate on how much longer it might continue.

"Now, we'll be using this IV rig to administer a cocktail of several agents to induce and maintain a light sleep, anxiety relief and short-term amnesia: Propofol and Midazolam, along with a narcotic/ systemic analgesic such as Demerol or Fentanyl. Of course, everyone responds differently, so we'll keep a close eye… but really, in most cases the dose is so perfectly calibrated that although you'll respond to vocal commands and light touch throughout, I very much doubt you'll even remember we've started, by the time you wake up."

"You've done this before, I take it."

"Many, many times. Shall we begin?"

I cast my eyes over the set-up again, so clinically neat and clean, especially when juxtaposed against the Modern Rustic interior of my family's cabin. It was built back in the 1920s by my great-grandfather Courbet, and re-done many times since. This latest iteration is my mother's work, mainly, and I think I may have spent more time here than anywhere else, over the years. It is bred as much from memory and dream as wood and stones, refuge crossed with mystery, a human oasis amidst the oddity of nature, its constant push and pull— all that life, and none of it your own. In an outcast world, it's as close as I've ever come to home.

What we do today may ruin that, I suppose. But frankly, I don't see any other way forward.

(Just do what it takes, Briony, I hear my father whisper, in my mind's ear. Seize charge, for Christ's sake; these people are experts, so let them do their job, and pay them for it. What else is money for?)

Soon enough I am laid back and tied down, ruffed like an Elizabethan, sinking fast. I feel the IV jack's needle prick as it goes in. Just past the cone's outermost edge, Karr turns the light on: 10,000 lux, green-bulb spectrum rather than blue, to manipulate melatonin and seratonin levels without doing damage to the photosensitive ganglion cells in my retina, or the cones behind my eye. Gauze provides a secondary lid of sorts, penetrable but protective, as Dr Karr murmurs that I need to try and keep my eyes open, but also remember to blink at regular intervals. Three breaths, Mrs Courbet...Briony. One, two, three, then blink. Repeat. Yes, that's right. One, two, three...

It may register as quite similar to daylight, she's told me, and it does, though not exactly; softer, hazed and vibrant, on the very edge of fading. That one last shred of bright, bravely overwhelmed, which comes before dark.

Like dusk, I think, and shiver.

This cabin is where almost every impression I have of Ontario outside Toronto was formed, over years of cyclic pilgrimage: the huge channels of moss-covered rock through which roads run like black-tarred veins, the foliage gummed with a year's worth of spiderwebs, pine needles carpeted ankle-deep upon the earth so they kick up like dirty brown snow with every step—a permanent shadow under every tree, air bitter with gnats and mosquitos that sip the corners of your eyes, where even the weeds can sting. And beyond all that the lake, overcast even on fine days, sun leached to white over grey water; sand and silt in the shallows admixed with great, trailing ropes of weed rooted deep in the dark portions, beyond the drop-off.

One time we accidentally arrived during caterpillar breeding season, and found the whole place boiling black and green with fuzzy, juicy, far too easily crushable crawlers: roof, walls, foundations all alike, the path itself squishing beneath our feet. Every morning we had to pound the screen door 'til it cleared, simply in order to see outside. But the next visit, the plague was gone, without a trace—vanished, nothing left behind but memory, and that fast-fading. As though it had never happened.

The silence, at night and otherwise. The complete darkness, once the porch-lights are off and the moths disperse. These are what stay with me. Time at the cabin has always been less a place, to me, than a method of being, never entirely lost, no matter how much distance put between; as though I leave part of myself there with each visit, to be recovered on return, if only briefly—rented, never regained. And I can never stay away for long.

To arrive here, always, is to step back into a dream I was born dreaming.

There is a thing you must watch for, Bri-oh-nee, Stana told me, as we sat near the lake together, the summer of my eighth year. The mrak, we call it. This means dark, or dusk—twilight. The time between.

She was a tall girl, Stana, very spare and severe, as if God had cut corners to make her: frowning lips, dark hair, cheekbones like eskers, set at a slant. A glorious bosom, kept well-leashed. Only later did I realize how she must have encoded herself onto my desire's DNA, forever pushing me towards women who looked like they might hurt me, if I only paid them enough for the privilege.

Stana came to Canada from Serbia, with her parents, and settled in Toronto. She had medical training, or so she said…not quite enough to requalify and complete her degree, but certainly enough to be somebody's glorified nursemaid. And she didn't hate children, though she often seemed indifferent. This in itself was so unlike my parents' attitude towards me that it probably would have made me think I loved her one way or the other, my eventual sexuality notwithstanding.

Does it live near here, the mrak? I asked her, mainly to keep her talking, as I spooned silty grey sand into my bucket, digging my toes deeper. Stana shook her queenly head, braids lightly swinging.

Here? I suppose so; it likes places neither one thing nor another, sand and shore, water and land. But everywhere else, too. The mrak is not bound by distances. It lives inside a moment, as sun dims and night comes on. Before the Morning Star rises.

Beneath the lake's shallows, my feet looked pale, green-tinged, faintly swollen. A ripple rolled back and forth over them, wetting me to mid-calf as the clouds massed overhead, turning the afternoon light sour.

We should go inside soon, she told me, while I upturned the bucket onto the shore beside me and made a teetery, decaying tower of its contents, already starting to wash away with the tide. This is no good time for you…for people like you. Of your age.

Because of the mrak?

The mrak likes to touch little children, or the things that belong to them. Sometimes it is a woman, huge and dark, sometimes a giant man with a rotten face, and always its hands are glowing—this is how it sees its way, in the darkness. And when it lays these long, bright hands on you, or even on your toys, your books, your clothes hung out on the line to dry, then you become not truly sick or ever truly well, not sleeping, but not waking. You fall between and stay there, for so long…

Here she broke off, staring out across the lake, where raindrops were beginning faintly to pock its waves. And I remember how I shivered, deliciously—frightened, or playing at it, for the sheer excitement of being so. Felt the wet hair rise up on my neck, my thighs all gooseflesh, as I asked her—

As long as what, Stana? Tell me, please.

As long as it takes, of course, Bri-oh-nee, little silly girl. For the mrak to eat you up, from the inside, like bugs eat a tree. Like ants in a hill, tunnelling in and in and in, 'til at last the hill falls down.

People tell children all sorts of things, I suppose, and who on earth ever knows why? She might have been angry with my parents, for exploiting her so shamefully, or with her parents, for making her play along. Perhaps she was home-sick, mourning the loss of her true place; Canada must have seemed strange to her, impermanent yet impossible to dismiss, a species of waking trance. Like being forced to dream someone else's dream.

She was gone by the new year, at any rate, just after Christmas holidays. My mother claimed she caught her stealing, but I never saw any proof that Stana coveted our possessions, and I'd spent far more time alone with her, at that point. In fact, I not only probably knew her better than either of them ever would, but also knew her better than I knew either of them...

This last truth, unfortunately for all of us, would never really change—not that they seemed to care at the time, or even later, when it was all too obvious I'd be their only child, their only heir. Cancer took my mother, then moved on to take my father, preventing him from running completely through the family fortune before I reached age of majority.

I didn't much care then, and I certainly don't care now it's all mine, to give or withold as I please to whomever I find least unfavourable. If I'd had the inclination, I might even have tried to track down Stana and deed some of it her way, instead of wasting my largesse on cheap imitations of her melancholy charm: my femme fataliste, dead end of all my childish fantasies. But...

No, it never seemed likely. What's past is past, gone forever, with no recall.

Yet here I am again, after all these years: up past Gravenhurst to Muskoka, back to familiar territory, the family cabin, the woods, the looming sky. The lake.

My wife didn't like the cabin, a difference of opinion that festered, the same as any other wound—the same as our marriage, in the end. And the infection left behind worked on me, slowly, in ways I became unable to ignore.

I brought her up here on our honeymoon, hoping she would love it, or at least come to understand why I did. But she never took to the place, not even at first, and later began to actively loathe it, lobbying me to do the same. It was as though she not only resented my affection for it, but eventually started to consider me just as innately toxic—poisoned, and therefore poisonous. My very touch tainted, by association.

It seems to watch you here, Briony, she told me, finally, by way of an explanation. To which I replied, perhaps foolishly: Yes, of course. And personally, I find that very comforting.

She dug her nails into her own palms, trying not to react, and failing. And right there, even so very early on…that was the death of us, summed up in a single moment. I watched our marriage wither, knowing it coffin-bound.

The truth is, I suppose, I've never felt entirely happy or entirely well, anywhere—not even here. But when I'm not at the cabin, I just feel so much worse. There's no comparison.

The cabin is where my mother chose to go, when she got her final diagnosis. It's what my father was on his way to, the night his chemo-therapy-weakened heart gave out at sixty miles an hour, spinning the car 'til it rammed a guard-rail and bloomed into a warm orange ball of flame. But when I unwisely chose to tell my wife how fitting I thought those two facts were, given my own deep love for our perch near the lake, recurrent centrepiece of our shared lives—how oddly beautiful, in context—she made a face, lips twisting. Her hand all but slapped up to cover her mouth, as though she were about to vomit.

Christ, Bri! she managed, eventually. That's just morbid. What the hell do you see in that place, anyway?

How well it sees me, I answered.

And that was that. As the old song says, I was alone again, naturally.

For some time before attempting this procedure, I only realized in retrospect, I'd slipped into some sort of all-over malaise with no apparent cause, but also no apparent cure. Constantly tired, I still couldn't sleep, or overslept, but took no particular good from making up for lost R.E.M. My dreams were multi-tiered and repetitive, forever revolving around commonplace moments somehow imbued with inexplicable terror, familiar faces rendered alien and malign, until inevitably I woke knotted from head to toe, in a cold sweat, suffering heart palpitations. Nothing pleased me, and I—in turn—felt incapable of pleasing anyone else.

Once it was my mother I dreamt of, washing dishes while discussing how disappointing my latest report card was even as her bald and nodding head raised a fresh crown of tumors, each pulsing slightly, a death-filled flesh-sac. Another time it was my estranged wife, dressing for some fundraiser, spraying perfume on her thighs and smiling at me in the mirror; I saw her pupils square themselves and catch fire, put forth a slick green nimbus that spread across her face like grave-mould, bearding her crown to chin with decay.

And once, predictably enough, it was Stana, faced into the sun with her back turned, shrunk to nothing but one long-braided shadow in the bright haze of its fast-eclipsing corona. Telling me, without much hurry—

You should go now, Bri-oh-nee. Before it comes, since it comes so soon, now. This is its time.

Bright Morning Star on the rise above and creeping dusk below, with the lake itself suddenly humping up all over like a submerged monster's back, dim water rolling free. The air itself one invisible chime of pixels and atoms, every particle set vibrating at the very same pace. A moment caught between, hovering on the knife-point verge of becoming something else.

The mrak, I thought, in the dream. You mean the mrak.

Yes, of course. What else?

(What else indeed?)

It knows you, you see. Your name, your face, and all of it because…I told it about you.

But why would you do that, Stana? I never did you any harm. I love you.

So easy to say, in a dream, but she simply nodded, or seemed to. Did I make her? Well, of course I did; it's not as though she was actually there, after all. Or me, either.

…perhaps that's why, then, she replied, after a moment. And stood there silent, no matter how I begged and pleaded, 'til I woke up.

"Sometimes I want to say my body isn't trying to kill me," I told Dr Karr, during our next session. "But whenever I stop to think about it, I remember that's really just accurate. Isn't it?"

"You could see it that way, Mrs Courbet," she agreed. "And—do you?"

"Increasingly."

"Well, we should probably talk about that."

The common cry, the human dilemma; animate meat, expiry dates encoded, all too aware for comfort. So we stave it off with various emollients, until (one day, inevitably) those become equally ineffective, necessitating something...more.

Nothing so very irreparable, in the end, Dr Karr hastened to assure me; nothing so very transformative, at least physically. And nothing, in the end, that money wouldn't solve—like most of my problems, I'd hitherto found. Yet probably best done in private nonetheless, I decided, once she'd outlined the idea in full—away from the public eye, with as few co-conspirators involved as possible.

"We could meet at my office, easily," Dr Karr pointed out. "Say three times a week, or even every other day, depending on how fast you want the treatment over with."

"I'd prefer not to, if you don't mind. I need to be absolutely sure this is kept discreet."

Polite as she was, she tried her best not to laugh, though I could see it was a bit of a struggle. "It's just light therapy, Mrs Courbet," she said, eventually. "Not exactly controversial."

"Oh, I understand, doctor. But you see, it's more about what the mere fact of any sort of therapy implies, to an outside eye."

"That you're unhappy?"

"Clinically so. It's not something I want widely known."

Here she narrowed her eyes slightly, and nodded. Because of your impending divorce, she might have said, if she'd been a different person. Because you fear the judge will think worse of you for being depressed, seasonally affected, sleepless to the point where you'd register as drunk on most tests, breathalyzer content notwithstanding. That you'll be forced to settle for less than you want to, because your wife will make it look as though you're not fit to handle other people's money anymore.

And: yes, doctor, I might have replied, without resentment. Given that's the only job—the only skill—I've ever really had.

But she didn't, and I didn't. Which, seeing how I'd never have employed that sort of person in the first place, if I could at all help it—the sadly frequent kind who apparently just has to open their mouth while thinking, or else their brain doesn't work quite as well—made me willing to trust her. On the matter of therapy, that is.

Eventually, we agreed on terms.

It's unseasonably warm and bright for an October weekend as we arrive at the cabin, yet still raining, as it almost never entirely ceases doing; typical fall, a border season, neither one thing nor the other. Within hours, this rainbow glitter will dull back down to a comfortable grey, but even now the air feels thick, smelling mildly of wet dust, or sodden, half-rotten pine-cones. You can taste it in the back of your mouth, a mint-wrapped stone. I haven't been here for nearly two years, though my people traveled up last week, stocking supplies, cleaning and airing out, the whole nine yards. Thanks to their efforts, we find the place in good repair, welcoming mat well-brushed, with deep drifts of dead leaves already gathered into piles for the mulch-pit.

Later, I stand at my bedroom window, sipping tea, listening to Karr's team set up her equipment, before the long drive back to Toronto. Soon enough, it'll be just her, me and the plan of therapy, or at least seem so—an easily-dispelled illusion, given that if you walk far enough in either direction you'll reach somebody else's dock, somebody else's beach, somebody else's equally "secluded" home away from home.

But this is the off-season, boats idle, lake stilled almost motionless whenever the rain slacks to drizzle. And while I might not feel entirely safe, given what's about to take place, I certainly don't feel observed, at least by human eyes.

In the chair, laid out, encollared, gauze over my eyes; the light snaps on, flooding my mind with sunshine. Then, what seems like mere seconds later—

"All right," I hear Karr say, from far away. "We're done for today."

I lick dry lips, tongue gone equally dry. "But...you haven't even started yet," I hear myself say, voice gone hoarse and querulous.

She laughs, closer now, fingers light on the ruff's fastening. "We started this morning, Mrs Courbet. That's the twilight sleep for you."

"No memories."

"As advertised. Now—be careful getting up, hold onto my arm. Here's some water, drink it slowly. Yes."

"I don't feel any different."

"You might not, immediately. It's not an exact science."

I take another sip, cough a bit to clear my throat, but the roughness doesn't go away. "That's…very reassuring," I manage, finally.

That night, when I close my eyes, I find myself back by the lake in full restraint, the base of Karr's chair plunged deep enough that my heels touch wet silt, with my face angled out towards open water. The straps dig my wrists 'til they start to numb, and through the cone's white flare I can just glimpse a silhouette I suspect must be Stana's to my left, hair unbound and whipping in the mounting wind.

Can you see it yet, Bri-oh-nee? she asks. Poor little girl. It is so close, now—very close.

The mrak? I ask, trying to crane my neck further, to finally see her, after all these years…all I have is memory, a bent mirror, and the warped reflection of her I've courted again and again, chasing it through a chain of equally unsatisfying women. And for a moment, fear grips me, bowel-deep: what if I do manage to catch a glimpse, at long last, only to find it's just yet another variation on a theme— so close to my wife, that unwittingly pale imitation, as makes no difference?

But: No one knows how the mrak is made, Stana continues, though we all wonder. Is it always the same? Or is it made anew over and over, every sunset, the same way day turns to dusk?

Perhaps it was a person, once. A child, even.

Perhaps it is the mrak's own touch, itself, that makes another mrak.

Out on the water are islands, the nearest of which sketches a cool curve furred with trees, a skeleton eyesocket of rock, a jutting cabin-cheekbone. And as the sun sets, as twilight falls and dusk creeps up, draining the world of colour—I watch the whole thing lurch and rumble, earthquake-shifting. See it re-orient itself, submerged portion slick and streaming, to form a massive, bisected face which turns my way, blindly seeking, like some sleeper fresh-awakened. Like a hunting animal, roused by the scent of prey, who sniffs into the wind to discover exactly which way it should turn, and pounce.

Phosphorescence spreading, a rotten green creeping up over its domed hillside skull, blooming all over. Its concave features, decay-blurred, algae-encrusted. Soon, I think, a pair of similarly glow-palmed hands will break from the lake, reach out to seize me, lift me whole and struggling to its gaping, rock-toothed shore-mouth…

The false sun that doctor shines will never keep it away, poor girl, Stana tells me. Only the Morning Star's true light can do that, and I do not see it rise, not now, not here. Not for you.

Oh, but surely, I want to shout in return, you will save me, Stana— you must. Because you love me, don't you, just a little? The same way I love you?

No reply. The straps bite deep; the mrak's green light fills my cone-collar like a cup, drowning me. I gasp and take it in, lungs filling cold as lake-waves, deep and murky, each lung set outlined and glowing in the red darkness of my chest—

—'til all at once, I feel Stana's hands on my shoulders, pressing me down, her hair falling 'round me, soft and dark, like earth into an open grave. Saying, as she does: But perhaps I should not have worried, Bri-oh-nee, all this time. For see, in its eyes—how it recognizes you? Perhaps it has touched you already, long before, without either of us knowing. This would explain much, yes?

So you belong to it already, and always have: never fully sick, never fully well. Never fully asleep, and never fully waking.

(Never fully loved, I think, helpless, at the same time—no, I know: unloved, loveless, unable to love. And never fully loving.)

At this, Stana nods, probably. Pronounces, as though passing sentence—

Now you are mrak, and this love you want so badly…this love you offer…pollution, only. Danger. Just as this hour is yours, this time between. Just as this place has always been your place.

Now, as then. Then, and always. Always, and forever.

(So I was right to send my wife away, after all, I think. I was being kind, keeping her safe. Because I loved her.)

(Because I still do, and always will.)

The island, looming, cliff-mouth wide, water streaming like a beard, and the lake opening too, right below it—lips of foam, teeth of bone, grim grey sky for a jaw-hinge, eternally poised to bite. A double devouring.

But before either mouth can quite close over me, I rocket up from sleep in one great, wracking leap, lie drenched and sleepless 'til dawn. Wait, with a pounding, skipping heart, for the moment when I can at last tell Dr. Karr: It wasn't enough.

—◄●►—

"I'll need to send you deeper," Karr says, as I frown. Explaining, gently: "In order to add auto-suggestions in on top, so I can guide you through the process. These dreams you describe—to me, they almost seem like your brain revolting against the twilight sleep, reframing your lack of new memories into some sort of phobia. I mean, you've been put out before, yes, completely? For surgery?"

"...now and then."

"And how did you react to the general anesthetic process, on those occasions?"

The frown spreads, becoming a full-bore shudder; I've always dreaded "going under," how consciousness simply drops away without warning, nothing left behind but a black hole of non-being. That total disappearance. That emptiness.

"I fought it," I tell her, finally. "The same way I would have fought death."

"Well, then."

I sigh. "But I've had these same dreams for years, doctor, especially here. It's all part of the pattern: nightmares, insomnia, depression..."

"Interesting that you chose to come to the cabin for therapy, then. Isn't it?"

(In context? Yes.)

"At any rate," she continues, "your body's obviously so used to these symptoms, it sees our attempts to cure them as an attack. Has it ever been this bad before?" I shake my head, reluctant. "So why do you think that is?"

"This place," I say, shrugging. "The situation... my divorce. Stress."

"Ah, yes—the prime exacerbation."

When looking for causation, always start with whatever's newest—Karr's not wrong about that. "My wife," I find myself saying, "had expectations, I think, about how matrimony would change things. Change me. I'm still not sure why. I was like this when she met me, after all. But..."

"Love cures all?"

I nod. "It doesn't, though."

"People are bad at distinguishing manageable behaviours from pathological ones," Karr agrees. "To grasp that it's not a question of 'getting well,' but of incremental steps towards long-term maintenance. It can be difficult to accept the essential uncertainty of that reality, especially when you have no opportunity to contribute. Significant others appreciate being given the chance to at least try to help—it makes them feel valued. Needed."

"But she couldn't help," I point out. "Nobody can. You can't fuck a crazy person sane. Why waste time trying?"

"It was hers to waste."

"I was trying to be…considerate."

Karr sighs. "I wonder if she'd think so."

Soon, twilight sleep gives way to twilight state. The lake, the grey sky, white sun hanging in dimness: so small, so bright. Is that the sun, or the Morning Star? It hurts my eyes to look at.

Deeper, Mrs Courbet, deeper. Briony. Can you hear my voice? Speak freely.

(Yes, doctor.)

Good. Can you move your head, your hands? Nod, if you can. Give me some sign.

Nothing happens. The lake laps the shore. Inside the cone's curve, my field of vision shrinks, restricted: lake, sky, star. My own shallow breath, my blood, my skull set singing, an empty shell's dull roar. My slack body, tied down, motionless as stone.

Speak freely. Are you awake, or asleep?

(I…don't know.)

Can you see?

(Only the lake.)

Can you move?

(…no.)

That's good. That's very good.

I hear Karr take a breath, then say: Open your eyes now, Briony. There's someone here who wants to speak to you.

So I do, and the first thing I see is a woman, standing over me: tall, spare and dark, curvaceous, queenly. She studies me the same way she did for most of our marriage, with a bitter fascination. As though I promised her something without meaning to, then never quite delivered on it.

"Hello, Bri," she says. "Been a while, hasn't it? You can answer freely."

"Hello, Heba," I reply, surprisingly unsurprised. But that's not enough for her, apparently. "Answer the question," she snaps back, an angry crack in her voice, as though she's testing something. Then relaxes just a bit when I answer, with only a second's pause—

"Yes, it has been."

Heba looks to Dr Karr, who's standing beside her; Karr nods, slightly. "Just like you wanted—total suggestibility, but without the amnesia, this time. Ask her anything."

"...all right."

Heba Gilroy Courbet, my wife—ex-wife to be, that is—takes a moment, maybe to think over what exactly "anything" should consist of; her hair hangs heavy, framing a pale, fatigue-smudged face set with eyes so deep blue they seem black. And: You don't look good, sweetheart, I catch myself thinking. Almost as bad as me, and that's saying something. Don't tell me you can't sleep now.

Heba leans in, studying me, as Dr Karr stands with arms crossed, nervously tapping one foot. I'm not sure what she thought would happen once Heba got what she must have paid for, access to me in this useless, curtailed state, but perhaps this wasn't it.

She's a hard one to trust, doctor, I try to project, unable even to meet her eyes. This circumstance alone should tell you that.

"Why do you think I'm here?" Heba asks me. "Speak freely."

My lips are so dry. "Therapy?"

"That's funny, but no." She sighs. "To find out why you're really here, I suppose. Mary told me you were sick, that you'd opted to come up to the cabin for treatment, and I...I remembered those stories you told me, about your parents. Stupid, right? But I know you, Bri. I know what this place is to you." She waits, as though expecting me to answer, then realizes her mistake. "Oh, for Christ's sake! Speak freely."

I clear my throat. "I don't know what you want from me, Heba."

"Four years, Briony. I just want what's mine."

"And what would that be exactly?"

"Think back: when we stood up in front of all those people, you promised me love, fidelity, loyalty...that we'd always be together. That we'd be like one person. So why did it take me reading Mary's session notes to get any sort of an idea about exactly how fucked you are, let alone why? You never even told me something was wrong, until it couldn't be fixed anymore. You never told me anything."

"Maybe I wanted to...protect you."

"From what?" I hesitate, drawing a bitter laugh from her. "You won't say, right? Even now. Well, Mary here can make you, if I tell her to, or even if I don't...make you do anything she wants. Hurt yourself, maybe. Stare in that stupid lightbox 'til you go blind. Jesus, Briony, how desperate would you have to be, to try a treatment this outlandish? To trust Mary couldn't be bought, when she very obviously can?"

(There's only one real weakness, Briony, I hear my father say, from somewhere down deep inside, universally shared, and nothing ever changes but the currency involved. That's why you have to hold onto money so tightly, because it'll leave you in a minute, for the first open hand. And all you really have is more of it than most people, at least to begin with.)

(But: No, Bri-oh-nee, Stana's voice points out. You do have one other thing, and always did, just as it has you. Even though you may not want it.)

The dusk deepens, clouds of mud roiling up through lakewater, disturbed by a delicate footstep; as much smell and sound as something seen, the susurration of wind on water, acrid tang of mouldering wood and leaves, an insectile buzz felt in the temples and fingertips... Oh but wait, no: that's Karr speaking, her too-calm clinical voice gone brittle, disturbed. Saying—

"...enough. Let me get her to sign the documents and send her back down; we can be over the border at Sault Ste. Marie in four hours—"

"Shut up, Mary." Heba is only a cut-out silhouette now, black on black on black, and I find myself smiling at her sharp command, realizing exactly where she must have learned that tone she's trying to mimic. "You'll get your money. Money's nothing. Briony taught me that—and I'm a fast learner, as even she'd agree." Swinging back to me, her bruised eyes suddenly visible again as they meet mine: "Wouldn't you, darling?"

"Very fast, yes."

"Thank you." Her shadow-self shifts, clenched fists kissing over her breastbone, as if to help her hold herself together. "Money's nothing, love is... well, it's something, but I was never going to get that, was I? So that doesn't matter either. Satisfaction, though... that's something, too."

"Do you want blood, Heba?" I ask without being prompted, and watch Dr. Karr jump, just a little—mouth opening and closing like a fish, making little o's, tongue-tied and maybe thinking: no no, this shouldn't be. She's breaking free, Heba, coming back up—anything could happen now—

"What I want is for you to look at me for once, straight on." I do. "Yes, just like that. Now tell me, for the last damn time, before you make me do something I'm really going to regret. Tell me..."

...what? I want to ask. But really, all I have to do it wait.

"…why I was never enough."

It's not that I don't want to answer; a blessed relief, in a way, simply not to care any more. Yet the words logjam my mouth, along with half a dozen others: Because/Because nobody could have been/Because I'm not enough, not you/Because you wanted to change me, or me you/Because neither of us could have known what "for better or for worse" might mean for us/For me…

Too much, and not enough, so in the end I don't say anything at all. Just let my eyes drift past her to the window, deep blue with autumn nightfall now, a cold yellow half-moon rising beyond the black curve of the islands—that one island, closer than any should be, already half-turned in its socket. Already humping up, poised to rise, and walk.

Heba doesn't see it, of course; she's far too busy suddenly shaking me hard by my shoulders, snapping my slack neck back and forth inside the plastic cone like a marble rolling 'round a funnel, shrieking: Talk, I said! Speak freely, goddammit! And Dr Karr at the same time, yelping over her, trying to break my trance: My voice, rise up, four three two one and wake, you will wake refreshed, you won't remember any of this, you won't remember—

Two sharp clicks. The therapy lights snap off, the living room track lighting on. But the dusk is thick now, everywhere, like air, covering both women in shapeless sacks through which I see only their eyes, beach mirage bright overtop as some bleak and alien desert. Sound bleeds out to silence. I stare past them, to the rising moon overlaid with sun, the silty sand, the lake.

And then I see the mrak, rising out of the water, stepping ashore. A mountain-tall figure, a giantess, yet still vaguely shaped like that girl I fell in love with, so very long ago: Stana, done up in draped and blurry shadow, reaching out, feeling her way by the uncertain, ten-fingered light of her own glowing hands. Her hair is ivy and pine needles, her skin weather-yellowed birch bark, her massive teeth made from the quartz-streaked sedimentary grey rock of the islands' shores, and she moves like rippling water as she strides silent towards the cabin, towering up into the dark.

Close enough, now, that those hands can light up its great face, so raw and unfinished. Close enough for me to finally see who it really does looks like: not Stana at all, in the end. No. Not even close.

I have never seen a mirror so tall, I think. Nor one so terribly, terribly…accurate.

Time has slowed, as it always does, in dreams. Heba and Dr. Karr move as if caught in treacle, turning upon one another so slowly that their conflict will not even have time to begin before this is over. And behind them, the mrak dips down, re-sizing itself; looks in through the window, a curious little girl surveying strange dolls. Without visible transition, it has already slipped sideways to the door, opening it, crossing the floor like a shadow. It climbs onto the chair to peer down at me, then slides down along my body, entwining with me, one glowing hand on my heart. Pressing down, hard, 'til it feels as though my breastbone will crack.

She kisses me, the mrak, with her rotting tongue. Pares the conical therapy ruff away gently, as her huge, bright hands brush me up and down. Then melts away, leaving me stretched out in its wake as a discarded husk, stuffed full and sodden. The straps holding me down burst, rotted instantly. I twist my hands free, raise them, and watch them start to glow—no surprise there. Just that sole unsteady, doubled light in the darkness, outside and within.

Sitting up, I seize Heba by her face, hauling her 'round; Dr Karr skitters back in shock, colliding with the wall, but I ignore her. Force Heba to look deep into my eyes, as I tell her, with the mrak's voice: "Answer? Oh, I can do much better than that."

She struggles, keening, a broken-winged gull, but those hands are irresistible. They bring her closer, closer. Until, at last, I can whisper, into her mouth—

"Let me show you."

The Morning Star rising, or perhaps setting, somewhere above. Impossible to tell which, from this angle: not here in this place, at this hour. Not that it really makes a difference.

What happens to Karr doesn't concern me, much; she stays stuck, I assume, unable to move, unable to flee. But you, my dear Heba—you will meet me halfway, from now on, as you always wanted. Absorb my tainted touch. You will stay with me forever, neither waking nor sleeping, neither sick nor well; I will give you what I can, and use you up 'til there is nothing left, for either of us.

That's love, isn't it? Or if it isn't, it should be. Since, after all…

…there's really nothing else.

Later, on the beach, I hear what might be Stana come up behind me. Maybe she'll put her hand on my shoulder, I think. Maybe we'll walk into the water together, submerge, never to be seen again. Sink until only the tops of our skulls are visible, just two more islands in a dim grey lake under a darkening sky, horizon lit by one bright sliver.

Where I come from, Stana's voice tells me, we use a certain herb with yellow flowers and leaves like rosemary as incense for a mrak-touched child's relief. But this does not grow here, unfortunately.

I know, Stana.

I would find some for you, Bri-oh-nee, if I only could.

I know.

On Krk, an island in the Adriatic, Stana continues, they tell how the mrak fights the sun, every day at dusk. How during the day the sun gets the better of his opponent, using flaming arrows to drive the mrak into the deepest, darkest gorges, but at night the mrak emerges once more, to chase the sun with a great net. But every time he is about to close the net over his prey, the Morning Star draws near, its light cutting the sun free.

So the mrak loses.

So far, yes. Yet the islanders know the mrak will win, eventually. And so the fight goes on.

I'm tired, Stana. So tired.

Then sleep, Bri-oh-nee, silly girl. Close your eyes. Let go…

(…until tomorrow.)

— HEARTBEAT —
Laura Anne Gilman

When we think of Kansas, many of us picture flat or gently rolling plains. In Gove County, the land is indeed fairly flat, with the exception of the Chalk Pyramids, also known as Monument Rocks. The rock formations are white or a light tan color—they look like the bones of a giant rising out of nowhere in shapes of towers and bridges and keyholes. The formations are up to seventy feet tall. They are the remnants of an inland sea, made of sediment and ancient seashells that accumulated during Cretaceous Period. To look at these formations is to look at some of the last remnants of an ocean floor from eighty million years ago.

The plains of Kansas were once the Niobrara Sea, densely populated with microscopic organisms called foraminera, giant oysters, fish, and sharks. Over time the calcium shells of the foraminera, along with other bones, mineral deposits, and sediment, fell to the bottom of the sea, and as the sea dried up the floor of this ocean became chalk. The Smoky Hill River carved through the chalk and left towering and bizarre formations behind. If you look at the tops of the formations, you are looking up at the last of the Niobrara Sea floor and the beings that inhabited it.

These formations are rich in fossils and are also a great place to see birds, particularly kestrels and pigeons (who were, after all, originally known as rock doves). Many Plains Indian tribes considered the site sacred and performed sun dances nearby. Travellers have used these formations as a landmark for centuries. In "Heartbeat", Laura Anne Gilman hints at a troubled link between travellers who would damage the rocks and the rocks themselves. Press your face against the ancient chalk. What do you hear?

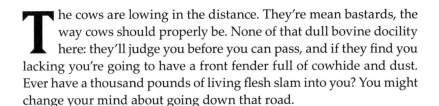

T he cows are lowing in the distance. They're mean bastards, the way cows should properly be. None of that dull bovine docility here: they'll judge you before you can pass, and if they find you lacking you're going to have a front fender full of cowhide and dust. Ever have a thousand pounds of living flesh slam into you? You might change your mind about going down that road.

Most, they don't bother. Most, they've got no reason to stop: it's none of their concern what humans do. Only the curious come down here, past the chestnut-red bulk of cows and the narrow ditches, down the long long road.

There are no signs, no stops, no guards, only the wind, low against the grasses, and the cows. That's all that's here, down this long road. And the remnants of the past, grey chalk pillars sculpted into the pale blue sky. It draws people, fascinates them, moths to a steady flame.

"You can hear your own heartbeat."

You can always hear your own heartbeat. You just have to stop and listen for it. The girl leans against the rock, fitting her body into the hollow worn by wind and time. She places a palm flat against her chest, tilts her head back, closes her eyes. Others have done the same, male and female, young and old. There are other niches worn into the rock, shallow and high, the surface rough against skin. Her hands are cool, spread where the sun's touched stone, and like so many others she thinks she can hear voices, some connection to the past.

There are no voices here.

The boy takes her picture. She smiles at him, and he leans in, presses his arm across her neck, pushes in. She watches him, lets him do it, her hands flat against the rock, chin tilted up. He smiles and steps back, looks up at the sky.

"I'm surprised nobody's tagged this," he says. "Nobody for miles, nothing to stop you from just walking up and doing it."

The girl smiles, her eyes closed now, listening to the wind and the cows and her heartbeat. "So do it."

"What?"

"You want to, don't you? Otherwise you wouldn't have mentioned it."

"I was just wondering...Jesus, no." The boy shakes his head. "No."

He's thinking about it. You can see it in his body, the way he's looking at the rock now, like a canvas, a tool. You can see when he thinks about what he'd write, where he'd place it. How it would feel. You can see when he decides that it would be a terrible idea.

They climb back into their car, too low-slung for the dirt road. They roll down the windows and drive off, taking their heartbeats and leaving the cows.

Every now and again, someone makes a different choice. Carving tools, spray paint, chalk, piss, blood. It's all been used against the stones, over time. Layer over layer of defiant human shouts, demanding to be remembered. To scream louder than a heartbeat.

Nothing lasts. The bison die off, domestic cattle eat their grass. The wind hollows the chalk, exposing new faces before calving the old into shards and dust, slowly finishing what the waters began, ages ago. Secrets are revealed and hidden again, sun bleaching bone-white and the moon cooling them to shadows.

There are secrets here, more than the casual visitor would think.

The silence hides the screaming. The wind wipes the marks away. The cows shit into the grasses, and the grasses cover the bones.

ABOUT THE AUTHORS

K. C. Norton's short fiction has appeared in publications such as Writers of the Future, Women Destroy Science Fiction, and Orson Scott Card's Intergalactic Medicine Show, among others. Although she has never spoken to a coral formation, she has gone on numerous dives and encountered many of the animals that appear in "Reef."

Former film critic and teacher turned award-winning horror author **Gemma Files** is best known for her Weird Western Hexslinger Series (A Book of Tongues, A Rope of Thorns and A Tree of Bones, all from ChiZine Publications). She has also written two collections of short fiction, a story cycle (We Will All Go Down Together, CZP), and two chapbooks of speculative poetry. Her next novel, Experimental Film, will be out in November. You can learn more about her than you probably want to know by reading *http://handful-ofdust. livejournal.com.*

Laura Anne Gilman is the Nebula-nominated author of more than 20 fantasy and SF novels and novellas, including the forthcoming *Silver on the Road*, Book 1 of The Devil's West (Saga Press/Simon & Schuster). Ms. Gilman also writes mysteries under the name L.A. Kornetsky. She hangs out on Twitter as LAGilman, and blogs at *http:// www.lauraannegilman.net*

Rebecca Campbell is a Canadian writer and academic. NeWest Press published her first novel, *The Paradise Engine* in 2013.

Mercedes M. Yardley is a dark fantastic who wears red lipstick and poisonous flowers in her hair. She writes short stories, nonfiction, novellas, and novels. She is the author of Beautiful Sorrows, Apocalyptic Montessa and Nuclear Lulu: A Tale of Atomic Love, Nameless, Little Dead Red, and her latest release, Pretty Little Dead Girls: A Novel of Murder and Whimsy, from Ragnarok Publications. Mercedes lives and works in Sin City, and you can reach her at *www.mercedesyardley.com.*

Sonya Taaffe's short fiction and poetry can be found in the collections *Ghost Signs* (Aqueduct Press), *A Mayse-Bikhl* (Papaveria Press), *Postcards from the Province of Hyphens* (Prime Books), and *Singing Innocence and Experience* (Prime Books), and in numerous anthologies including *The Humanity of Monsters, Dreams from the Witch-House:*

Female Voices of Lovecraftian Horror, Aliens: Recent Encounters, Beyond Binary: Genderqueer and Sexually Fluid Speculative Fiction, The Moment of Change: An Anthology of Feminist Speculative Poetry, People of the Book: A Decade of Jewish Science Fiction & Fantasy, The Year's Best Fantasy and Horror, The Alchemy of Stars: Rhysling Award Winners Showcase, and *The Best of Not One of Us.* She is currently senior poetry editor at Strange Horizons; she holds master's degrees in Classics from Brandeis and Yale and once named a Kuiper belt object. She lives in Somerville with her husband and two cats.

Caroline Ratajski is a writer and software engineer currently living in Silicon Valley, California, USA. Previously published as Morgan Dempsey, her short fiction is currently available in Broken Time Blues and Danse Macabre, as well as at Redstone Science Fiction. She is represented by Barry Goldblatt of Barry Goldblatt Literary, LLC.

zm quỳnh huddles in a room tinged with blue nursing calloused hands worn down from the chronic transcription of restless dreams. past lives have included scattered jaunts through urban minefields with each misstep hinting at a life less easily mapped out by this amateur cartographer. irrationally drawn to moving mountains one stone at a time, quỳnh has tackled the tasks of labor organizer, juvenile hall literacy coordinator, artistic director of a guerrilla feminist theatre troupe, mother, mentor and best friend (all rolled up in one), civil rights advocate, guardian ad litem for foster care youth, waitstaff at one too many late night diners (hey...free food—what?), slam poet, urban horticulturalist, visual junk artist, passionate lover, and cocktail server/candy salesperson at all night rave parties (hungry people pay $5 for candy bars!).

J. Daniel Batt is a recovering high school English teacher with a degree in Language Arts. He is finishing his MFA in creative Writing through National University. Jason and his wife Karen have three children: two boys, Tristan and Keaghan, and one girl, Aisleyn. He works with the 100 Year Starship as their Creative and Editorial Director. In this role, he works to bridge the gap between scientists and science fiction writers. He is also the editor for the 2012, 2013, and 2014 Symposium conference Proceedings, a collection of nearly 2000 pages of the latest research and thought about interstellar exploration and travel. He is the organizer of their annual Science Fiction Night, "Telling the Story," bringing science fiction authors and scientists together to discuss the impact of science fiction on space exploration, and the lead for the upcoming Canopus Awards, celebrating the best in interstellar writing, both fiction and non-fiction.

He serves on the Advisory Board for the Lifeboat Foundation with their Media/Arts Board, Futurism Board, and the Space Settlement Board. He served as a judge for the Lifeboat to the Stars award for science fiction literature presented at the 2013 Campbell Conference. Through the Lifeboat Foundation, he is currently editing their science fiction anthology titled Visions of the Future with stories from a wide array of authors.

His short fiction has appeared in *Bastion Magazine* and *Bewildering Stories*. He also does marketing writing for television and film. He is on Twitter at *twitter.com/jdanielbatt* and online at *jdanielbatt.com*

John Barth described **Cat Rambo's** writings as "works of urban mythopoeia" — her stories take place in a universe where chickens aid the lovelorn, Death is just another face on the train, and Bigfoot gives interviews to the media on a daily basis. She has worked as a programmer-writer for Microsoft and a Tarot card reader, professions which, she claims, both involve a certain combination of technical knowledge and willingness to go with the flow.

Among the places in which her 200+ fiction publications have appeared are *Asimov's*, *Clarkesworld*, and *Beneath Ceaseless Skies*. Her collection, *Eyes Like Sky and Coal and Moonlight* was an Endeavour Award finalist in 2010 and followed her collaboration with Jeff VanderMeer, *The Surgeon's Tale and Other Stories*. Her most recent collection is *Near + Far*, from Hydra House Books, which contains Nebula-nominated "Five Ways to Fall in Love on Planet Porcelain". She was nominated for a World Fantasy Award in 2014 for her work with *Fantasy Magazine*. Her nonfiction work includes *Ad Astra: The SFWA 50th Anniversary Cookbook* (co-edited with Fran Wilde) and *Creating an Online Presence For Writers*. Her fiction includes novel *Hearts of Tabat* and fantasy collection *Neither Here nor There*.

B. Morris Allen grew up in a house full of books that traveled the world. Nowadays, they're e-books, and lighter to carry, but they're still multiplying. He's been a biochemist, an activist, and a lawyer, and now works as a foreign aid consultant. When he's not roaming the world fighting corruption, he's on the Oregon coast, chatting with seals. In the occasional free moment, he works on his own speculative stories of love and disaster. Find out more at *www.BMorrisAllen.com*

Seanan McGuire writes things. It is difficult to make her stop. She spends a lot of time neck-deep in swamps, and is very fond of frogs. So fond that sometimes, she's the reason there's a frog in the kitchen. You're welcome. Keep track of her at *www.seananmcguire.com*.

Wendy N. Wagner is the author of *Skinwalkers*, a Pathfinder Tales novel inspired by Viking lore. Her short fiction has appeared in many successful anthologies, including *Shattered Shields*, *Armored*, and *The Way of the Wizard*, and magazines like *Beneath Ceaseless Skies* and *The Lovecraft eZine*. She is the Nonfiction Editor of *Women Destroy Science Fiction!*, which was named one of NPR's Best Books of 2014. She lives in Oregon with her very understanding family.

Damien Angelica Walters' short fiction has appeared or is forthcoming in various anthologies and magazines, including *The Year's Best Dark Fantasy & Horror 2015*, *Year's Best Weird Fiction Volume One*, *Cassilda's Song*, *Nightmare*, and *Apex*. "The Floating Girls: A Documentary," originally published in Jamais Vu, is on the 2014 Bram Stoker Award ballot for Superior Achievement in Short Fiction.

Sing Me Your Scars, a collection of her short fiction, is out now from Apex Publications, and *Paper Tigers*, a novel, is available from Dark House Press. You can find her on Twitter @DamienAWalters or online at *http://damienangelicawalters.com*.

Heather Clitheroe lives and works in Calgary, Alberta. Her work has previously appeared in *Beneath Ceaseless Skies* and *Lightspeed Magazine's 'Women Destroy Science Fiction.'*

Stina Leicht is a Hugo award-nominated sf/fantasy writer and podcaster. When she was small, she wanted to grow up to be like Vincent Price. Unfortunately, there are no basements in Texas—thus, making it impossible to wall up anyone alive under the house. Alas, she'll have to resign herself to going quietly mad while wearing a smoking jacket. Too bad Texas is hot, she doesn't smoke, and therefore, doesn't own a smoking jacket. Her next project is *Persephone Station*, a Feminist SF novel due from Saga Press in 2020.